SOUL
OF THE
BUTTERFLY

The Conclusion to the
BUTTERFLY
Trilogy

Scott Carruba

Soul of the Butterfly

©2019 Scott Carruba

First Edition

Edited by Christina Hargis Smith

Cover art by Jeffrey Kosh Graphics

Published by Optimus Maximus Publishing, LLC

ISBN- 10: 1-944732-44-6

ISBN- 13: 978-1-944732-44-8

Words shall not be hid, nor spells buried. Might shall not sink underground, though the mighty go.

\- The Kalevala

SOUL
OF THE
BUTTERFLY

A Novel by

Scott Carruba

Optimus Maximus Publishing, LLC

Brick, New Jersey

Chapter One

The large house stands nestled deep within the grounds, trees lining the private, gravel road, growing lusher as one moves from that avenue until they become as dense as a forest. The architecture is Second Empire, the floorplan asymmetrical, the top of a darker shade than the overall rich coloring of the structure. A single tower rises up, only taller than the roof by its own cap, the home showing three floors with many bay windows, and a modest balcony emerging from one side.

Lilja notes the late afternoon sun is even more obscured as they slowly progress along the way, nearing the mansion. She leans forward a bit in the driver's seat, peering, then spares a glance to her passenger. The junior girl, Zoe, slouches in place, one hand up to somewhat prop her head. She also looks outside the vehicle, though judging from her expression, she is none too pleased.

During the short time of this assignment, the Felcraft woman has not been shy about her displeasure. Though she is about five years younger than her partner, she has been trained in the hunting of demons for most of her life. Despite this, Lilja had been put in charge and given lead for interacting and investigation. Zoe figures it's because she is the girlfriend of the Head of the Family, Skothiam. She's heard things about the redhead, heard tales of what she's done as well as seen some of her skills in training exercises. There's no denying those abilities, but Zoe still stews, feeling passed over for one less experienced, one who is not even family. Lilja does not press Zoe to talk.

There are a few other vehicles noticeable as Lilja brings their rental into a decent parking place on the circular drive. Lethal and exotic equipment waits in the trunk, but it remains there for now. They are not unarmed and would not be without some skill even if bereft of conventional weapons, but a measure of subtlety and secrecy is still called for. As they mount the impressive steps to the front door, an older, quite refined woman waits for them.

"Good afternoon, Mrs. Barrington," Lilja greets as the other woman stares down the angle of her sharp nose at the two arrivals. Zoe remains as taciturn as on the drive. "We spoke on the phone?" She gently presses, then fishes into the pocket of her light, waist-length jacket, producing a sleek identification. "We're the Special Investigators."

She doesn't know exactly how the Felcrafts have come by these ID's or the obvious back-up to give them quasi-legitimacy, but they are impressive, even if the agency for which they purportedly work is so obscure as to make one wonder if it exists at all. Fortunately, the Barringtons, though quite well-off, are not so wealthy as to possess the types of connections and power to have made this angle of approach more difficult than it already proves.

"Why does someone from England care about what's happening on my private property?" Mrs. Barrington asks, eyes peering, her voice issuing forth with its own regional, cultured accent.

"I'm not from England, ma'am," Lilja informs, returning the elder woman's gaze. "I explained this on the phone, and I presume you checked this out before agreeing to our visit."

Of course, the woman had not readily agreed, but again the Felcraft resources had proven sufficient to compel her to feel like she had no other choice but to allow it. Lilja is not entirely comfortable with the subterfuge, however lacking in outright abrasiveness it may be, but she understands the necessity.

Mrs. Barrington just stares, seeming to give but the barest examination to the ID, more taking measure of the visitor. She then moves her eyes to Zoe who returns the look with one that seems apathetic. The staring continues until Zoe seems to get the point, producing her own credentials.

"You two don't look like Special Investigators," Mrs. Barrington comments.

Lilja glances around, displaying a cool exterior, before setting her eyes back on the woman. "Do you mind if we take a look around your property before the sun sets?"

"I don't think you care if I mind," the woman retorts after a bit of a pause.

"I am sorry for the inconvenience, Mrs. Barrington," Lilja replies, keeping her even, soothing tone, "but it would be best if everything went as smoothly as possible."

The woman narrows her eyes, and Lilja notes as some wrinkles gather there. She obviously takes care of herself, but the vestiges of aging are visible. The lips are painted, turned slightly down in the hint of a permanent frown. Lilja waits a moment more, then gives a single nod, eyes then gone to Zoe as silent beckon before she heads out.

It doesn't take them long before they find the small stream, the gurgling of the water like a lure in the gentle noise of the area. Lilja finds herself enjoying it, though the heat and humidity are far more than what she is used to. This trek appeals to her love of nature. She stands beside the narrow vein of water, then turns and heads to follow it upstream. Zoe proceeds in the redhead's wake, her silence quite adeptly relaying her discontent.

The bubbling brook veers languidly right, and eventually the foliage and trees part, giving way to a manmade structure. Lilja halts, just observing, as Zoe slowly walks up, stopping beside her.

"A cemetery," the younger Hunter remarks, seeming to have finally regained the use of her voice.

Lilja nods, noting that not only are there markers which indicate the sites of graves, but there is also a small building that looks like a church. The place, though, stands in obvious disrepair, weeds and vines tangled up in some areas, and the structure itself shows signs of fire and neglect. Judging from the overgrowth and rot, the damage did not happen recently.

They walk toward the area, dead leaves crunching under their boots. One side of the building bears a large opening from the fire, and Lilja uses this rather than moving about to what is left of the door. Once inside, she sees the remnants of pews, the wood looking to have been of very good quality- dark, highly polished, the cushioning now dotted with mold and tears. She produces her small flashlight, turning it on to better see, for though a portion of the roof is gone, the angle of the setting sun does not offer much illumination. She halts the scan rather quickly, noticing a drawing on the wall.

"Hey, I found something outsi-" Zoe begins, coming into the room, but her voice stops as she peers at what is captured in the focus of Lilja's torch. "What's that supposed to be?" She asks, getting up a bit closer, then stopping to study the markings.

"I don't know," Lilja admits, also staring.

The work is crude, looking like graffiti, the broad swathes of paint seeming as though done by a child, thick with a charcoal-like texture. The form is obviously that of a bound woman, though the head metamorphoses into something like a deer, crowned with an impressive display of crooked antlers.

"It looks primitive," Zoe remarks, "like it's been here forever." She bends a bit at the knee, getting closer, bringing one hand up to gently wipe at it, giving way to a brief fall of gossamer dust.

She steps back, fishing out her mobile, holding it up to take a few quick snapshots. Once done, she glances at the device, eyes narrowing a bit, muttering, "Reception is poor out here."

"Do you think it has anything to do with what's been going on?" Lilja asks, still focused on the strange artwork.

Zoe cuts her eyes to the other Huntress, just looking.

"I don't know. You're lead."

Lilja fights to not roll her eyes. Zoe keeps making it painfully obvious she is upset at not being given the top role, but the job still needs doing. Lilja wishes Zoe would suck it up, act professional, and help them both to accomplish just that.

"You found something outside?" she asks, voice calm, expression rather bland.

"Oh, yeah," the shorn-haired girl recalls. "Check this out."

Lilja follows as they move out to the gravesites, noting where Zoe gives a casual point as she catches up.

"Fresh flowers," Lilja remarks, giving a slit to her eyes to belie her curiosity.

"Yeah. Over there, too."

She glances in the newly indicated direction, then looks about, noticing several places where fresh flowers have been left near certain markers.

"Pretty weird if you ask me," Zoe manages, the words seeming to tumble from her mouth as though more of thought.

Lilja blinks, looking over. "Is it not a custom in this country?"

Zoe gives a slight turn of her face, resolving into her own expression of confusion. She then shakes her head. "Nah, I mean the whole thing. This place has been burnt-out, left to rot, and that strange drawing in the church, but then fresh flowers on the graves, as if everything is *normal* ..."

Lilja gives a contemplative nod, then looks about further, wondering what else she may find. The foliage may not be as dense yet here in the cemetery, but the area is far from clear. She notices something in the near distance, something dark and gray.

"What's that?" She peers, standing on tiptoes, moving about as though to better see.

Zoe does similar, though seeming with less enthusiasm, and she gives another curt glance to her partner's back as Lilja heads off.

It proves to be a fountain, one somewhat large and giving memories of impressiveness. As it stands, the angel holding court in the center shows broken wings, lines of discoloration painting its face as though the stains of tears. Lilja steps nearer, noting the smaller statues, sentinels holding place at the four cardinal points. They prove so weathered, she cannot exactly tell what they are supposed to depict. The water within is still, stagnant, dark. Zoe leans down, sniffing, then wrinkles her nose, going back to her standing position.

"It's polluted." She gives to Lilja's casual, inquiring glance.

Lilja blinks, looking back, wondering what all this implies. The fountain should be clean, alive, vibrant, gurgling with a steady flow of water taken from the lifelines of this land, but it reposes within rot. She stares into the liquid, somewhat losing her focus, thoughts flowing out in a manner in which the soiled waters of the fountain do not. There is a bit of a shimmer from the reflection of the nearly set sun, a glimpse into the darkness of that fluid. She sees something, blinks again, rapidly.

"Did you-?" she begins, her eyes now narrowed, set, her body tense. "Did you see that?"

"See what?" Zoe is quick to respond, her tone a bit defensive.

"I thought …" Lilja begins, voice trailing off as she continues staring into the dark waters, her voice then resuming, though a whisper, "I thought I saw something."

When she finally moves her eyes away, turning to look at Zoe, the younger girl is just staring. She unloads silent judgment in that gaze.

"Let's head on back," Lilja finally says.

They make return to the house, no words exchanged during the short trek, and Lilja sees that more cars have arrived. She knows that this evening is some sort of soirée. The information had been gleaned, and they had deliberately come on this night. The small party happening the same evening gave Mrs. Barrington even more reason to be upset. She did not wish this intrusion during a social gathering to discuss and show her dead husband's artwork, but it had been chosen to use the fête as a diversion. There was also the general concern that the Infernal would be more prone to inflict one of their attacks during a night with many potential victims.

The history of these grounds shows a spotted, though irregular picture, no rash of recent murders, but the trail shines out plain enough to be seen. The Felcrafts had decided it was time to take action, and Lilja hopes to discern the nature of the infestation and deal with it in a manner resulting in as few casualties as possible.

A trio of well-dressed guests disappears through the open front door just as the two Hunters are meeting the bottom of the staircase. Lilja bounds up with a dancer's agility.

"Mrs. Barrington?" she calls to get attention, and the woman of the house halts, the congenial smile on her lips dropping as smoothly as she turns.

"Are you done, then?" she clips, and her guests seem to somewhat notice the change in demeanor, proceeding toward the innards of the house.

"No, ma'am. We're just getting started."

"Why can this not wait until another time?" the widow hisses, stepping closer to meet this unwanted pair on the porch, pulling the door somewhat closed as though a shield. "You can see I have guests," she adds, perking her penciled-on eyebrows.

"We found the cemetery on your property, ma'am," Lilja persists, "it looks as though the … *church*," she adds a question mark to the word, "had been burnt …?"

"That's correct. It was arson," Mrs. Barrington elaborates, somewhat defiantly, "but that is a matter of public record. It was a long time ago."

"Never bothered to rebuild?" Zoe tags in, her aspect much less diplomatic.

Mrs. Barrington gives the younger, less professional looking 'investigator' a very long look, one from which Zoe is not inclined to avert her eyes.

"No," she finally answers.

"There was a drawing of a woman to look like a deer. She had antlers," Lilja states.

"That's a buck. If they have antlers, they're male."

"This drawing depicted a person with obvious female characteristics," she presses.

"Like she was a sacrifice," Zoe interjects.

The older woman stares, seeming to almost become a statue. Lilja is not sure what part of the drawing may have drawn Zoe to this conclusion, but she just as quickly wonders if the statement was not made to ruffle feathers, to merely gauge reaction.

"We read about Imogene Wright, the thirteen-year-old girl who went missing and turned up on your property." Lilja shifts, and those eyes slip slowly to hers, the expression all but bleeding displeasure into the very air.

"That had nothing to do with us. They caught that man who did it. He dumped …" the hostess pauses, lips steeled into a straight line, a nearly imperceptible shake of her head, "the body on our land, yes, but we had nothing at all to do with it."

Lilja nods, ponderously, more seeming to offer mourning than agreement. When she returns her eyes to the woman, she notes the firm gaze and slightly raised chin. She all but feels the powerful will trying to get them to leave. It shall not work, as both Lilja and Zoe have faced much worse, but it is telling nonetheless. She begins to wonder if the woman has something to hide or perhaps has been unduly influenced.

Just then, more guests arrive, a dark, sleek automobile pulling into another place on the broad driveway.

"Come in, then, if you must," Mrs. Barrington coldly invites, "but I ask you to please be discreet, and please have a care for my property."

"Of course, ma'am, we'll be very-" Lilja begins, but the woman rudely walks through the duo, heading down to meet her most recent guests.

When Lilja looks over at Zoe, she gets a casual shrug as commentary, though she had half-expected some self-satisfied smirk. They head inside.

The place seems as grand within as without, the ceilings quite tall, the walls painted rich, dark colors, giving an overall ambience of warmth and shadow. The draperies on the front windows have been pulled aside, allowing some of the dwindling natural light to slip in. The illumination inside carries a deliberate affectation of gaslights and candles. They move through the small foyer, Lilja noting the fine marble tiles just there at the entrance, heading left into a spacious living room.

There are but a few guests here, and Lilja spies what seems a servant of some sort, holding a tray of beverages. The young woman looks rather smart in her dark, long skirt, if not somewhat old-fashioned. She visibly halts upon spying the two others as if realizing they are not here for the party. Lilja gives the girl a short look then turns away.

They meander to the large fireplace, eyes upon the quite sizable piece of art hanging above it, the canvas displaying a somewhat abstract, boldly painted figure within a sort of miasma. Some of the colors and shapes are quite distinct, but the overall impression is one of chaos.

"Does that remind you of anything?" Lilja asks, pitching her voice low, as if they were in a museum or library.

"Yeah, it looks like something a bunch of students would argue over in art history."

Lilja presses her lips together, moving her eyes away from her colleague to study the piece. It reminds her of the Infernal, and something in it also makes her think of the image on the wall of the burnt-out church. She recalls Skothiam once mentioning that sometimes people with an artistic bent may be more prone to sensitivity to the Infernal. She wonders if that may have been the case here. Perhaps Mr. Barrington had been a lure.

She glances over, noticing the hostess entering with the most recent arrivals, so she blinks her eyes to Zoe. "Let's go," she murmurs, giving a slight tilt of the head and making way out of the room.

The heels of their boots resound over the wood floor in the main hallway, pace slow, dictated by Lilja. More pieces of art are displayed, some framed canvases on the walls, pedestals supporting sculptures. They spare some time in perusal. Lilja feels captivated by the otherworldliness of the work. She rises up from a closer look at a tiny piece, the detail stunning, to see Zoe looking like a bored teenager.

They pass by another room, peeking in to notice several guests milling. A few heads turn their way, and she can all but feel the sneers. They end up in another chamber that holds no occupants.

"Lots of fireplaces in the house."

Lilja blinks her eyes to Zoe, nodding to the assessment. Though it may seem premature, all the rooms thus far seen have borne impressive such sections. Lilja is reminded of the time she found a secret passage in such a one. She wanders to the mantle, moving her hands along it, not disturbing any of the trinkets and décor resting atop the wood. She finds no hidden switches, but she still feels this place brims with secrets.

"Ah, hello."

They both turn to see a well-dressed man of likely holding age somewhere in his third decade. He carries himself with a certain, obvious degree of confidence and charm, the light curl of his lips adding to this.

"Hello," Lilja finally returns after some time of the two women just looking at him. Zoe continues to hold her tongue, seeming more taciturn than the generally quiet Finn.

"You two are here for the showing?" he tries, perking dark eyebrows as he shifts focus between them, the warm smile still on his mouth.

"Not exactly," Zoe grates.

"I … see," he obviously doesn't, but he continues, resetting himself, "I wonder what Mr. Barrington would think of all this."

Lilja just looks back, her manner one like stone. She finally blinks, the fraction of a motion and tilt to her head as response.

"Aaahh, he wasn't much for social gatherings," the man elaborates.

Lilja nods slowly, feeling the same.

"It's like a haunted house."

Both slip their eyes to Zoe.

"Mm, yes, I suppose it is," the man admits after a short silence, then almost musing, something of sincerity finally catching in his solicitous demeanor. "Full of memories."

"Hmm?" Lilja responds.

"A haunted house is full of ghosts, yes? Well, some, at least, and ghosts are memories," he elaborates, then extending his arms a bit, palms upward, gesturing like a salesman to encompass the room. "All of this is his memory … uh, Mr. Barrington's."

"It's like a funeral," Zoe continues her dry commentary.

It takes a short moment, but the grin snaps back to the man's face. "I suppose it somewhat is. Mr. Barrington was one for the somber and dark, that's for sure. You ought to see the rest," he adds, giving a little teasing twist to the final words.

"We intend to," Lilja remarks, then heads out.

Zoe gives the man a smirk, a silent taunt regarding the one that got away, then she heads to follow.

They find more rooms, some with fireplaces, confirming Zoe's speculation. They locate the kitchen, gaining some looks of confusion and surprise from the few workers there. One approaches, beginning effuse apologies and direction to points other than the work space, but Lilja gives a light, warm smile and single nod, leaving with a silent passage of comprehension. Such aimless wandering is how they end up in the dark, narrow hallway.

It doesn't seem like the rest of the house, from what they have explored. It is lit by spaced-out, recessed lights, the glow soft yet without the feeling of warmth found in the rooms comprising the party. This light is utilitarian, and there is not much of it. The hallway does not come to a dead end, but it does show a simple wooden door at a bend. Lilja tries it, but it proves locked. She stands there a moment, pondering.

"I've got it," Zoe murmurs, moving in, managing to displace her partner without any untoward collision.

Lilja watches, quickly noticing Zoe's intent. The younger girl merely picks the lock, quite adeptly, then slips the tools back into her pocket, standing and looking at Lilja as though the most mundane of chores has been done. Opening the door reveals a set of stairs heading down into a basement.

The area is quite dark, large, though they locate switches that lead to similar illumination as the hallway that brought them here. The chambers are vast, and they do not hold the sort of dank incompleteness one might expect from a basement. There is also the artwork.

"Wow, this guy really was weird," Zoe breathes as the two examine the pieces.

Lilja had spied the first shape when the lights had come on, wondering for a split second if someone else lurked down here, but they realize it is a strange collection of sorts. First the one, then another, yet another, and more – all held in acrylic glass cases, as though to keep them from escaping, showing predominately anthropomorphic shape, though obviously not entirely identical to humans.

One is of a woman, wearing a dark gray, nondescript dress that covers from wrists to ankle, but her face hides behind a mid-twentieth century gas mask. Close examination shows the mask to actually be part of her face, giving forth a meld that is quite out of the ordinary. Her hair is stringy in some places but others seem of ridged rubber. The combination is so well done as to somewhat trick the eye.

"Look at her fingernails," Zoe mentions, giving further personification to the statue.

Lilja notes the cracks and chips, the detail again as she had seen in the smaller works.

"It's like she tried to get free."

The redhead glances at her companion, noting a mingling of interest and awe that Zoe has not yet shown. She thinks back to the remark that the drawing in the church might depict a sacrifice.

"I think *he* was trying to escape."

"What?" Zoe asks, eyes narrowing a bit.

"I think this house is not just haunted, but it may have been his prison. Maybe he felt strangled by whatever visions compelled him to create."

"Yeah, well, I guess he's free now."

Lilja does not care for the quip, but she says nothing further, moving to examine more of the curious mannequins.

She finds one set up to appear as a ballerina, toes of the left foot *en pointe*, right tucked up and held just so. The form seems quite perfect, and though the piece holds beauty, the grotesquery shows as abundant as all of them down here. She begins to realize the displays they saw on the ground floor found themselves chosen due to being more palatable, this lower "dungeon" locked to hide the more disturbing things.

"It looks like skin…" she barely whispers, close enough to the transparent box that her nose almost touches, and she wonders if such material had indeed been used.

In her life as a librarian and curator of rare books, she knows of human skin being used as cover in bindings. It might not be the most lauded method, but she is not even sure if it would be against the law, depending on how one acquired such. Still, certainty hides behind the glass, examination prohibited. She snaps from the near-hypnotic study, remembering she is also not here as an admirer of art. Surely, if the dead artist proves a lure, his work may hold some clue, but they are not sure of that.

She turns, then, hearing Zoe calling, and judging from the intensity, it is likely not the initial summons. She heads over, giving a rapid pace to her steps to make up for getting lost in thought.

"What is it?"

"Check this out," the other girl replies, pointing to an open section in a wood wall.

Zoe has found a hardly hidden secret portal, opening it to reveal a small room, the area tight like a restrictive closet. Though one may be inclined to perhaps even think of the tiny chamber as such a room for storage, its innards tell otherwise.

There hang no clothes, stand no shoes, clutter no other forgotten objects. The space is empty. The wall, though, holds a drawing that appears at first blush to be by the same hand as painted the bound deer-woman in the burnt-out church. The lines are again thick, showing discontinuity as though of a careless or rushed manner, but something in the overall appearance screams deliberate intent.

The main attraction is a large star, covering a goodly portion of the back wall. It is crudely done, some of the points careening out further than others, though the topmost holds the most prominence. A quick scan counts seven points, and Lilja's mind immediately begins to seek for references. The one that hurls to the fore regards using such a symbol for the summoning and controlling of spirits.

But the star is not alone. Covering nearly the remainder of all walls is a word, repeated over and over. The manner of it feels unsettling, both in the appearance and its repetition. The scrawl of the letters holds aesthetic of its own, seeming the hand of one with as precarious a hold on sanity as the brush. Her memories again find Ernst as well as more of what she has learned of those who hold sensitivity to the hidden world populated by the Infernal and such mysteries. Without proper training or fortitude, mental unbalance often results.

"Do you know what it means?" Zoe asks, her voice a whisper, as though she has finally encountered something requiring care.

"No." Lilja slowly shakes her head.

She reads the word, over and over, taking it in, etching it into memory, but even with her background, recognition eludes her. What does *ananael* mean?

"It looks fresh," Zoe remarks, stepping in closer, her small flashlight picking up the shine on the markings. She even dares to dab a fingertip on one portion, and Lilja finds herself suddenly tense, ready to forbid the action. When Zoe pulls the digit back, it shows nothing.

They snap some quick photos with their phones, moving away from the cramped chamber.

"I'm going to send this to Skot now and see if he ..." but Lilja's voice trails off, face pinching up a bit as she looks at her phone.

"Yeah, the reception's pretty much gone down here," Zoe informs.

The underground level does indeed prove to be as large as those above, and for a time, they seem to be lost in another world. The sudden rise of a clomping noise pauses them instantly, eyes shooting upwards then slowly looking at one another.

"Maybe we should get back upstairs," Lilja suggests.

Sher turns to head to the stairs but pauses after nary a few steps, looking back to see Zoe just standing there.

"What is it?"

Zoe does not answer. She seems rapt with some concentration. She moves her light, angling the torch to the side, then back, then away, bringing it to bear on Lilja each time. She finally ceases with it away, leaving only the meager light from the bulbs in the ceiling.

"Lilja," she says, voice not quite a whisper but husky with some alarm, "your shadow is upside down."

The redhead freezes for an instant, then shifts her face to the cast from the lights. Her eyes widen, tension taking her form as she spies her silhouette. It stands on its head.

"We have to get to the car, get our gear," she begins, still staring at the inverted form, but her calmly issued orders are interrupted by further noise.

There comes another thump from above, and they hear reactionary cries. A louder, sharper sound then chews on the heels of this one, a brash strike and resultant crack followed by similar. This has arisen from down here in the basement.

Both pull their sidearms, Lilja expertly gripping a Glock 19 while Zoe holds her Kahr P9, each loaded with the specially crafted and treated rounds which promise pain to demons. Not rushing, handheld lights shine the way, sweeping gently for threats as they move back toward the staircase. More noises from above, thumps and shouts, even a crash. Zoe's eyes veer upwards momentarily only to return to the path ahead. A light catches something, stopping in its motion as does the carrier, knees bending a bit as feet hold place, eyes studying.

"What is it?" Zoe asks, moving in closer, her own light staying in a different direction, increasing coverage.

"One of them got out," Lilja mutters, and Zoe then looks over, seeing what had recently caused the ruckus here- a container holding one of the many disturbing-looking mannequins has been broken, its occupant nowhere in sight.

The younger Huntress does not bring her light around to add to the glow, instead keeping it angled away as she steps forward, eyes narrowing a bit then widening with outré intent. She sees now with more than normal sight, scanning. Lilja has moved her own torch aside, knowing that such is not needed for Zoe to engage this ability. She continues to sweep the area, offering protection.

"Nothing," Zoe finally whispers, gaining a quick glance. "I don't see any signs. Maybe this whole … thing," she opts, looking up for the word, "is just some distraction to steal this art."

"No," Lilja calmly assesses, still looking around the dark room, "something else is going on."

Zoe's shrug shows slightly, but Lilja does not see, for she continues her careful movement. Though she does not entirely agree with her own flippant suggestion, Zoe wonders what really is happening here. She holds a singular adeptness at tracking and finds it odd that she sees nothing coming from the case. This makes her think there is nothing of the Infernal involved. Just because something odd or dangerous is happening doesn't mean it has to be them. Still, there was Lilja's shadow.

But it seems they are not the only ones gifted at tracking and silence, and only because she had turned back to speak to Lilja does Zoe spy the motion in the direction from whence they have come. Whatever it is must have circled around in pursuit.

"Contact rear!" Zoe cries out, firing quickly, two rounds shooting in the direction of that motion, brief lines of amber tracing the path and giving hint of the bullet's imbuement.

Lilja reacts instantly, instinctively, bending at her knees, turning in the direction of the possible threat. She sees something in the flash from the shots, some motion in the darkness, something dark itself. She hears the noise, a whispered skittering, and she also opens fire as Zoe adds more bullets.

Both now have flashlights shining unerringly on the attacker, and as they step closer, Lilja feels confusion rising from the seeping leak of adrenalin. She is nearer, and she sees quite well the form of the mannequin, sprawled now down on the ground, a portion of its upper body and one arm up along the wall. There doesn't seem to be any fluid of any kind, but there is obvious damage. It looks as though they merely shot the inanimate thing, leaving it broken and ruined.

17

"What's going on?" she dares to whisper, hesitant to even utter the question.

Zoe glances at her, and even if this scenario were not doubtful enough, there still emerges the clamor from above.

"We'd better get upstairs."

Lilja nods, turning to lead the way, Zoe keeping a sharp eye behind as they mount the steps.

The ruckus comes louder here, but it still proves somewhat muted by the distance created by the narrow hallway. They carefully traverse the length, noticing more than a rise to the chaotic sounds.

"It's warmer," Lilja mentions, and she thinks she knows why.

She peers about a corner, keeping low. A scream peels forth from somewhere, then rapid footsteps, those closer. She shifts her eyes about, hoping to catch a glimpse of something. She hears whimpering. A motion of her head serves as silent command, and they move, walking into a nearby room to find a woman crouched behind an overturned, antique-looking sofa.

The desperate, repeated words of denial flutter up like dancing petals on puffs of coiling wind. The woman is so lost in her fear, she does not realize someone else is right there.

"Ma'am?" Lilja tries, voice calm, though she maintains some distance. She knows that people in the grip of such panic may also prove a threat, even if unintended.

The woman sucks in a sharp breath, eyes opening, going back, head following in stuttered motion, and when finally seeing the other two, she screams, scampering to her feet, heels giving poor purchase on the hard floorboards.

"It's okay," Lilja delivers, but the woman's wide eyes seem to gulp in more terror than anything her ears might hear. "We're here to help. Everything is going to be okay."

She gets closer, both their handguns diverted. Though there may linger the nagging doubt of possible possession, the woman shows none of the signs they've learned to seek. Lilja holds up a hand, leaning a bit closer to give a placating touch. The woman's trembling grows, head shaking slowly, as though breaking free from some frozen hold. She then exhales a forced, stuttering breath through her mouth, air crashing over bared teeth, and she turns to flee.

"Hey, wait, stop!"

The woman does not heed, but her escape is short-lived as she collides with a window so harshly as to render herself unconscious. Lilja rushes over, crouching to the crumbled form, checking for a pulse. She then looks up at Zoe.

No words are exchanged, for both recognize the signs of sheer panic and ruin, mental instability that comes with a demon attack. Confusion still clamors regarding the encounter in the basement, for it did not show what they'd consider the usual signs, and were it not for the situation in these other parts of the manor, they might think themselves the butt of a practical joke.

"Let's get to the car," Lilja says, gaining a single nod of compliance from Zoe.

They make it some ways down the main hallway before the ceiling collapses.

The noises had risen from the floor above, growing louder, more imminent, giving way to an increased pace, but they had been too slow, too careful. The sound ripped forth, squeezes and breaks growing to a roar, the wound showing, wood, debris, and burnt furniture pouring out like so much strange viscera, blocking the front door.

"Fire," Zoe breathes, the comment almost a question, and both realize they now have a much more critical situation to resolve.

Footsteps from above announce the continued presence of others, seeming to indicate fleeing if not possible fighting. Yelling pitches out further signs, panic as well as challenge. The two Hunters exchange another look, turning to head to the staircase. Going up in a burning building may prove a bad idea, but they wish to confront whatever is causing this as well as save as many people as they can.

The heat intensifies halfway up, flickers of light indicating the flames. They must hurry. Further noises guide them as well as merely navigating the obvious path away from the fire, and they find three people cowering in a room. One man looks out the window, likely gauging it as a possible escape route, while the other stands guard over the third, a woman. He holds a piece of wood in his hand, what looks like the polished and curved leg of a chair. He starts when the two Hunters enter, legs flexing, his hand going up to brandish the makeshift weapon. The other man turns from the window, bracing his back against it.

"We're here to help," Lilja says, gun again averted, free hand held up in a warding gesture.

Zoe immediately scans the room, taking a few steps in, eyes briefly noticing the occupants before taking a position that allows her to cover the door.

"I saw you two earlier. You're not guests," the man says, his notice finding their weapons as he continues to hold up his own. "Who are you?"

"I'm Lilja, and this is Zoe. We're Special Investigators, sent here exactly because of this situation."

"The fire?" the woman pitches.

An awkward silence takes the moment.

"You going to put out the fire with that?" Zoe grates out.

The man glances at the piece of wood in his hand.

"There's more going on here than a fire," Lilja says, trying to gain better control of the situation. "Everyone calm down, and, sir, put the weapon down."

A tense few moments arise as the man contemplates compliance. Lilja and Zoe stand ready, too far for him to be any seeming threat. They have handguns to back up their force, but Lilja knows this may merely add to their perceived danger. Seeming with little choice, the man drops the wood, backing away, though he remains in a position of protection near the other woman.

Lilja casts her eyes on them for a quick moment then moves to the window. The man steps back as she peers out, not taking her full attention away from those in the room.

"Can we get out that way?" Zoe asks.

"It's risky. Someone would get hurt."

"Did you kill those people?"

Lilja turns her eyes to the man by the window, noticing the insistent fright that has crept over him.

"What people? What happened?" Lilja asks.

"Two people," the man who had lately been armed replies. "I don't even remember their names. One … she had her throat cut, and the guy-" He takes in a deep breath. "His head was twisted around."

"We didn't do that," Lilja speaks quickly, though calmly, on the heels of the man's announcement.

"Janice," comes a whisper, and everyone looks to the woman, her makeup smeared from tears. "That was her name. I- I don't know the man's name." She swallows, tension showing in her throat, seeming to have to force the words. "Bu- ... but her name was Janice."

Lilja nods, no more eulogy given.

"Do any of you know this house well, or where Mrs. Barrington might be?" she asks. "We need to get everyone and find a way out. The front door is blocked, but we can all get down the stairs and out another way. We need to get moving."

The three just look back, reluctance and fear showing itself. Lilja realizes they likely did not know the front door is blocked, and yet even with the fire, they were hiding away up here in this room.

"I know you're afraid, but we-" and she halts her words at a crisp shush from Zoe, looking over.

The Huntress stares ahead at nothing, merely listening, moving very slowly toward the open doorway. Lilja hears it, too, then, though she knows her senses are not as sharp as Zoe's preternatural abilities. Rapidly approaching footsteps resound from the hallway.

The other three hear it, eyes going wide with alarm, and just as Lilja commands, "Get back!" the figure bursts into the room.

It is a large man, his suit jacket open, clothing showing disheveled, torn, bloodstained, and if the darkly-coated butcher knife in his fist were not sign enough, his eyes bleed out with a strange, red hue. Those orbs see Lilja, and he roars, eating a few precious seconds before he launches himself at his prey.

During that short time, Lilja not only sizes him up, but she sees something, something within him, like cracks, tiny fractures in the foundation likely long forgotten yet not gone, and now they seep with the damage of a red flood. Contemplation, though, is not a luxury, and she strikes out with a pressing front kick to the man's knee, causing it to buckle and bend the wrong way. He seems to hardly register what ought to be shooting pain, though it does slow his advance, but his momentum proves unstoppable. Lilja raises her arms into an A-block, protecting her head from the attack, feeling the collision of the man's arm as he tries to stab her, his force bringing them both to the ground, the Glock knocked out of her hand.

The attacks come in a savage fury, and she is tied up with using both hands to try to stop or mitigate the blows. Lilja feels the scratch of the blade a few times, knowing these are superficial wounds, but her attacker seems unwilling to let up, huffing and heaving with the enraging passion that fills him. He comes down with a two-handed stab directly at her face, putting all his body weight behind it. She resists, summoning all her strength, and then in that instant, it stops.

The knife falls free, and she feels the weight from the man increase. Zoe is there, having given the assailant a knock to the base of the skull with her gun, and the two of them shove him over. Heavy breathing and a certain look from Lilja's eyes suffices for thanks, acknowledged by the single nod from Zoe. The redhead looks about, seeing her sidearm none too far away, retrieving it.

"We have to restrain him," she manages between gulps of air, noticing the man's tie.

It seems much less worse for wear than the rest of his suit, and as she grabs it, she feels that it is silk. Good. It provides a suitable binding for his wrists, and she turns to see the man who had lately held the makeshift weapon of wood handing over his leather belt to help. She uses it to bind the ankles, then stands.

"What just happened?" the other man asks, voice full of shock. "Why would Ronald attack us like that?"

"We-we're not going to leave him here, are we?" the woman adds.

Lilja looks about, noting the continued promise of the growing flames, hungry flickers of light from down the hall. Then she sees another type of movement.

"Zoe," she gives out a quick word, eyes moving from the girl to the open doorway.

They make themselves ready, but this does not prove a similar sort of attack, instead the lady of the house comes into the room, seeming to still hold some of her stately poise. Lilja takes a step nearer, hoping the woman is alright, but she is halted by a gaze that holds as much flame as the encroaching blaze.

"You!"

She does not point, but the steel of her unblinking gaze suffices, her body gone rigid.

"Mrs. Barrington-" Lilja begins, her voice coated in soft, soothing tones.

"Do *not* address me," the woman clips Lilja's words, "*you* have done this."

A quick scan shows both hands held in front, and though the aged fingers curl as though the beginning of claws, she is unarmed. Lilja does not think the woman would be much of a threat, but she is clearly agitated.

"Calm do-" she begins, and again, is quickly interrupted.

"You did this! You brought this here. *You* are the curse."

"Charlotte? What are you talking about?"

Lilja notices as the once-armed man steps forward. She moves away a bit, watching closely.

"The stories," the hostess replies. "We've all heard those *damnable* tales. I've endured them for the sake of my husband and home, but look." She gazes about, the carnage evident and mounting, and it seems a crack begins in her controlled exterior.

Lilja stares, trying to use her own sense to detect if something worse is about to happen, something similar to the motive force that once possessed the large, bound man. "We have to get out of this house," she says.

This seems to fuel Mrs. Barrington, her composure returning, eyes narrowing as they pinpoint on the speaker.

"What good will that do?" she challenges. "You've already brought ruin here. This is *your* fault!"

Lilja remains calm, though urgency still claws at them. She can hardly believe what she hears, but as she casts her eyes over, she notices that the others have moved away. "How could I possibly-"

"Look *around* you," Mrs. Barrington interrupts. "My beautiful home. My party. People are *dead*. This is no coincidence. You are unwanted here. Look what you've done."

"Why are you two here exactly?"

Lilja turns to the man, the one who seems more possessed of will and courage than the other.

"We're Special Investigators-" she manages before he cuts her off.

"Investigating what? What agency are you with?"

"We don't have time for-"

"You!" Mrs. Barrington points, looking ready to come unhinged, "You've brought *ruin* unto me."

Another glance shows the other woman has moved further away, tucking herself against the wall, even giving glances to the door as though she may flee.

"I did not cause this," Lilja says, retaining her calm, even tone, "I'm here to help."

"I don't think it's a good idea for us to do anything you say," the man speaks.

Mrs. Barrington gives a curt nod, moving closer to Lilja, puffing out her chest a bit. "This is *my* house, and I will-"

Zoe steps forward. "Look, lady, the fucking house is burning down around us, and people are dying. We're in deep shit, and we're here to help you out of it. Your legs aren't broken, so use them and let's get out while we still can."

The moment lengthens. Zoe glares at the older woman, and she cowers. It's subtle but noticeable. No one else does anything until Lilja speaks.

"Mrs. Barrington, the front door is blocked. We need another way out of the house." She is pleased, at least, that this time she was not interrupted.

"What about Ronald?" one of the others asks.

"I am not leaving someone in a burning house. Phones are not working in here. We need to get out. We can call for help from our car," Lilja states, giving a brief pause to let it all sink in as she sets her eyes on each person. "Now, let's get moving."

Heading to the doorway, giving a cautious peer into the hall, she feels more heat from the fire, a passing moment given to wondering of its cause. Lilja steps out, moving more quickly, checking the stairway. When she looks back, the others are trailing, Zoe in the rear.

"Mrs. Barrington," she summons, standing close to the woman, "you'll take them downstairs and out another way than the front door."

"I know my own house," the woman clips, eyes still holding anger, preparing to head down.

"Mrs. Barrington?" Lilja halts her, and the woman turns, reluctant, seething. "There have to be more people in here. Do you have any idea where they are?"

"The ones that aren't *dead*?" she challenges, and the redhead merely stares back. "Try the third floor." She gives a dismissive shake of the head, then turns and moves downwards.

Zoe stops after the others have gotten on the staircase, looking at Lilja. "You want me to go with them?"

"Yes. Make sure they get out, and call emergency services."

She gives a single nod, then sets forth.

Fire, darkness, and ash hold sway now. Lilja wipes at her brow with the sleeve of her light jacket, then takes hold of her pistol with both hands, moving out to check what she can of this floor and find the stairway leading up.

She keeps a wary eye. She knows something odd happened in the basement, even if it did not seem like a familiar sort of demonic attack. Ronald's possession had been textbook, and thinking of this makes Lilja realize she needs to hurry. She had hoped the man would regain consciousness rather quickly.

She stumbles on more remains before finding any access to the topmost floor. Three corpses, all showing signs of death by physical trauma as opposed to the fire, blood spewed about in further evidence. She wonders if these are more of Ronald's kills and frowns a bit, thinking of the horrible path lying ahead for the poor man, if he even survives.

She hears a crashing in the distance, sounding like more of the third floor giving way. She has already discerned the part of the house most consumed by the raging fire. It's quite possible the stairs to the third floor are already gone. Lilja pauses, then, holding place, listening. She thought she heard a scream coming on the tail of the crash. She doesn't hear anything else, but she moves off in that direction.

She finds a room, the door ajar. She peeks in, slowly opening it further, trying to gain more vantage on the chamber. It seems relatively intact, except for the gaping hole in the far wall that opens into an adjoining room. She spies flames beyond that as she steps further inside. Then she hears it- whimpering.

She follows, finding a small, dark figure huddled in a corner, rocking in place. It proves to be a woman, one of the staff, judging by her clothing.

"Hey," Lilja calls out, gaining a quick rise of a head, as though a fidgety bird on the lookout for predators. "It's okay. I'm here to help."

"Oh, god." The woman turns wide, teary eyes on Lilja. "I thought everyone else was dead. I saw them," she continues, scooting back a bit, bumping against the exterior wall. "Their faces were melting from the heat," she speaks through a hitching breath, "from the fire, and then ... Why do you have a gun?"

Lilja averts the barrel further, somewhat obscuring the weapon aside her hip, holding up her other hand, displaying its emptiness. "I'm a Special Investigator. My name is Lilja. I'm here to help."

"You're a cop?"

"I'm ..." She inhales, feeling the tinge of heat in it. "Something like that, yes. Let's get out of here. Come on."

The woman does not move, somehow finding a way to mash more of herself against the wall. "But ... the fire, and the ... the people. Everyone's going crazy," she says, and Lilja hears that threat of unhinging in the woman's voice.

"Calm down," she soothes, moving closer. "I can get you out of here, okay? Okay?"

The woman finally gives a jittery nod.

"I'm Lilja," she repeats, "what's your name?"

"Vicki."

"You work here, right, Vicki?"

"Y-yes, for the party."

"You know the house, then? You can help us find a way out?"

"W-what?" she replies, seeming stymied even as Lilja uses the conversation to try to further soothe the woman, holding out her hand now as bid to take it and rise.

Showing on the verge of such, her hand held up somewhat, Lilja takes the opportunity to grab the woman and pull her to her feet.

"The front door is blocked because of the fire. We'll need another way out."

"Oh." Vicki seems somewhat lost, then she nods. "There are other doors. I know of other doors."

"Okay. Let's go, but we need to check for others first. How do we get upstairs?"

"No!" Vicki jerks her hand free, moving back to the wall.

Lilja furrows her brow.

"The- the- *no!*" She rapidly shakes her head. "The fire. The stairs are gone. Everyone up there is dead. I saw. I saw."

"Okay, okay," Lilja calms. "Let's get out of here while we still can, okay?"

Vicki gives a rapid nod. "There's a service entrance, or that's what Mrs. Barrington called it," Vicki explains once they make it back to the ground floor, "maybe we can use that."

"Which way?"

Seeming to have regained some of her composure, Vicki makes to step forward, but Lilja halts her with a light hand to her arm.

"I'll lead. Just tell me which way."

Vicki nods, seeming to understand, and she points, giving a few directions. Lilja recalls her and Zoe's earlier accidental walk into the kitchen area. It would make sense to have a door there leading outside.

The heat seems thankfully abated here, giving more credence to the supposition that it started above. Lilja knows, though, they haven't much time. She hopes Zoe and the others made it out safe and that emergency services rush even now to get here. Her thoughts snap back to sharper focus when she hears the sounds of struggling.

"Wait," she commands Vicki, then creeps forward to the kitchen.

The place shows its own expected amount of disarray, though this seems more chaos than fire, as if someone merely went through all the cabinets and drawers and caused a whirlwind. She thinks she knows the culprit.

"He's choking!" comes the voice behind her, and it seems Vicki's curiosity has given her to not exactly wait. "It's smoke from the fire!"

The fire has not crept this far, but Lilja understands why the other woman might make this assessment. She sees the figure of a man on the ground, struggling for breath, but she also sees what Vicki does not – the dark, indistinct shape of a demon atop him.

It sits there, perched on his chest, diabolical weight no doubt hindering the man's lungs. It holds a globular form, seeming more a heavy bag of thick fluid. It does possess appendages though, like a many-armed spider. Those limbs work to keep the victim restrained, skeletal thin with stretched flesh barely containing them, ending in all too human-looking hands. As if this were not enough, it is bent over, its own face, if it even possesses such a thing, attached to that of the man, sucking the life away.

Lilja hears a stifled yelp and glances back to see that Vicki stares wide-eyed, hand over her mouth as if to protect her from the life-threatening smoke.

"Stand back," the redhead warns, then she takes aim.

Those eyes go wider, the other woman unsure what is happening. Lilja knows the confusion that must clamor through Vicki's mind, and she needs to act fast. Not only does she not want to invite interference, but she'd also prefer not to have to make explanations. Giving another brief moment to settle her aim, she fires.

The bullet sinks into the thing's bulbous body, almost as if sucked in and absorbed like a sandbag deterring a shot. Lilja fires again, following with two more, and the thing finally breaks its hold. She sees that it does have a face – a rugose crowd of fallow flesh held in some semblance of form, and it screams at her, showing a crowd of tiny hooks lining the inside of that maw. It releases the man, using arms and the suddenly quite capable motion of its sickening body to launch itself at her.

She holds her ground, pulling the trigger rapidly, aim unflinching, as she empties the magazine into the thing. It lies there, then, defeated and diffusing, seeming more a dark stain than anything animate. She smoothly ejects the magazine, loading another and putting away the empty.

"What?" comes a huffed call, and she knows it is Vicki, though hearing is temporarily hindered for them both. "What?" again coming on the pauses between gulped breaths. "I saw something."

Lilja ignores it, rushing to the man, seeing it is the one who tried to flirt with her when they first were exploring the house.

"Wake up," she says, giving him a shake at his shoulders, and when this has no effect, she delivers some light slaps to his cheeks.

This works, and he begins to come around.

"Careful," she offers, sending a quick glance to Vicki who has slipped over. "You were unconscious," she adds, placing a supportive hand on the man's back, helping him to turn to his side.

"Wha-?" he tries, coughing and gasping, the word squeezing off in his sore throat.

"You were unconscious. We're at the party at the Barrington house. There's been a fire. We need to get out."

He takes in a few more breaths, shaking his head somewhat, eyes blinking, then he nods.

"Okay," he manages, then looks up, recognition floating over his face, and his lips twitch into the hint of a grin. "Thanks."

"What's your name?" she asks, her tone calm.

"Haran."

"Haran, I'm Lilja. This is Vicki."

"Hi," he somewhat manages, coughing.

"We need to get you out of here."

"I don't feel so well."

"I know, and I wish I didn't have to move you, but we need to get going," she repeats, looking about for any further signs of the Infernal, then glancing to Vicki. "The service door?"

"It's right there." She indicates, and indeed there is a door none too far from them.

Lilja breathes a sigh of relief, then gets the other woman's help in standing and supporting their charge.

"Lilja!"

She looks up from the shambling cadence they use to hold Haran, the man seeming more weakened by the demonic attack than they initially thought, to see Zoe running to her. She quickly displaces Vicki, proving better assistance.

"I called 911. They'll be here any minute. I hear sirens."

Lilja doesn't, but that also doesn't surprise her.

"This is far enough," she says, and they help to set Haran on the soft grass of the yard. "You rest here," she orders, removing her jacket and draping it over him.

"I-" he coughs out a short, embarrassed chuckle, "don't need this."

"Yes, you do. You might even need to lie down. Take it easy until the paramedics get here."

"What are you doing?" Zoe asks, noticing a particular set to her colleague.

"There are more people inside. That woman we first found and the guy who attacked us. I'm not leaving them in there."

She glances across the way, seeing the accusatory eyes of Mrs. Barrington on her.

"Right," Zoe nods once, "let's get to it, then."

They turn to head back inside, going to a jog.

"I also saw a de-" Lilja begins, but her words stop as an explosion erupts from within the house, shooting glass and wood splinters out from the first floor.

They both freeze, not close enough to experience any damage, then rush toward the spot. There, in the distance, is a shape, shrouded in darkness and the flickering shadows from flame. A survivor. Lilja picks up the pace. The figure rises, seeming incapable of normal movement, perhaps wounded. She wants to cry out for them to not move, to just wait, but something halts her tongue. The shape gets to its feet, still wobbly, but it looks uncanny, wrong, and then as it turns, focusing on her, she realizes it is another of the mannequins from the basement. It begins walking toward her, stunted and bobbling.

Lilja stops, bringing her weapon up and aiming. She freezes, feeling a sudden creep boiling up like a lingering flame finally reaching crescendo – she recognizes the figure.

Zoe rushes up beside her, settling into a shooting stance, but then she glances at her partner, confusion inking onto her features.

"Lilja," she hisses out a whisper, "what is it?"

"We don't just lurk in shadow ... we also live in dust."

Zoe slowly moves her eyes over, realizing this has come from the mannequin. The voice is somewhat high-pitched, strangled, though still managing a deeper undertone, hinting at being carried on a foul wind. Lilja still stands in place, eyes wide, unblinking, as though latched onto the thing against her will. The mannequin continues its shamble, stumbling ever closer.

Whispered words finally fall from Lilja's lips. "But ... you're supposed to be dead."

"Varjolilja ... you are bound to me. You *owe* me," the thing speaks again.

Zoe does not exactly remember this one, for it bears the appearance of a young man, though still cracked and distorted, but it looks more human on its face than the others.

Zoe experiences a moment of further confusion and hesitation. She does not understand how the Infernal manage to possess these dolls; the oddity of the whole thing gives her pause. She continues glancing back and forth between Lilja and the encroaching mannequin. Why Lilja seems so suddenly stunned? Even though it chapped her to not be given lead on this assignment, she knows Lilja to be very controlled and to the point, unhesitating even as she displays a great deal of calm. Zoe also knows the Infernal have tricks they've never encountered.

Zoe pulls the trigger of her pistol, firing continuously. The thing takes four shots before it crumbles. She glances at Lilja, the redhead still unmoving, so she walks carefully toward the target. It lies on the ground, twitching a bit, so she puts two more rounds in its head, not exactly sure if that makes a huge difference, but it does stop the moving. She then trots back over to Lilja.

"What was that all about?" she demands, noticing that the emergency vehicles are now pulling up.

"I …" Lilja begins, the word seeming to come from the depths of her, robbed of its volume and strength.

"Are you alright?" Zoe presses, eyes narrowing.

Lilja blinks, then nods.

"Good. We need to put our guns away and let them handle this now, right?" She gives an indication behind Lilja with a jab of her chin.

Further blinks, then a breath, and Lilja turns, seeing several vehicles have arrived. The people within quickly begin to take control, lengths of hoses being pulled out in preparation of dealing with the fire, paramedics seeing to the milling people. She also notices Mrs. Barrington speaking to a police officer, a meaningful glare sent their way.

"Right," she finally responds.

"It seems her sense is coming along."

Skothiam looks over at his sister. Nicole-Angeline wears, as usual, something gossamer, ethereal, looking less and less like a conventional occupant of this corporeal world. He is dressed in one of his many bespoke suits, having spent time today in more conventional dealings. He'd felt distracted as his thoughts often meandered to Lilja. They'd conducted the formal debriefing as soon as possible when the two had arrived back at the manor. From business to debriefing to this, and the day escapes. He holds a crystal glass of fine scotch in his hand, taking a lingering sip.

"You know this?" he asks.

She gives a steady look of her eyes, then a single nod.

Anxiety gnawed him after the fact. Had he made an incorrect decision in sending only those two? He knows they are capable, and he knows there are always risks. Still, sending the woman he loves on such operations fills him with conflict. He is proud of her, fully confident in her abilities, and yet, every assignment could be the last. It seems she is developing another talent that will make her even more valuable, thus putting her more and more in the face of danger.

"You must realize the attack was for her."

His eyes move over again to his younger sister. He exhales deeply, then glances into his drink as if he might scry some solution from the contents.

"Varjolilja," his sister intones, reminding him that answers await, open and before them, ripe for the plucking.

"Yes, she told us everything that happened."

"I am not attacking her, Skot."

He sighs again.

"Your love for her tempts you to compromise."

"I know," he finally admits, "I'm also worried because of what they said about Dad."

The message sent by the Infernal had come nearly a year ago now, but it still remained emblazoned in their concern, raw like a fresh brand.

"We cannot know if their taunt is true," Nicole says, moving nearer, her own features now laced with sorrow, for she had been very close to their father.

"And it is their way to do just this sort of thing. They want to gut us, weaken or kill us all."

"*That*, we do know."

"So, her dead ex-boyfriend shows up in the face of an animated mannequin and calls her 'Shadow' Lilja. Both she and Zoe saw her shadow inverted." Skot has a deep taste of his drink. "What are we supposed to make of that?"

"First of all, it was not her dead ex-boyfriend."

"I know," he clips, gaining a stare from his sibling.

"But it means they are aware of this piece of her past, and they feel it is a weak link they can exploit."

He nods to the words, knowing they are something of an apology for the quip.

"We had thought once that she was bothered by paranoia. She is," Nicole continues, gaining a pointed look from her brother. "Not the kind we originally assumed. She worries of hurting those she cares about. One way to absolve that is to stop letting people close. To not overly care about anyone."

"She is not heartless."

"I am not saying that." Nicole returns the stare, the link acting as though it may shift to a challenge. "You act as you do out of defense for her. You know that does no good. I am not the one attacking her."

Skothiam releases a deep sigh, looking away. He has more of his drink, noting it is nearly gone. He refrains from making another.

"There is more," Nicole resumes, then adding as though the coax of a sharp needle, "Whatever she saw in the waters of the fountain."

"What?"

"She saw something in those waters."

"How do you know? She didn't say anything about that."

"Zoe did."

Though it sometimes feels like mistrust, they generally conduct debriefings as a team and then individually. Not only are their different senses and vantages to consider, but the very nature of what they do is mysterious, even compromising. Zoe had said little during the group meeting, but she had found her voice when away from Lilja.

"You were there when Zoe gave her version of the events. You know she mentioned the fountain and the effect it had on Lilja. You are still acting in blind defense of her. If it bothers you so much, then stop-"

"I won't remove her from field work," Skot quickly says, then more contemplatively, perhaps even sorrowfully, "we both know she'd carry on independently, anyway."

"Which is even more dangerous."

Skothiam nods.

Time stretches, a weighty quiet. Nicole studies her brother, the Head of the Family. She looks to almost go into a trance, such is her unblinking focus. He does not notice, lost in his own mental travels.

"They are targeting her," he finally speaks, musing. "Why? Zoe is much more experienced and a blood member of the family-"

"And Zoe is more stalwart in the face of such attempts." Nicole cuts into his thoughts.

Skothiam looks over, another small battle of stares.

"I begin to worry of many things," Nicole speaks, her words floating like a prophecy.

"What is that supposed to mean?"

"Lilja is marked," she expands, holding place like a statue, studying her brother closely. "For whatever reason, they are laying traps for her. Such effort cannot be dismissed."

He exhales into a nod, then decides to refill his drink. He moves to the bar service, taking his time with the selection of ice cubes and pouring of fine scotch. Nicole sees it, knowing he is trying to buy time, trying to avoid the picture being painted before him.

"The heptagram ... and the strange word they found – *ananael*," he leads.

"It is Enochian."

"The language of the Angels?"

"If one is inclined to believe Edward Kelley. Not the most reputable fellow, according to several sources," Nicole remarks.

Skothiam nods, familiar enough with this but not familiar enough to have so immediately recognized the word.

"What does it mean?"

"Secret wisdom."

He nods, slowly, thoughts careening through his mind.

"It would be simple enough for the artist to have known of this and painted the word of his own volition."

"Of course."

"But there is something else."

"Hmm?" He looks over to his sister, the silence having again grown.

"Allow me some time to check into these things, then I will tell you more."

Water. Droplets falling like a natural metronome. They create a soothing rhythm, one that speaks of calm even as it acts a herald to change unseen and unseeing.

Varjolilja. Why was he even there? Why did that demon take on his face?

Lilja strikes the punching bag with a particularly powerful blow, following it up with several more. Her hands are taped, but they will end this exercise bloody. She is not conducting class, nor having one of her post-class workouts. This is exercise she craved, hoping to face the whispers in her own mind, or at least perhaps elude them.

What did it mean for them to invert her shadow? Varjolilja ...

She bounces lightly on her feet, hardly thinking of such movements, face seeming calm, but furrows take it as the doubts take her. Her lips barely part, showing clenched teeth, and she strikes the bag again and again and again.

She is not a bad person.

She teaches her classes to help women. She is a good girlfriend to Skot. She protects the book!

Lilja lashes out again, hoping to punctuate each point, rising forth with a knee, then a kick. It is as if each hit hopes to dig a trench for her resolve. Yet doubt proves a merciless adversary.

Still, she has been approached to expand her classes, to teach men, to teach emergency workers, police, even military personnel. She has declined all of those. Why?

And Skot ... Skot has been very patient with her, though she knows he wants more commitment. He doesn't press, but she knows he remains here in the City for her, not for the Book. He would marry her if given the chance. He'd welcome her back in their palatial manor in the United States. She avoids all of those. Why?

The chains holding the punching bag rattle out their resistance as her strikes again intensify. She dances about, the only breath given forth coming from her exertions. She does not call out any of her hits, though she also does not care if anyone is about that might hear her. She is focused, determined, still working on a dual front of conquering and evading. She knows in the back of her mind that those two do not work together, but she is not exactly sure how to rectify the situation. She has run before, fled, escaped, or so she thought.

Why was his face on that demon?

And she hears the name again, like a petal fluttering on warm winds, the edge tickling at her flesh as it tumbles by – Varjolilja.

She is not a shadow! Punch, punch, punch!

The bag does not move of its own accord. It is not a cogent opponent. She fights the whispers, she flings her fist in an effort to smash that tickling petal, to destroy it.

They inverted her shadow. Did they take a part of her and taint it? Do they merely show what is already there? Punch, punch, punch!

She finally stops, realizing tears have welled up and fallen in streaks down her face. She also bears a sheen of sweat. She is thankful no one has seen. She grabs a nearby towel, wiping her face. She heads to the shower, knowing a good, long time beneath the blast of the hot water will do her good.

Other things do not clean so easily.

Therese has done as asked. It had been a strange request. She had been eager for something, she had to admit, having heard nothing from the elusive vigilante for some time. She had watched the news, her electronic sniffers doing a better job than the normal outlets, and nothing of note had been found. The City, for once, seemed to be enjoying a calm.

She knew it was something worth celebrating, but she missed the work.

She also knew that was not entirely honest. She missed the vigilante.

That even was not entirely honest.

She missed her self-defense instructor, Lilja, the one whom she felt all but certain was the shadowy crusader. Therese never learned why Lilja's apartment was in the state it had been when she broke in those months ago. She never got her confirmation if the reason Lilja had been absent was because she was indeed the vigilante and under pressure from the police. It nags her, wondering if - if Lilja really is who she thinks she is, and if Therese even did the right thing by going to the apartment.

Classes had been on hold for a while. This had happened before, and just as with other times, the underground network that fed the vigilante information seemed in a lull. Therese knows she is not the only cog in the machine, so she tries not to assume too much from the lack of activity, but she cannot help but be drawn to the correlation.

So many seeming coincidences, yet none of them are enough to be sure.

And then the request for information had cropped up in that most secretive of emails.

Despite the oddity of the bid, she pursued it as she did all others, tackling it with a verve that spoke of trying to impress. She generally approaches her work with an aloof assurance. She knows she is one of the best at what she does, and she does not feel the need to prove it to anyone. Well, almost anyone, but the more she becomes convinced that Lilja is the vigilante, the more she puts into each opportunity to find and present information. This came along with her greater dedication to the self-defense classes. The woman *inspires* her.

She'd found the expected when checking on that strange word, *ananael*. It came up in something called Enochian, the Angelic Language. She'd also found a link to a metaphysical system whereby the world was divided between the celestial and the infernal. The word "chthonic" had even cropped up, suggesting a more literal interpretation of "beneath the earth".

Everywhere she looked, the initial information talked of Angels and hidden knowledge. Therese found it all somewhat pretentious and new age. Most of the people using it had found it from the same source and were just applying it as some sort of tag. Those sorts of things might shape a meaning, but she felt there was little value in such results. Her contact had not specified an area for conclusions, but Therese mostly ignored those, digging deeper.

She'd discovered information about the man who supposedly "discovered" the language, one Edward Kelley, associate of John Dee, astrologer and possible spy for Queen Elizabeth I. Dee had been one of the earliest to suggest an officially sanctioned library, and when denied, he'd kept an impressive collection of his own. One that eventually fell to arson.

A library might certainly be considered "secret wisdom", and if one were particularly needful of keeping such secrets, destroying the source might be one way to do so. Still, she kept such conjecture out of the report. She also couldn't help to make the association between this sudden information about libraries and the fact Lilja is a librarian. She knows she is reaching, but nothing sufficient has happened to keep her from such thoughts.

Ananael is a word in Enochian, an occult language discovered by Edward Kelley and used by the Angels, were one to believe the claims. Therese put this aside, trying to find mention of the word in the City, perhaps used as some code or other by criminal elements. She, of course, finds nothing, and when she finally compiles her report, readying to send it off to the vigilante, she feels as though she has done a poor job.

But she cannot dislodge this nagging feeling of oddity, that the assignment hints at something else, even as it seems to harbor the very concept of secrecy and ciphers.

Chapter Two

Fog lurks thickly, impeding sight, enhancing sound. A sibilant cadence shifts throughout like a dissonant orchestra teasing at ear drums. Some find it calming. For others, it is a constant torture.

"Does the time finally near?" asks one of those here, one who is possessed of voice, fortitude, drive.

"Time is not the same for us," remarks the other, a rise to the flesh of the brow.

Satariel says nothing. He, for this one is indeed a male, possesses power in this realm. As befitting, he also holds wisdom, and such does he restrain his tongue.

"Everyday has its dawn," she says, realizing Satariel will not speak. There is still the perch to the brow, the haughtiness, distasteful even if deserved. "Motherhood teaches one patience. Who knows more of that than I?"

He dips his head but a bare bit. She notices, and it is enough.

"You are quite worshiped by them." He finds his voice. "Loviatar."

An expression that may pass for a grin takes her lips. He calls her by the name she most prefers. A gift.

She is not blind, and as much as she may be capable of causing death, her purview is motherhood. Her prolificacy is well known amongst them. Though the expression may be different, reverence finds her here as well as in other places.

"Do we seek worship from *them*?"

"No," he answers after a brief time of thought, "but it may provide opportunities all the same."

She angles her gaze upon him. "I am aware of the various expressions of power, and you did not come here to discuss religion."

Again, the tongue holds.

Her fingers weave as a spider's limbs, movement brought unto them as a deliberate wave only to find otherworldly stillness once posed. The fog, this entire realm, is their haunt. The jagged cracks and dark, glassy surfaces might stab at the minds of other beings, but they have learned to survive within.

"We are familiar with the hunt. Mayhap overly so," she intones. "We learn to wait, to linger, to watch. I am the patient fisherman."

The winds waft, the hissing brought over as though an audience pained with curiosity. Time is indeed not the same for them, and a portion of it passes with no more discourse.

"And do you have a bite?" Satariel finally asks.

The grin takes her lips again. She knew he would speak first. Silence does not discomfit her. She thinks of it as a treasure.

"I do," she allows. "It will be as I have foreseen. One of them will be the gateway."

He does not ask. She will tell him if she so sees fit. For now, they merely ponder the possibilities.

Asenath Malkuth sits at the table with her cousin, Denman. Neither of them favor rising early, but the demands of life have given them to understand that sometimes one must do what may be considered unpleasant. Judging from the sumptuous breakfast arrayed on the circular table, they are not the only ones aroused and working at this hour.

Asenath sips at her coffee, lips unpainted and holding that seeming constant hint of sensuality as they close upon the edge of the fine cup. She feels the urge to grin when catching her cousin's eyes on her but suppresses the expression.

Denman idly wonders why she has summoned him, just as he does with all such meetings. He won't ask, so he also samples the brew. It is exquisite, as expected. He does not live at their family manor. He finds the visits to be bittersweet, having spent much time here growing up. He covets living here as the master and Head of the Family. Asenath's hold, though, proves iron strong. Some such ambitions are expected of him, but he knows she would never want him to succeed.

"One book in the library," she mentions after another sip of the coffee. Neither have yet touched the ample food that waits, steaming.

"The other two still out there," he adds to the conversation.

He finally looks over to see her cut glance upon him. His eyebrows perk as question.

"I presume you mean 'out there', waiting to be found," she leads. "All we can be sure of is that we don't know where they are. For all we know, the Felcrafts have them both."

"You don't think they would let us know?"

She gives a subtle shrug.

"I think Skothiam retains a modicum of naïve optimism. Oh, he harbors cynicism, no doubt, but I think he truly believes there is always a chance that we may evolve beyond what he considers petty greed and create some sort of miraculous cooperative." Her lips find a smirk as she completes the observation.

"You know him far better than I," Denman gives.

"We need better information from their home. Why has it been so difficult to insert an agent? Their staff *is* quite large."

He nods, swallowing another taste of the fine coffee. "Their vetting procedure is very thorough. They've never actually caught us in the act, but none of our candidates have made it in."

She ponders. The seeming depth of it makes him feel a scratching encroachment of nervousness.

"Have you sensed something?" he finally dares.

"A hint. I am not sure if it is portent or memory or something else. It could be that someone has a lock on the location of one of the books."

"Someone?"

"The Infernal is always a threat. Always," she replies, slowly looking over to him. "Even with all the security we may ever hope to bring to bear. So long as they exist, they are a threat."

He exhales, catching himself partway through, controlling, limiting the audible nature of the breath.

"They are a worthy fear."

He wonders at the sincerity of this, a bit shocked by what actually feels like sympathy coming from her. Still, subtle layers of manipulation may lie beneath the genuine.

"Caution is prudent, but fear would paralyze us."

"You do have a flair for the melodramatic." She grins, gaining nothing but a stony stare in return. "It might compromise us, but it need not paralyze. Some measure of fear may prove useful."

"What use?" he retorts. "We will either win or lose. Fear doesn't help."

"Then we need to find the books. If it turns out they are all three held in utmost security by the Felcrafts, then so be it, but I want to *know*. This ... *feeling* I have had does not make me secure."

"What is it, Asenath?"

She notes the sincerity, still finding it possible to plumb him. Though as he matures, he becomes more and more formidable. In any other family, he might have risen to the rank of a global leader of industry, but here, he walks in her shadow. She thinks he'd have been wasted otherwise.

He also lacks the sensitive attunement she has to the realm of magick. She is not on par with Nicole-Angeline Felcraft, but her power is not without its potency.

"You may wonder why I asked you here at this ungodly hour."

He lets slip a light grin onto his lips, wondering why she plays at casual conversation.

"I depart soon to pick up my son. The jet should be arriving shortly."

"Ah, he is coming for a visit, then?"

She does not answer, instead, "He seems to be doing well in school. I hope his diligence emerges. He has great potential."

"Do you think he might be any help to us?" Denman asks, the question taking some time to come forth, for he had not thought such a thing would ever be.

"I'm not sure. He made his choice some time ago, even if he was not fully aware of it. I expect such matters as *this*-" she waves a hand, "-to be put aside when he is around."

Denman nods, fully understanding.

"I'd like your attention to it, of course, but do not let these concerns vex you in his presence."

He gives another nod.

Once their meeting has ended, and he is left alone with the remnants of breakfast, his thoughts drift over what has been exchanged. He has met Asenath's son before, and though the young man is charming and intelligent, he seemed unwilling to engage the Malkuth business. Denman wonders now what may be changing. He also wonders if this may finally be a chink in his cousin's nigh impenetrable armor.

"It means 'school'."

Skot looks over at his sister. They have gathered here for a sharing of information. His expression implies he had not expected this.

"School? I thought you said 'secret wisdom'."

Nicole merely nods.

He glances at Lilja, the only other person present, as if seeking confirmation from her for the lack of loquaciousness on the part of his sibling. Lilja says nothing, silence being very familiar to her.

"So, we send Lilja and Zoe to investigate a place with activity, and they find it, along with a closet bearing a word in a supposedly Angelic language that means 'school'. Why?"

"We don't know," Nicole finally says in the growing quiet.

She wonders if her brother has asked the question rhetorically, perhaps to stimulate their thoughts, or if he actually expected her to have an answer.

"We may assume the artist was touched by the Infernal."

"Like Ernst." Lilja finally speaks, her nigh-whispered tone almost interrupting Nicole.

Both look over at her, but her eyes gaze in another direction. Skot knows that expression, knows she is lost in her own thoughts.

"How did Mr. Barrington come to know that word?" Lilja asks, turning her attention back to them, seeming unaware of why they might be scrutinizing her.

"Are we sure he wrote it?" Skot advocates.

"I don't think it was his wife," the redhead continues. "She was living off his success, but something about it bothered her. I could tell. She probably rarely even went into the basement."

"The place was left to fester," Nicole comments.

"Skot ..." Lilja begins, the hesitancy causing another gathering of concern from the others. "When you closed that gateway, you spoke some strange words that sounded like Latin."

"That was not Enochian," he is quick to say. "There are many languages at play here."

"We actually know little of this one," Nicole expands, "that is one reason it took us some time to truly decipher the word. It is not the most highly regarded of occult languages."

Lilja nods. "There are some who think Edward Kelley invented it as a scam."

Skot perks his eyebrows. "You've done some of your own research."

A self-conscious smile graces her lips for but a moment, her eyes shifting away then back. "You know I like to do research, so I did some checking."

He smiles warmly, walking over and taking the seat next to her on the couch. "What did you find?"

"Well," Lilja begins, eyes shifting between Skot and Nicole, "John Dee is quite a figure, and he was associated with intelligence gathering for Queen Elizabeth. I suppose the language could just as well have been a cipher as a scam."

"Yes, but if so, then why does a word from it appear in the artist's closet?"

She sets her eyes on Skot. "We know of the language. We found out about it. Mr. Barrington could have done the same."

"She's right," Nicole intones. "We have no evidence that the Infernal whispered it into his ear. We know they were there, but we mustn't jump to further conclusions."

"How can we discern that?" Skot returns. "We're investigating as many avenues as we can. Some are sure to be dead ends. Regardless, there is something about that closet and the markings inside it. Isn't there?" This last comes with a firm set of his eyes on Lilja.

It takes her a moment, but she blinks, then looks over at Nicole to find a degree of focus from the woman.

"What?"

Nicole drifts closer. She continues looking at Lilja but takes on a gentler aspect. Lilja has been around Skot's sister enough to be wary of such expression.

"The attack was for you. I doubt it was initially laid for you, but it happened when and how it did for *you*."

Lilja begins to sit up straighter, leaning back slowly, almost imperceptibly.

"This is not news to any of us," Nicole continues, still wearing that light, calm smile. "It behooves us to consider whatever felt meaningful to you."

"I ..." Lilja begins. "The closet ..." She stops, sitting in silence.

Skot knows what is happening now, and he doesn't want to push too much. "It's worth checking. Even if Mr. Barrington did his own research and found Enochian, why did he have that closet, and what of the star? It must have been important to him, and we know the Infernal were there, quite probably influencing him. So, why did he do it? What is it supposed to mean?"

"It means 'school'," Nicole repeats, moving away from Lilja, returning to her usual demeanor. "Why use that word except to relay such meaning? Mr. Barrington felt his work, or where he worked, might be a place of education. Or he was referring to a specific such institute."

Skot shakes his head lightly. "How are we supposed to find that out?"

"He used Enochian for a reason," Nicole carries on. "He could have used Latin or Sanskrit or any number of other languages, but he chose Enochian. Why?"

"It must be for the connection with Edward Kelley and John Dee," Lilja tries.

"Alright, then what school?" Skot asks. "Was there a school where the occult teachings of Dee were taught? I haven't heard of such."

"Nor have I," Nicole adds, "but I did find information of a particular school of magick that John Dee sought."

"Oh?"

Nicole meets Skot's eyes. "Scholomance."

"Has the Elusive Vigilante Finally Met His End?" "Is the Infamous Vigilante Merely a Hired Gun for Criminals?" "Should the Police take Lessons from the Vigilante?"

Therese scours over old news reports she keeps in her records. She ignores the sensationalistic aspects, but she culls from all of them for that most important of commodities – information. She is impressed that the vigilante has managed to continue operating and remain undiscovered, but she is learning things from the patterns. More than once now, the vigilante has gone enough off the radar, and the news outlets assume an end. Whether dead, captured, or merely on vacation, no one knows. These times correlate with occasions when Lilja has been out of town, the self-defense classes on hold. It is still circumstantial, but it nibbles at her notice with a stubborn insistence. The hacker digs deeper.

Nothing conclusive had come of that night when the police received the anonymous tip and were converging on what they thought was the vigilante. Freshly slain corpses had been found inside, an avenue of ingress from a smashed window, but that was all. Therese is also not proud of breaking into Lilja's apartment, and though it left her with a demanding slew of questions, she still lacks those answers. She now finds herself doing more she is not proud of, things for which she possesses the talent and skill.

It had taken some time, but it occurred to her to check the university's library. Maybe Lilja had been working that evening. Her cyber-digging had resulted in finding something more interesting, for the library reported a break-in and possible vandalism and assault from students that very night. Coincidence? Records show that such acts do not come up often within that somewhat small and elite student body.

One thing, though, sprung out at her, and so now she sits on her motorcycle, waiting. She is not far from the gym, but far enough to hopefully avoid any undue notice. She is also not hiding. On the contrary, she is hoping to find someone. And there he is.

"Billy?"

The security guard looks over when his name is called. He finds the slender, punk-looking woman who has called his name. He peers with confusion, obviously not recognizing her, but he does walk over.

"I'm Therese. I'm a student in Lilja Perhonen's self-defense class."

"Oh." Billy nods, still trying to figure this out.

"We talked once before, but it was a while back."

"We ..." Billy grins, a stunted chuckle escaping like an impatient breath. "We did?"

Therese smiles, an expression she generally finds alien. She hopes her unpracticed one doesn't scare him off.

"Yeah. I was out here, after class, and you came over to make sure I was okay."

"Oh, right, right," he says, but Therese thinks he still doesn't remember. He looks around, as though taking stock of their surroundings. "So, how are you? You didn't just get out of a class, did you?"

"No," she answers. "I am curious, though, about the school. I'm considering trying to become a formal student. I know it's very expensive and all that, but I've saved up a good chunk. I wanted to ask you, since you're a guard and in the know, is it pretty safe here?"

She notices how Billy gains more focus, nodding, looking quite serious, even showing a slight reaction to her mentioning of his inner knowledge. She's manipulating him, and she is pleased to see it working.

"Oh, yeah, it's very safe. The security here is top notch."

She keeps her eyes on him, stilling giving that smile. She hopes she looks more like a potential victim than a criminal.

"Well, I'm pretty good with investigating information, it's sort of my job, so I did a little digging just to look through reports of incidents and what not."

Billy nods, seeming to take this in good stride. He actually holds one arm up, elbow resting in his hand, as he taps his lips with his bent index finger. Therese realizes how into it he is, so she decides to dare.

"I read about something that happened at the library a few months back. Some kids, maybe, students, broke in and vandalized the place and even assaulted some security guards?"

"I was there!" Billy exuberantly declares.

Therese, of course, knew he was, having found his name in the reports and realizing the potential angle she might pursue.

"Wow." She blinks, letting her grin grow. "So, what happened?"

"Oh, it was nothing." He presses his lips together, shaking his head. "Some kids got in after hours and were messing with us. They knocked over some books then made some noise, trying to scare us. It was silly."

"That's it? What about the assault?"

"Well," Billy begins, hesitant, "yeah. One of them got me. Well, they got both of us. We saw a guy, but he was a distraction, then they got us. They might have used gas."

"Gas?" she replies, knowing how silly that sounds. She figures he must be saying this to excuse what he feels is a personal failing.

"Yeah." Billy nods, seeming very casual in the face of Therese's incredulity. "They're just kids, you know? But they're really smart."

"Were they ever caught?"

"Nah." And again comes the casual expression.

"That's where Miss Perhonen works, right?"

"Oh, yeah. Yeah."

"Was she there?" she asks, giving a stretch to her eyes to convey concern.

"No. If she had been ..." Billy's voice trails off, a smirk taking his lips.

"What?" Therese presses.

"Oh, well, you take her class. Can you imagine? Those poor students would have been in serious trouble."

"Yeah, I guess so." Therese manages to reply, but she is just as quickly lost in thought. "So, there are some pretty valuable books in the library, right?"

"Well, yes, there are." Billy looks at her, and Therese finally sees something she thought would be immediate in the guard – suspicion.

"You don't think, maybe, someone broke in to try to steal something valuable and then knocked you out and fled when you found them?"

Billy turns his lips down, giving a sort of shrug. "Not really. I guess it's *possible*, but the really valuable stuff is kept in its own room, and that was never broken into."

Therese nods. "Separate security there. That's smart."

"Not our thing," Billy explains. "The library has that set up on its own, and it even has outside monitoring."

"Wow. There must be some really important books in there."

"You have no idea."

The sound reports with a dull thud, quickly followed by another, then again. It changes, still a solid hit but flatter, sharper. The others arise again, faster, and the punctuating grunts can now be heard. There comes the slight jangle of the thick chains. All of it like a crescendo that will not break, but it does eventually stop.

She stands there, catching her breath, the sheen of sweat evident.

"Your technique is very good."

Her eyes slip over, not darting as might those of prey.

"I thought I was alone," Lilja remarks.

"I'm not trying to disturb you," the woman says.

Lilja just looks, then she goes to remove the wrap from her hands. She cringes inwardly as the material peels forth from her bruised and bloodied flesh.

"Oh my," the observer states, "you sure are serious."

Lilja glances up again. She doesn't feel like engaging in conversation. All she wants to do now is go have a long, hot shower.

"I must be bothering you."

The redhead grabs a towel, dabbing at her face and neck.

"You teach, don't you?"

"Yes."

The other woman gives a smile, whether from the answer or just getting Lilja to respond is unknown.

"Everyone could benefit from learning."

Lilja agrees, but she says nothing. She stands, firmly, facing the visitor, exuding an aura of wanting to leave.

"I find that one mistake too many people make in life is thinking they are done … or just letting it happen. Even if we learned all we could in one lifetime, we'd barely scratch the surface of what all is out there."

Lilja sets her piercing blue eyes on the stranger, wondering more why these things are being said than who the person is. She feels a vague hint of suspicion, a whisper of discomfort. She studies the woman with more intent, her brow furrowing. Her deepening line of thought is interrupted.

"Are you accepting new students?"

"Not at this time."

"A pity. I am sure there are many who could benefit from your instruction, but there is only so much one person may do."

"I'm very busy."

"Of course, you are." The woman pulls back from the conversation, giving one polite dip of her head.

Lilja takes the looked-for cue and goes to have her shower.

Chapter Three

"Thank you both for coming."

Gaspare Duilio follows Denman Malkuth into the dimly-lit chamber. The place bears all the trappings of what Duilio would consider a charlatan's take on fortune telling. There is a tall bookcase populated with worn tomes and curious objects, dust and cobwebs in a meaningful array. The condition displays a deliberate attempt, more like a movie set than any true sign of neglect. The art on the walls paints more of the same picture. The woman receiving them forwards herself as some 'Madame Blutasky', an obvious play on Helena Blavatsky of occult fame. Whatever faux accent the woman might thickly lay on for other clients, she has abandoned for this engagement.

Denman takes one of two chairs at the small, circular table, interrupting the woman as she goes to find another for Duilio. He gives a short, sure shake of his head then an undeniable gesture with his hand for her to sit.

"What have you found?"

She glances briefly to Duilio, unfamiliar with him, but the air of command from the Malkuth suffers no lack of intensity despite the man's grin. She spares a short moment, seeming to collect herself and perhaps also her courage.

"It's the City," she begins, somewhat hesitantly, "the gateway, the attacks, the sacrifices. There is a great deal of power there. It has been chosen."

"For what?" Denman asks, and Duilio hears the hint of impatience.

"I-I don't know," the woman responds, eyes again searching over her guests as though imploring of a reprieve.

Denman bores into her with his eyes, the light, congenial curve still to his lips. He waves his hand casually as bid for her to continue.

"It is all so strong; I can easily feel it here."

"Still?"

"Yes!" She is eager to finally give a solid answer. "It has fluctuated, of course, but it has never completely gone away."

"What do you sense?"

"It's ... it's not entirely clear, but ..."

Silence descends. The two men watch. Denman finally pierces the stillness. "But?"

"The vibrancy is almost blinding. It's not colors, but a light. It's difficult for me to see it, like staring into the sun."

Duilio furrows his brow, lost, wondering how any of this makes sense, wondering even why they are here.

"Yes, but it is not the sun. You see *something*."

She nods. "I do, yes. There is something beneath the light."

"What is it?" Denman asks after another short wait.

"A shadow."

He rises from the chair, the sound of the legs scooting back over the wood floor like an intruding scrape. The other two watch as he takes a few meandering steps away from the table. He then looks back at the fortune teller, eyebrows rising. She returns the gaze with a questioning one of her own. Duilio senses the underlying simmer of fear.

"What is casting the shadow?"

"I don't know," she quickly answers. "The light is too bright."

"You said the power fluctuates, and I presume that means it has waned since the failed attacks. Was it blindingly bright before, and now is only *somewhat* blinding?"

The woman blinks. She glances again to Duilio then back to Denman. Duilio knows how intimidating the Malkuths may be. He sometimes wonders how he maintains his own sense of calm in not only being employed by them but also with the continually growing knowledge of the demonic threat hungry to consume humanity. He supposes it is a defense mechanism to keep from going insane or suicidal.

52

"I …" she tries, sitting up a bit as her spine stiffens. "I can … tell that there are changes, but it's still insubstantial in the details."

"That sort of …" Denman speaks, waving a hand casually, "*shit* may work on your customers, but I need more."

"This is not a con," the woman says, and Duilio continues to sense the pleading nature.

What have the Malkuths done to you, he wonders. Sympathy creeps in. He begins to think he might pay the woman a visit once this is done.

"Oh, I don't think it is," Denman replies, his charming smile doing nothing to placate the tension. He moves back over to the woman, standing behind her now, placing his hands on her shoulders. "I need you to really think about this. I know it isn't easy, but I need more."

She gives a hesitant nod, taking in some breaths, trying to calm herself.

"There is a force." She finds some words. "It's also difficult to see, difficult to separate from the others."

"Something of the Infernal?"

"I … I can't be sure. It seems in opposition to it, but it's difficult to separate."

Denman pats the woman's shoulder, leaning down to whisper, "You said that already. What else?"

"It was also drawn there … to the City."

"Why?"

"I …" she begins, but her voice is cut off as Denman squeezes those shoulders, an unspoken warning to voicing ignorance. "There is fear *and* strength. A drive to hide and be in the thick of it, trying to help."

Duilio watches as Denman alters the pressure of his hands, as though now milking the woman for information.

"It's there, right in the heart, right in the light."

"Perhaps *it* is casting the shadow?" Denman leads.

The woman looks at him, nodding, eagerly. "Yes, yes, that must be it!"

"What stands at the place of power, the place of *danger*?"

"A guardian."

Both look at Duilio as he speaks the word. The woman looks enraptured, as though hypnotized by this answer. Denman merely studies the man, his eyes drilling into those of the former Interpol inspector. Still holding that gaze, he speaks to the woman. "Is that it? A protecting force?"

"Yes." She nods, again eager to latch onto answers, all in hope of assuaging the Malkuth and getting closer to his departure.

"But you said you could not easily discern details, that you were not even sure if this power was not of the Infernal."

"It's all so muddy. I want to see. I want to know, but this power is ... shadowy."

"I thought it was casting the shadow."

"I ... it is! But ... but. It *is* casting the shadow. It is *very* strong."

Silence descends. Denman stands there, ruminating. Duilio notices the woman is staring intently at him, perhaps hoping for some assistance. He has none to offer. He is still unclear why he was even brought along to this. Unable to maintain the interchange, he looks away.

His eye is caught by more of the enigmatic knickknacks, an arrangement on a small shelf hanging in one corner of the room. He looks at some others. He feels certain there are secrets here amidst the foppery. Perhaps he will ask her about that if he comes back. Such thoughts running through his head, he looks over just in time to see Denman produce something dark and glassy from his coat, an obsidian dagger, and he smoothly drags it across the woman's neck.

Duilio cringes in shock and sympathy as Denman casually steps away. The fortune teller's eyes have gone wide, a trembling quake to her body. She swallows. It as if she does not realize her throat has been opened, her rich blood leaking and spurting free with the insistent pounding of her heart. A few more stunted gasps and grunts emerge, the sounds sickeningly wet, and she collapses onto the table.

"Why did you do that?" Duilio demands, his voice a hissing whisper.

Denman moves closer. "I owe you no explanation." The response is not a challenge, not laden with any threat, merely uttered with the same casual confidence and disregard he generally shows.

He pauses, though, on his way past Duilio and to the exit. "If you were more astute, you'd know."

Anger effuses from Duilio. He does not even realize how much had been brewing throughout this engagement. He tenses, stepping closer to his employer. Denman looks him over, slightly surprised.

"She was talking about the guardian. *You* figured that out."

"And?"

"It's the librarian, Lilja Perhonen. She's casting the shadow."

"Who is Lilja Perhonen?"

"Someone more dangerous than I realized."

Scholomance, a place steeped in folklore and rumor. A place of the sort of renown that hides beneath scarce shadows in deeply recessed areas. Most have not heard of it, or their knowledge is incorrect, held in the grip of misinformation or popular culture.

It is said that Merlin studied there before gaining his strength and wisdom and becoming companion and advisor to King Arthur. It is also said that the school would impart deep secrets and great abilities, but all at a steep price. Each class of ten would sacrifice its lowest graduating student to Lucifer. Some sources say the number was thirteen, but there was always the single offering as payment.

The others would go on to become powerful practitioners, even rumored to ride on fire-breathing dragons, making themselves into great masters or the elite support thereof. The dragon's breath is a thing known to those familiar with Merlin. Some say Dracula studied there, and the link between dragons and that infamous name is undeniable.

Was it ever real? And if so, where was it located?

Some sources say Spain, others say Romania, still others, Russia.

John Dee sought it, but with a man of his proclivities, one may not always be sure of the literal nature of his journals and writings. This fog of conjecture sometimes claims he even attended the school, but by all accounts, it was no longer intact by the time of the Elizabethan man's days.

It is known that Dee traveled to Central Europe later in his life, accompanied by Edward Kelley. During these travels, he spent time in the courts of Krakow and Prague. Being a serious man of letters and the preservation of knowledge, Dee also promoted cartography, commissioning maps of his journeys.

"Assuming he found the school, is there a map?" Skothiam asks.

"We have discerned something of interest from *Liber Os*," Nicole says.

"*Liber Os* is a real book?" Lilja interjects.

Skot smiles somewhat apologetically. "Yes, and we have it in our collection."

Lilja just looks at him, the unspoken dialogue of her striking eyes seeming to both implore and demand.

"I presume you have heard of the *Book of Soyga*, then?" Nicole asks, somewhat diffusing the situation.

Lilja nods, a pondering moment passing quickly for the usually taciturn Finn. "The book once possessed by John Dee that talks of various aspects of the occult. It was thought lost but then found in the late Twentieth Century in the Bodleian Library."

"Yes. The manuscript has been thoroughly examined and is accepted," Skot intones.

"And you're saying the Felcrafts possess a book cited in *Soyga* as one of its sources?"

Skot again finds his lips tracing into that subtly sheepish smile. Nicole watches the interplay of the two, noting not only the charm but also how differently her powerful brother reacts to the woman he loves. She again interjects.

"We do," she flatly states. "As you may know, the *Book of Soyga* was found to also possess many of Dee's usual tricks at cryptography. It also contains tables that appear to be a code of some sort. This was also not unusual for him or occult scholars of the time.

"After a great deal of examination, a cipher was developed, but it seemed … inadequate."

Lilja replies through a slow nod, "Yes, errors were found that were assumed to have been copied from the source." She looks between the siblings, hopeful of some verification.

"We have been able to piece together the correct cipher."

Lilja blinks, eyes on Nicole. She then looks at Skot.

"You've had it all this time?"

"Oh, no," Skot quickly replies, "Though *Liber Os* is a tremendously rare book, we were not terribly compelled to study it much more than we already knew. Recent developments, of course, changed that."

"You figured out the cipher in a few days!"

Skot's own blue eyes look to his sister, as though desirous of aid. Lilja follows the gaze to see Nicole give a single nod.

"Dee supposedly spoke to angels about his information," Lilja mentions, "which I doubted before ... all of this happened. Is there any truth to his having had interaction with supernatural entities?"

"We don't know, but he may well have been sensitive to it."

"Or mayhap Kelley was," Nicole offers.

"Or both?" Lilja tries. "Were they Hunters?"

"Again, not that we know," Skot says. "Back then, we presume that people who showed the sort of insight and abilities possessed by those with the correct genes were thought of as wizards."

"Or witches."

Lilja looks to see Nicole staring with steely eyes.

"We sometimes wonder how many potential Hunters were burned at the stake, though countless innocents were set to that self-righteous and despicable fire." Once uttered, Nicole returns to her usual appearance of uncanny calm, as though having spit out a poison. "Of course, not all places treated witches the same, as you well know from your own homeland."

The Finn quickly nods, and though many more questions crowd the forefront of her mind, she waits.

"Yes, we are digressing," Nicole says, offering a brief, subtle grin. "It would seem the location of the school is indeed mentioned in *Liber Os*. There are several maps in the book, of course, but the cipher has allowed us to determine what we need.

"Scholomance is in one of its likely places – near Sibiu in Transylvania."

"How can that be?" Lilja asks. "Sibiu is a tourist center."

"We're looking into it. We did not give Scholomance nearly the attention it deserved before."

"And we're still not sure it deserves that attention," Skot advocates.

Nicole gives a single nod before continuing. "We shall find out more soon, and then we will know how to proceed."

Therese has dressed herself as conservatively and non-threatening looking as possible. She knows she has not done too well in the past with her offline detective work, and she hopes to raise the bar with this effort.

What is *this effort?*

She still wrestles with herself. Why is she so adamant about proving whether or not Lilja is the vigilante? She's obsessed with it, and she usually finds herself too apathetic to be that concerned with anything. She begins to feel the realization that her obsession centers about the woman herself.

She's removed or replaced much of her jewelry, taking out her brow and nose piercings, replacing the more ostentatious adornments in her ears with things less weighty. She has also brushed her hair back, giving full view of her lightly made-up face, and dressed in a long sleeve shirt and plain trousers, no jeans, no leather. The colors are solid but not black. She feels awkward.

The woman answers the door, and even though Therese has spoken with her a bit via e-mail and text, she senses hesitancy. She wonders if the door is about to be closed in her face. She puts on a smile and begins.

"Amanda Honeycutt? I'm Yan Stendahl," she introduces, having decided to complete her quasi-disguise by using her real first name. The irony is not lost on her.

"Of course." Amanda finally replies after giving the slight woman a brief once-over. Therese notices that Amanda puts on her own smile, opening the door further, acting as if everything is fine.

Therese had found the former assistant through her usual methods. She had wanted to speak to people who worked directly with Lilja, and she had found that to be a short list. She also figured speaking to an ex-employee might yield more results than talking to the young man currently holding that position.

She follows into Amanda's modest flat, noticing that everything seems in its place. The woman is rather plain overall, not really standing out in any obvious way. Therese meets her two cats, one of which seems less than inclined to greet guests. She also notices quite a bit of feline paraphernalia acting as décor throughout the apartment.

"Would you like coffee or tea?"

Therese resists her instinctive urge to decline, wanting to seem as normal and receptive as possible.

"Coffee, please," she replies, another of those practiced smiles on her lips.

She takes a seat, and one of the cats immediately begins rubbing against her legs. Therese absently scratches it atop the head.

"Olive! Get!"

The cat gives a pleasant-enough sounding meow, trotting off as Amanda arrives unto the room, setting down a small, plastic tray holding two mugs of steaming coffee. Therese is reminded of her own mismatched cups, though these are without stains.

"Thanks," she offers, taking up the drink, which she notices is colored from cream or milk. A quick tastes slightly shocks her, but she suppresses her reaction.

"I hope you like it sweet," the hostess says.

Therese nods, quickly swallowing.

"So, you're doing this for a research project, or is it a thesis?"

Therese nods again, trying to remain as nebulous as possible in her 'cover'. "Rare books fascinate me."

"Are you wanting to become a librarian?" Amanda asks, her brow furrowing as a smirk takes her lips. "No money in that unless you get the *important* position."

Therese notes the rolling of the eyes.

"No, I'm not. I'm interested in the whole concept. Why're they highly valued? Is it just because they are rare, or is it the knowledge inside them? How is that knowledge hidden? That sort of thing."

Therese notices that Amanda has narrowed her eyes. She wonders if the woman is naturally suspicious.

"It's not really hidden. Why did you come to talk to me, anyway?"

"Well, I was hoping to get further insight," Therese tries. "I'm not just writing a paper but also trying to impress my professor, you know? I figured talking to you would show more initiative."

"Hmph." Amanda throws out another smirk. "I sure do know my stuff. I was on track to take over the collection before ... well, you know."

Therese doesn't, but she hopes to find out.

"You worked for ...?" Therese plays at searching her notes and memory, swiping through information on her tablet.

"Lilja Perhonen."

"Right." Therese nods, and she notes the way Amanda pronounces the surname, giving the 'o' a long sound instead of the less inflected way she has heard Lilja say it.

"Have you talked to her?"

The challenge is palpable. Therese had guessed there might be some bad blood, and she would have to admit to herself that she hopes to capitalize on it. "Nooo?" Therese blinks, her eyebrows lightly perked.

"Hmph."

An awkward silence descends. Therese senses the possibility escaping, so she plunges on. "You had a lot of interaction with the rare books?"

"Oh, yes, I had *full* access."

"Were any of them written in code or a strange language?"

"No." Amanda again wrinkles her brow. "Why would they be?"

Therese gives another smile, hoping this is working.

"I'm still in the early stages of my research, so I'm just pursuing all sorts of possibilities. I expect many of them to not pan out. I've noticed, though, that sometimes the knowledge in these books is considered privileged or maybe even controversial, so some of it is hidden behind codes or secret languages."

"I don't remember anything like that in our books."

"So, they were just valuable because they were rare?"

"Why else would they be?"

"That's what I'm trying to figure out. Exactly why we consider valuable books valuable."

"Because they're old and rare." Amanda shrugs.

"So, it has nothing to do with their contents?"

"Well, I guess it could, but it's not like they went to great lengths to hide it. The most valuable book in the collection was written in Latin."

"Did you read it?"

"Well, no," Amanda admits with a moment's hesitation, "but I had access to it. It's the only one in existence, no other copies, *very* valuable."

"And it's entirely written in Latin?"

"Yes," Amanda quips, coating herself in a slight sense of affront at being so questioned. Therese makes ready to diffuse the situation with a different tact, but Amanda carries on. "Some man used to come in all the time to do research on it. Rich, too. His family has one of the world's most valued private collection of rare books."

"Oh?"

Amanda nods, seeming proud of herself to know this. "The Felcraft family."

"I've never heard of them."

"They aren't *celebrities*," Amanda informs the obvious, giving a slight roll of her eyes. "That book is why I lost my job. The university won't admit that, but I know it is."

Therese just looks at her. She isn't sure what to say, thinking this line of information is not really getting her anywhere.

"One of the faculty came to look at it. A *very* handsome professor. I mean, he could have been a male model, he was *so* good looking."

Therese continues with her open regarding of the woman, still not sure what else to say.

"I showed it to him, but he kept coming around for *other* reasons."

Therese slowly nods.

"We had a fling," Amanda adds, throwing this out with a casual flair. "He was also into books. He knew his stuff. I don't think that book impressed him, really."

"He was … into *rare* books?" Therese tries to rejoin the conversation.

Amanda nods, giving the motion a somewhat conspiratorial edge. "He might still be at the university. I don't think they fired him like they did me. Hmph. Discrimination, right?"

"Right."

"Look him up. He can probably help you a lot better than I can."

"What's his name?"

"Denman Malkuth."

Therese adds the name to her notes.

"If you see him, tell him *I* sent you."

Chapter Four

"So, you think John Dee knew about the Books?"

Skot looks at Lilja, her striking blue eyes like an eager thirst. Her curiosity shows the temperance of skepticism, but that does not hinder the intensity.

"Nicole has been doing more research, and we're finding evidence to suggest this."

"How is this possible?" she asks after a moment of silence. "Your family has massive resources available to it, and you've been looking for these books for many years?"

He nods, the motion a subtle expression, slowly inhaling.

"Yes, but, frankly, we were somewhat dismissive of Dee before, or even with our resources, we didn't prioritize it. We're also at the moment of discovery, and it's an exciting thing. It seems unreal, and it's a good idea for us to maintain levelheadedness, but the pieces are suddenly fitting into place."

"So, that's it? You finally know where to look, and the answers have been there all along?"

"No. We're still following trails. We don't have answers, yet. Even if we found a listing of Dee's that mentioned the titles specifically, we'd still not feel like they were answers until we found the actual books. Besides, from what we can gather, Dee suggests all three are at Scholomance, and we know that isn't true."

"And this is all based on interpreting the code."

"Yes, so it could be wrong, but from what we've found … and because of what's happened, we need to give it the necessary attention."

Lilja doesn't speak. She knows what he is referring to. She can see it in him - that worry. She doesn't want him to worry about her, and even as much as he knows that, such a thing is difficult to suppress.

"Do you think this is all a trap?" she finally asks.

"No," he says. "If the Infernal had left this on purpose, then they could trace the same information. They'd go after the Book."

"Or they're luring us to where it once was."

He sighs, finally giving forth a slow nod. "That is possible."

"I'm going," she states after seeing a certain look in his eyes.

"It might be better if you didn't."

He can feel her powerful will as she looks back at him. Their interaction is not contentious, and he is possessed of a great willpower of his own. There is debate here, a mountain of possibilities being expressed with no words.

"This is not about me."

"Lilja, that attack was clearly directed at you. The Infernal are aware of you and that you guard one of the books."

"So? A guardian's job is to face attacks."

"Not to run off to Romania. Who guards the book while you're away?"

He can see it. It's slight, for she is not one to largely convey emotion, but they have been together long enough now, that he knows. In her own way, she becomes perturbed.

"I have left before on assignments. You know that. I would be of value."

"I know," he says, resisting the urge to pull her into a hug, "but I'm still … concerned about what happened."

"The Infernal are aware of you. Does that stop you?"

He waits longer than he should to supply an answer of which they are both aware. "No, it doesn't."

"We have measures in place for when I'm absent, so you know it shouldn't matter if I'm gone for a short time."

He wishes she'd say that she wants to go because he is also going, but somewhere inside, he knows that won't happen.

"Why did you go back to Finland?" He shifts, mentioning the trip she took not too many months past.

"I told you about it," she clips, immediately becoming defensive.

"You said you went to face your own personal demons."

She does not reply, merely meeting his gaze.

"You faced them, but did you dispel them?"

The moment stretches. He knows her self-control. He cannot recall a time when she truly gave over to anger, even when she has had ample reason. He worries now that he is pushing her in just that way, but he feels a more compelling sense of concern. She does not answer, and he wonders if she will leave the conversation. In her own way, she does.

"I want to go. I know it's ultimately your call, and I won't undermine your decision, but I want to go."

He already knows his answer, and he hopes it will prove the correct one.

The staff here is generally permissive, but even they have their standards. Those seem more relaxation during the less used times, and so the disheveled person is not turned away. It helps that he has money, however small an amount that may be. Bone-thin fingers move over the keyboard, the tips dark with faded and chipped black polish but also showing small bruises and grime. He sits tucked in close, hoodie up and shadowing most of his face. He emits a low burp that catches a short bit of the attendant's attention.

It is less than a quarter hour past three in the morning, and they are the only two in this twenty-four-hour cybercafé.

He accesses e-mail, and a new message comes up, encrypted. He stares at the code, willing memory to work and allow him to decipher it. His forehead bears a pale sheen, labored breath accentuating his concentration. That brow furrows, and his throat works with a dry swallow, teeth then partially shown in a light grimace. Another belch escapes.

The attendant stays focused on reading a graphic novel. He doesn't feel entirely comfortable with the patron, but he's seen him before. As unpleasant as he is, he's never caused any trouble in his recent regularity, and he is usually out quickly. As though this thought serves as cue, the disheveled young man pushes back from the desk, the chair's scraping legs reporting the motion. He glances once at the attendant then leaves.

His trek along the early morning streets goes generally unnoticed. He is a dirty dweller here in the City, and the others out and about know of his ilk. He spies some policeman across and down a block, talking to some others. He carries on, not wanting to garner any attention of his own by suddenly changing direction or appearing to hide. He's no fool, though he is often taken as such. People tend to make generalized assumptions on a snapshot. He hasn't been in this situation his whole life.

He comes to a particular fork in the road, following the gently sloping downward angle until going further off the lit path. He sees the flicker of light coming from fire instead of publicly-provided lamps. He notes the dark shapes huddled in various positions about the flame licking up from the rusted barrel. He knows most of them, and they know him. He finds one of particular import, taking a seat on the ground beside him.

"There was a message," he informs.

"What was it?"

"Something about someone else digging into things."

"Someone else?"

He nods. "Another 'seeker', the message said."

The other one studies him. He finally breaks the focus, looking around. Many of those here are watching.

"What are we supposed to do about it?" he asks, eyes again finding the messenger.

"Wait. Watch."

"That's it?"

"Look, Lance, I'm in this just like you are. You've read the messages before. We're-" and his voice stops as he cringes, forcing a swallow. He looks away, producing a loud burp which resolves into a series of unsettling coughs.

"Pierce?"

He looks over to Lance tapping his own lip. He takes this to mean something is on his, so he checks, and his grimy fingertips come back with the reflective mark of blood.

"Getting worse?" Lance asks.

"I don't know," comes out too defensive, but he relents. "Maybe."

Lance rises to his feet, evincing his own pain and soreness as he winces and groans. Both are in their twenties, but this life ages them. Lance presses a hand into his own lower back, trying to stretch, but the pain takes him again.

"I'll check with some of the others. See if they've noticed anything." He begins to walk away, a noticeable limp to his stride.

Pierce watches, trying to focus, ignore the signs. His head feels fuzzy, pressured. He needs to find something to take the edge off.

They all have their masters. He's not entirely sure who pulls their strings, but he knows this life is shit. No matter what he does, no matter the charities he visits, his condition just continues to worsen. Still, the compulsions are undeniable, so just like Lance, he carries on.

Though the City indeed has its share of a history of crime, she is only concerned with the past couple of years at most. Having narrowed the search and used some custom scripts to pick and sort the data, she has come across some interesting things.

She's been a victim of crime, herself, twice kidnapped and twice rescued by the vigilante. She recalls the serial killer that once haunted the City and when she trailed the spooky-seeming man into the strip joint. That was the first time she was attacked, and she felt sure it meant that guy was the killer. Thinking back on it now, though, it makes no sense. She supposes it never did, but the overwhelming mysterious nature obscures like a fog.

Therese finds a disturbingly imaginative description of one murder, calling it a "demonic killing", and she uses the key words, finding others. Such colorful language was eagerly used by the more provocative news outlets in describing the condition of the victims of that serial killer. No one was ever arrested, but the murders did stop.

She does more digging, hacking, trying to find out if the police ever came up with something they did not report to the news outlets. She doesn't find anything. She hates coming upon such dead ends. She trusts her scripts and searches and realizes there is nothing more. She stares, as though using force of will to plumb an answer. As expected, nothing more happens. She gets up to make more coffee.

The City is enjoying a record low of particular violent crimes, just the sort to draw the vigilante's attention. Therese has to admit that just because she finds nothing of late concerning the shadowy crusader's activity doesn't mean they're gone from the City. That work may finally just be paying off. Criminals may be finding other places more agreeable to their pursuits.

The microwave beeps, and she takes out the mug of water, casually spooning in the instant coffee. She doesn't even watch as she does, thoughts off exploring other avenues as ceaselessly as her programs constantly search the internet. She goes back to the computer, sifting through other data.

She easily found more on Denman Malkuth, searching through the faculty records at the University. He is a very attractive man, possessed of many academic accomplishments. He is also, apparently, on leave. She wonders if there's much of a point of tracking the man down. She's trying to garner more information on Lilja, trying to put this whole vigilante business to bed once and for all. What knowledge might this professor have?

Based on Amanda Honeycutt's claims, Professor Malkuth holds knowledge on valuable books. According to his curriculum vitae, he also possesses a good deal of understanding on other subjects. None of it seems germane to Therese's pursuits, but she is nothing if not meticulous. She'd rather rule a source out than leave it hanging. Sometimes the threads of the web are indistinct. Such is the nature of mystery.

She leans closer, her practiced fingers flying over the keys as she puts together a script to do some virtual digging on Denman Malkuth. Perhaps she'll find something interesting.

Lilja strolls casually about the campus grounds. The days are hot, of course, during this mid-summer month, but this one holds an alluring pleasantness. Work is also not as demanding during the break, so she enjoys the times to get away and just experience nature. She ponders a more involved hike, perhaps adding in some rock climbing. Her lips subconsciously take a light curve as she thinks on such activities.

There are few people about, and she meanders to an area off the beaten path, feeling the well-cultivated grass beneath her shoes. She stops atop the gentle hill, looking out over the city. From this vantage, she cannot make out much before other buildings obscure. She begins to look more inward, letting thoughts swirl about as they may. She does hold some concern about the upcoming trip. It is all being sorted, and mostly, it seems, without her input. She'd like to participate more, but her main worry lies in going at all. Though Skot has told her they want her along, Lilja harbors some anxiety that this may not come to pass.

"Lovely day, isn't it?"

Lilja blinks, looking over to see another person here. How could she not have heard the approach? She must have been too deep in her own musings. She recognizes her as the one who appeared that time when she was working out. The one who inquired if she was accepting new students.

"Yes," Lilja finally agrees.

The woman stares off in the direction lately observed by Lilja, though the librarian gives her more of a study. She is obviously older than Lilja, but she has that appearance and bearing of one whose age is difficult to pin, as though she carries her years well.

"It's important to stop and smell the roses."

Lilja is also inclined to agree with this, but something about the woman makes her more hesitant than usual to engage in conversation. She's also never been much for small talk. The woman turns her eyes on Lilja.

"I think too many people forget that. Our time is limited, and all of this is so fragile. We should enjoy it while we can."

Though delivered conversationally, the words come across as a warning, even showing a hint of self-righteousness. Lilja does not like it. She turns to leave.

"All done with your smelling?"

She pauses, not liking the woman's implication one bit, yet she has halted her egress. She gives a casual-seeming glance. "I have to get back to work."

"Oh, you work here, too?" the woman asks, having the audacity to walk over to Lilja, accompanying her as the redhead again tries to walk away.

"Yes," she gives.

"Oh, it must be nice. You're a professor?"

"Librarian."

"Oh, how interesting."

Lilja finds the woman more and more irritating, not only from her forwardness but also her repeated use of the word 'oh'. She sees no reason why these "revelations" about herself should be any sort of a big deal at all.

"I'd imagine this library has a great many interesting books," the woman carries on. "Still, with the internet, I do wonder if such things are not on their way to obsolescence."

"I doubt it."

"Ah, an optimist."

Lilja glances at the woman, noticing a deep grin on her lips.

"It's very easy to get lost in all of it."

She gives another brief look.

"The internet," the woman answers the unspoken question. "So much information can be like a fog. I'm sure it's nice to come to a place like a library and have it all laid out, especially with someone to help find those books you need."

Lilja nods once, non-committal.

"One might say that librarians are like shepherds."

Lilja stops. The woman does so, too, and Lilja looks at her. "It's not like that at all."

"No?" she asks, keeping up that infuriatingly pleasant smile.

"The students mainly handle it all themselves. They don't usually need help finding anything."

"Oh, no." The woman emits a soft chuckle. "I meant more as you shepherding the books."

Lilja blinks, staring.

"And you teach those lovely self-defense classes, don't you?" the woman carries on. Lilja says nothing to this, just stands and looks. The woman, of course, speaks. "There must be some reason you teach those, yes? It's not just for exercise, is it?"

"There are risks and threats out there."

"And you want to protect everyone from them."

"No, I want to help people to help themselves."

The woman's smile shallows somewhat. She cocks her head, staring right back at Lilja. She finally nods, contemplatively.

"Yes, humans are terrible monsters, aren't they?"

"Some can be," Lilja gives, though so many other things crowd her mind. She thinks of the conflicting things with how people act, how some truly do treat others in horrible ways. She feels the burning rise of memory that reminds her of the children that died at the hands of that horrible human trafficker. He may be dead now, but he was clearly not the only one.

She snaps out of it, eyes refocusing on the woman.

"Are you alright?"

"Yes," she quips.

She then turns and heads to the library doors. She wonders if the woman will follow. She wonders if she might have to be firm about being left alone. As it turns out, the woman just watches as Lilja departs. She does glance at the large library building, then back to the redhead. The smile is gone.

She produces a cigarette from her pocketbook, setting it aflame with the flick of a silver-plated lighter. She stands there, just looking in that direction, taking a lengthy drag. The cigarette burns down quickly, and the woman squats, flicking the length of ash onto the concrete, then running the butt through it as though making sure to put it out. She does not look at this, her eyes kept on the library.

She stands, taking her leave. The ashen smear on the ground holds a shape beyond a mere abstract mess. It holds the suggestion of a portrait, and it looks like Lilja.

Chapter Five

She holds the compact assault rifle close to her body with a practiced ease. Her grip and poise do not compromise safety, everything about her showing a relaxed focus. The signal given, she moves. She comes about, raising the weapon from its downward angle to sight-in and fire quickly, giving off light pops of single-round deliberation. The rapidly responding pings announce direct hits on the metal targets. She moves within the complicated cover, dipping and side-stepping, coming out to aim and fire again, fluid, quick, accurate.

The magazine expended, she slides the rifle behind her, the strap holding it taut, and whips out a sidearm, bracing properly, both hands on the gun. She continues the quick squeezes of the trigger, so fast as to perhaps make an inexperienced observer think the handgun fires in fully automatic mode. This magazine also finds itself shortly emptied.

She has come to a point in the training course to find a shotgun conveniently resting atop a stack of plastic bins. It is semi-automatic, unloaded, and she retrieves it, sliding the shells in with nary a glance. She racks the first with a casual slip of her left hand, then unloads the barrage, striking targets at varying distances. Large holes opening in the cardboard brook no question.

She weaves about some more, using her petite form to keep to cover unless she is shooting or changing position. She drops the shotgun, bringing her handgun back out, reloading a fresh magazine and unleashing these bullets. She leans out from thin cover, firing multiple rounds, then stepping out further to empty the remainder.

Now without ballistics, she unsheathes the gleaming bladed weapon from her back, the length having waited patiently beside the assault rifle. She cries out, face a grimace of determination, striking the target. These are denser, made to better mimic the fleshly bodies of an opponent. Broad tears appear as she swipes, cutting into the material. She lodges her weapon sharply into one's neck, not beheading it, but she pulls free instantly, twirling and giving another lethal cut. She moves through this collection of "enemies", dodging, ducking, delivering hit after hit until she finally comes to the end.

She stands, gasping, catching her breath. The sun has witnessed it all, casting its bright rays onto the field. She squints, looking up toward it, then turns to the approach of feet.

"Thanks," she says, taking the offered water bottle and having a lengthy taste.

"That was good, Zoe."

"How good?"

David gives a half-grin, hinting at apologetic.

"Shit," the young Hunter replies. "How slow?"

"Oh, come on, now," her cousin chides, "you were only off by a half second or so."

"Or so?" she pushes, giving a steely-eyed stare.

"Drink your water," the senior Hunter suggests, walking back to cover from the sun.

Zoe does so, guzzling more before joining the others at their station.

This land is owned by the Felcrafts, and they use it often for training and practice. Though they have this temporary shelter and many boxes, obstacles, and targets, they'll have it all gone when they're done. Unwanted observation out here seems unlikely at best, but they are in the habit of cleaning up after themselves when out in the open.

"I should have been faster," Zoe comments, then tipping up the water bottle to finish it.

David looks up from giving his S&W 500 revolver a final wipe down before they get to cleaning and packing up. The others here are already out collecting items, even picking up as many spent shells as they can find.

"Why are you pushing yourself so hard? You're about the fastest one of us."

"About?"

He glances at Zoe, then continues with his gun, giving a smirking chuckle. "Are you so worried about beating her?"

"This isn't about jealousy."

He slips the cleaned and gleaming weapon into its holster then gives her a more serious stare. "Then what is it, Zoe? This whole *rivalry* thing you've got going on with Lilja needs to stop. Some competition is healthy, but-"

"Look." She steps closer to him. "I'll admit to some jealousy. She comes in here and suddenly is *numero uno* Hunter, and that chaps a bit."

"Come on, Zoe, she's not-" David tries, but he's cut off again, this time with a raised hand.

"Whatever. That's not the point." She looks at him, waiting, and he does so, too. "You weren't there at the Barrington House. Something bad happened."

"I read the reports."

"That attack was because of *her*. Taking her along on this next mission is a bad idea."

"Maybe," he gives, "but that's not our call."

"It's Skot's."

David nods.

"Lilja's *boyfriend*."

"Yes," David agrees. "And the Head of the Family."

"That doesn't mean he's infallible."

"No one thinks that."

A moment stretches, the two caught in a stare, friction beginning to all but sizzle between their gazes. Some of the others pick up on it, giving them a wide berth as the clean-up continues.

"Do you think his judgment is compromised when it comes to her?" David presses. "Do you think he's incapable of making those sort of decisions?"

"Maybe," Zoe finally gives, but her usual forceful tone is much reduced.

"None of us are perfect, Zoe. But we *are* family. This isn't the first time the Head and their spouse are both Hunters. Can you

74

imagine how difficult it is to make these sort of command decisions when the people are your kin?"

"She's not kin."

"Oh, stow that shit. Jericho isn't, either, technically, but you go tell him he's not part of the family."

Zoe gives back silence to this. David turns to continue packing.

"Yeah, well, what about the attack at Barrington House?" Zoe pitches.

"What about it?" David replies, still putting things away.

"If it was against Lilja, then sending her on this mission may be a bad idea."

David stops, looking over, noting the careful diplomacy of the young woman's chosen words.

"That's not how the Infernal work. We know they're patient. Hell, they have longevity we don't, but what they did was launch an attack from a place they'd already seeded, and they twisted it against Lilja."

"Well? Isn't that enough reason to be cautious?"

"I'm going to ask you again, Zoe – do you really think Skot's not being cautious? Do you really think he hasn't considered all of this? You know Nicole is probably his closest advisor. Do you think *she's* not all over this?"

Zoe contemplates, looking away for a moment.

"I do, but Skot doesn't always take her advice."

David throws up his hands.

"You're insisting on finding fault. There's always a way to poke holes. Always. We're always up against bad odds. We just do our best to do our best. That's it."

"What if it's not enough?"

"Then we're all screwed."

Lilja slowly turns the pages of the book, her washed and thoroughly dried hands moving with a smooth sense of delicacy. She has already inspected the calf leather binding, finding it in generally good condition. The non-descript cover gives way to the vignette, an etching depicting the burning of St. Paul's Cathedral in 1666. She continues moving through the pages, not bothering to read the script of the 17th Century book. She searches for blemishes.

"What do you think?"

She glances up at the dealer, a man with whom she has limited familiarity, one Rosendo Costa. He gives her a light smile. He is not an unattractive person, but something about him gives Lilja to think of a rodent.

"It's in very good condition."

"*The Causes of Decay of Christian Piety,*" he intones, "by Richard Allestree. First Edition."

She looks at him, and he maintains that small grin. She has seen the book's imprimatur and title page.

"Six hundred and sixty-five euros," she says.

"The book is pristine and authenticated."

She gives a slight nod, looking down at the book, pondering.

"Though small, your collection is known to contain many impressive pieces."

"It's not my collection."

"Of course," he grins more, "but you are its curator, and obviously, its procurer."

"The University has given me limited authority to make such decisions."

He leans forward, as though suddenly ensconcing them in conspiracy. "I'm sure you give consultation and advice on all acquisitions."

She blinks once, slowly, fixing him with an unwavering glance. "I do."

"Well, then," he speaks first after some measure of quiet. "What do you think?"

"I will let you know."

She begins to gather up her things. The book is in wonderful condition, and she'd like to have it in the collection, but there are other considerations.

"The book is in demand, Ms. Perhonen. It won't be available forever."

No book ever is, she thinks, but instead she merely gives him a polite grin and heads out.

She stops at a casual restaurant on her way back to the City, having taken this short business trip to view the book. She expects to make it back before her work day would normally end, but she is in no hurry. She also knows the importance of lunch, so she makes time to have the meal, even if it is somewhat later than usual for it.

The place is not empty, seeming somewhat busy. She expects it is because of its location on this highway. There aren't too many choices around. She assesses the place, noticing a group of people at the counter seats, and she takes a table next to a wall. She quickly scans the menu, placing an order when the waitress comes over to ask about a drink. It doesn't take her long to notice what is going on.

"So, you support immigration?"

The young lady glances around, seeming somewhat defensive. She is outnumbered, the four guys all but surrounding her.

"I don't see any reason to ban it."

The guy smirks, standing rather close to her. As Lilja observes, she notices more of the agitation. She had at first though they were all friends here together, judging from their manner of dress and similar-seeming ages, but it shows clear that they are not friends. Lilja sees bloodshot eyes on the questioner along with his awkward grin.

"All these immigrants are coming in here, raping women," he persists.

Lilja looks over his companions, noticing a slightly slumping posture on two of them. The last one hangs back, looking a touch worried. He blinks slowly then finds a nearby seat.

"They're not *all* raping women," the young lady retorts, her face tensing, and she moves back, trying to find distance from the man, though she is against the counter. "And not all rapists are immigrants."

"You might as well say you want to be a victim of rape."

The woman recoils at this, lips parting, forehead furrowing.

"Immigrants rape women when they get here. Those guys see women as objects, and they think it's okay to do whatever they want to them."

"And how are you showing respect for women by bullying this one?"

The guy turns, seeing Lilja standing there. She sees as he moves his glassy eyes over her, that grin staying on his lips. She notices a collection of saliva at one corner of his mouth.

"Ooooh. Are you here to protect her?" he challenges, smirking to one of his friends.

This one looks her over, too, and though none show proper balance, she can sense the rise to them. One gives her more of a dreamy look, and he sways the slightest bit. The fourth stays seated.

"They'll rape you, too," the guy states. "Do you want that?"

"All of you calm down, have a seat, and leave this woman alone," she says, using a more commanding tone of voice.

The wobbly guy widens his eyes a bit and shuffles back, sitting across from his friend. The speaker, though, curls his top lip, looking more determined.

"What's wrong with you?" he all but yells. "Do all you women really just want a guy to force himself on you? Huh?" The grin comes back to his lips, taking on a sinister, hungry cast, his eyes moving over Lilja's body.

"You!" Lilja points at him, raising her own voice. He blinks, pausing in motion. "Go *sit* down and be quiet."

He stands there for a second, then he begins laughing. The only one of his buddies still on his feet adds his own titters. The guy then reaches out, surprisingly fast for one so obviously under the effects of alcohol. Lilja shifts back, dodging, but he keeps pressing.

"Don't touch me! Go sit down," she continues.

He doesn't listen, reaching out with his other hand to try to grab her rear now that she has turned a touch sideways to avoid his initial accosting. She pivots on her right foot, now facing him fully, and she brings up her left leg, delivering a strong front kick. It comes off as more of a shove, but the force is undeniable, and he quickly ends up on his own ass.

Most everyone reacts with a stunned expression. The guy turns to his side, cradling his solar plexus, moaning. The sounds turns into coughs. Lilja wonders if he might vomit.

"I – I called the police."

She looks up to see the proprietor. He appears apologetic, obviously worried Lilja might get in trouble for her efforts. She gives a single nod, then looks back at the young guys. The wobbler has gone to help his friend, getting him to his feet with some effort. They look at her, some possible fire still in the main antagonist. Lilja slowly narrows her eyes, keeping balanced and ready. They opt to slip into the booth with their friends, heads tucked down, though some muttering emerges from the pained one. She watches them for a moment longer before going back to her table.

She'll wait for the police. She's dealt with such before. She'll give them a very concise report of what happened. She also still needs her lunch.

He keeps his head down for several reasons. He feels the driving focus from within him, but he also doesn't want to give the world any reason to intrude. He has the hood up on his jacket, the edges frayed, the material discolored. The weather tells a different tale than one generally requiring such a covering, but he doesn't do so to ward off cold. He plods onward, steady steps finally interrupted as a light coughing wracks his body.

It grows, and he moves to the edge of the sidewalk. The people out at this late evening hour ignore him. He's just another denizen on the dregs of society. He does draw some looks when the coughing erupts and peaks with a loud burp. He tries to conceal it, but the sound rings undenied. His body goes through a quick shiver, then he looks around. He takes a more attentive posture, peering. He finally sees what he looks for, going to a skittering sort of jog-shuffle as he makes way back down from where he has come.

"Lance," he hisses, leaning in close to his limping companion, "Keep up!"

"I'm trying," Lance replies to Pierce. "The pain's really bad today. Can't we take a break?"

"A brea-?" Pierce raises his hands in exasperation. "No, we can't take a break!"

Lance gives a hurtful look, brow furrowed deeply, though he continues on, favoring his one foot. Pierce walks beside, impatience coloring his fallow features. They cut through one alley, coming up on another, busier thoroughfare. Pierce acts something like a driver trying to whip his horse to faster speed, using his right hand to deliver harmless, yet regular prods to his companion. They turn another corner then Pierce's eyes go wide, and he uses that same hand to grab Lance.

"Wait!"

Lance glances quickly to his partner then down the street and back. "What?"

"There they are," Pierce hisses through clamped teeth, and he pulls them over beside a nearby building.

Lance watches, not sure what is going on. He continues shifting his rheumy eyes from Pierce to down the way, trying to see "them".

"Stop looking!" Pierce swats at his associate.

"I don't see anyone," Lance whispers, head now tucked down, both facing each other and the wall, trying to become unobtrusive.

"Are you going *blind*? There are people all over the place."

Lance rolls his eyes, shaking his head. "I mean *them*. I don't see who we're looking for."

"You're not supposed to. I know who they are. You don't."

"Then why am I here?"

"Because you're *supposed* to be."

This gets another roll of the eyes, but Lance holds in place. Pierce eventually looks up, giving his own concentrated peer. He presses at his partner.

"Okay, come on. Let's go."

Still unsure who they are trailing or why, Lance follows, the compulsion that moves them both proving unyielding.

Therese's mode of dress might also seem much for the weather. Some might even say she looks better suited to mingle with those like Pierce and Lance as opposed to "regular" people. She'd agree.

She practically stomps down the sidewalk, her heavy boots reporting each step. She walks with a purpose, hands stuffed in the pockets of her black, denim vest, hoodie pulled up, though a few, spikey strays of her black hair peek out.

She's out to meet a new contact, one she's exchanged information with. She's vetted that information, too, never assuming trust with anyone. Her feelers paid off, and she had been reached regarding Professor Denman Malkuth. Enough has been proven to lead to this – an evening meeting at a public coffeehouse.

Doubt continues to nibble at her like a constant, coiling worm. She knows she feeds that life, giving it fuel to further grow and nag her. What does she hope to accomplish with this meeting? All of this had begun as part of her effort to prove if Lilja is the vigilante, but it seems to be going further. Her life, though, is one of investigation, and though she still holds much less experience with this off-line variety, she feels better suited than when she first tried.

She makes it to the place, Infusion. She's heard of it, but this is her first visit. It's more avant-garde than the typical cafés, owing to its industrial feel, the bold, abstract art on the walls, and the unconventional seating offered along with the wood and metal tables. The place is also dark and sparsely populated.

Therese glances at one of the two patrons in here – a woman who looks to be in her thirties. She gives Therese the typical quick look and away that most do. She's not the contact. Therese sets her eyes on the older man. He doesn't look up at all from his newspaper. She figures she's the first to arrive to this rendezvous, so she wanders up to the barista, the spectacled girl offering a friendly smile.

Therese gives nothing more than her typical, dry expression, then looks up to study the large menu that hangs on the wall. She knows these brews, not sure why she is even bothering to read the thing. She'll just get a typical coffee and find a seat. Footsteps arise behind her.

"Hello, Therese."

She turns sharply, recognizing the voice, and there stands ex-inspector Gaspare Duilio. He wears a light blazer over a button-down shirt, his slacks close to the dark color of the jacket. His hands are both held down at his sides, but he moves his right toward Therese.

She reacts in a flash, grabbing his wrist with her right hand. She twists, moving closer, then around him, shoving his arm up behind his back, pushing with her momentum. He cries out, dropping to a knee, and she puts more weight on him.

"I am not here to harm you!" he declares.

The barista watches with shock, already reaching for her phone. The other two patrons have also become like beacons, watching the display with wide eyes and growing agitation.

"What the fuck are you doing here?" Therese demands, not relinquishing her hold.

Duilio does nothing physical to extricate himself.

"I came to meet you. I am the one who was speaking to you via the e-mails."

"You set me up," she growls, putting force on his arm, gaining a short, grunting cry of pain from him.

"I did not. I swear. I didn't even know it was you until I saw you just now." He actually emits a short chuckle. "I should have known."

"Stop lying to me."

"Therese, *please*. I am not here to harm you." He tries to look back at her, then his eyes spy the barista. "I think the police have been called. We don't need them to interrupt us."

Therese glances at the young lady then looks around, seeming to remember others are here. She releases Duilio, stepping back.

"Thank you," he breathes, then stands, rubbing his arm. "Therese, wait!"

She has already left the place. He mutters a quick apology to the barista, then rushes out in pursuit.

"Therese!" he looks around, spying her none too far, and he goes to a trot. "Please, wait! I need to talk to you."

She is not running, but her steps come with a rapidity bordering on it. He picks up his own pace, still pursuing. People out here begin to take notice. She finally stops, turning, confronting him with her eyes. Her hands are out of her pockets, ready.

He halts at this, keeping his distance, hands held up in a placating gesture.

"I do not intend you any harm."

"Ma'am, do you need help?"

Therese barely looks at the man who has stopped to offer this. "No," she finally grates out, and Duilio sighs in relief, dropping his hands. The man lingers a moment, looking between them, but then he leaves.

"You keep your distance," Therese says. "I can hurt you."

"Yes, yes." Duilio shows the flash of a grin. "You seem to have gained new skills since last we met."

"Getting kidnapped a couple of times seemed like a good reason to learn some self-defense."

He stares at her, finally giving a short nod. It becomes more emphatic. "Yes, of course. Good for you."

"What do you want?"

"Must we do this here?"

She glances around, noticing a well-lit bus stop. She turns, heading to it. Duilio follows.

"Thank you," he offers once they have settled. No one else currently waits here, but there is the light and other pedestrians are not too far off.

"What do you want?"

He glances about, then back to her. He fishes out a pack of cigarettes, offering one to her. She slowly moves her head side to side. He lights up, taking a deep drag before exhaling a thick plume. He massages his upper arm, giving her a sheepish glance and another of his short, breathy chuckles. He then suddenly looks serious.

"You are looking for Denman Malkuth."

Silence returns. A pedestrian walks by.

"He is a very dangerous man."

"He's a philosophy professor."

"He ..." Duilio begins, the word almost sounding like a question, then his grin emerges. "Of course, he is." He takes another lung-filling drag on the cigarette then fixes his eyes on Therese. "I don't know how much you know, and I don't think I want to know, but I will tell you this, Therese, you are heading to a place that likely ends with your death."

"Fuck you."

Therese turns to leave.

Duilio starts after her, speaking quickly: "I am *not* threatening you."

She turns, again projecting a force of will that is near palpable. "It sure sounds like it."

He trades stares with her, then looks away, huffing. He gives her another sheepish cut of his eyes.

"I... work... for Denman Malkuth."

"What?" She blinks in confusion, giving a quick shake of her head.

"They found out you were looking for him, so they, of course, wanted to know why. I was sent to find out the why... and the who."

"You didn't know it was me?"

"No, Therese, I did not," Duilio says, his voice giving forth sincerity laden with insistence. "I was as surprised as you." He offers another of his brief grins, then again takes on a more serious tone. "If I wanted to harm you, why would I have gone up and greeted you in a public place?"

"That warehouse parking lot wasn't exactly private."

"Fair enough," he gives, again holding up his hands to demonstrate a lack of threat. "Why are you trying to find Denman Malkuth?"

"You said you didn't want to know."

"Yes, I did, but that is not what I mean," he somewhat stammers, "I ... care." She rolls her eyes, but she does not give another turn and attempt to depart. "I am worried. I was worried before I knew it was you."

"And now you're more worried?"

"Yes, I guess I am. I feel guilty for what I did, Therese, as difficult as that may be for you to believe. I will protect you if I can."

"I don't need your protection."

She expects him to offer some rebuttal, some typical thing that men do when they decide that a woman is a prize to be held and controlled. Instead, he just looks at her, grinning. But instead of one of his usual, quick and disarming smiles, this one hints at a devious knowledge. She finds herself feeling a creep of fright.

"Oh, yes. You do. The problem is that I am not sure I'm up to the task."

"What?" she asks, confused. "Then ... why are you here?"

"I'm here to caution you. To hopefully get you to stop, because if you do become a problem for the Malkuths, they *will* kill you. They will not kidnap you or use you as bait. They will kill you."

She parts her lips, going to speak, but no words come out. She gives a jerky shake of her head.

"I … his name just came up with something I'm investigating regarding libraries and rare books. That's it. He's a tangent. He's not even the main thing I'm investigating."

He has another drag on his almost forgotten cigarette. He nods, contemplatively, as he delivers another forceful exhale of smoke.

"Libraries and rare books." He then looks at her. "Knowledge."

She blinks, eyes studying him anew.

"How sure are you that Denman Malkuth is just a tangent in this *investigation* of yours?"

She hangs, inverted, legs wrapped tightly about the punching back. She brings herself up again, feeling that burn in her abdominal muscles. She's lost count of how many she's done, but somewhere in her subconscious, she has a familiarity when enough is enough. She pushes, feeling the simmer of pain. This is what she wants, and she is not ready to stop yet. Her face is a flushed sheen of perspiration, her breathing an audible accompaniment to each curl of her body. She finally stops, reaching up to hold the chain and use that leverage to drop back to her feet.

"Amazing."

Lilja looks over to see the same woman from before again encroaching on her supposed private exercise.

"Pardon my bothering you again, but I just could not stay away."

The redhead goes into some push-ups, trying to ignore the intrusion. The woman does not get to a workout of her own, just watches. Lilja finds it difficult, so she finally gives up, rising to her feet, looking the woman in the eye.

"May I help you?"

"I'm just watching. You're amazing."

"It's just exercise. Anyone can do it."

"Well, not like you do. I am sure many benefit from your instruction."

Lilja narrows her eyes a bit. The woman makes her feel defensive, but there seems no reason to react that way.

"I hope so," she finally gives.

"Self-defense is important. Self-reliance." The woman nods as though having proven the point. "When will your classes resume?"

"I don't know." Lilja does have an idea, but she isn't going to tell.

"Surely it's not for lack of interest?"

"No."

Lilja moves back to the punching bag, turning to better face the woman. She begins striking the bag.

"Is there some other reason, then?"

Obviously, Lilja thinks, wanting to just evict the intruder.

"I'll be going out of town soon." Just as she says this, she wonders why she's offered it.

"Oh?" The woman perks her eyebrows, acting as having sniffed a juicy morsel. "Having a holiday?"

Lilja bobs and dances on her feet, moving with a fluid effortlessness. She hammers several punches into the bag.

"I guess that's none of my business," the woman accedes.

The snapping and thumping reports of the punches have become the instructor's language as Lilja continues to refrain from any reply.

"Still, you'll be coming back. Won't you?"

Lilja pauses, looking over. Something in the woman's tone halts her. This doesn't feel like the cloying attempts at casual conversation typically thrown out by this visitor. The last sentence has been pitched almost as a dare. Lilja peers at the woman, furrowing her brow.

"Of course, I'll be coming back," she finally declares, immediately wondering why she has again let more be drawn from her than she likes.

"Mmm." The woman nods, slowly, staring back in an unabashed way.

Lilja moves about, taking a few steps toward the woman.

"I hope you have a fruitful trip," the woman says, giving a pleasant smile and cant of her head. She then turns and exits the room.

It is some time later when she is visited again, and she just sits there, quietly.

"Lily?"

It takes a moment for the sound to register, but she finally looks over, head moving slowly. She blinks, then gives Skot a shallow smile.

"Hmm?"

"You've been in here a while. I was just checking on you. It got too quiet." He smiles.

She rises to her feet, grabbing a towel and patting herself with it. She picks up her large glass of water, drinking down a good portion. When she glances back over, he is still there, just looking at her.

"I'm all finished up. I think I'll have a shower."

He moves closer, grinning, reaching out for her. "Would you like some company?"

"I'm fine," she says, giving him a quick hug before leaving.

Skot watches as Lilja leaves. Something feels off to him. Things have certainly been tense since the operation at Barrington House, but Lilja feels decidedly distant. He glances about the area, hoping to perhaps garner some clue as to her behavior, but nothing looks out of place here in the training room in their house.

Chapter Six

"The man is a murderer."

Therese drills Duilio with her eyes, plumbing his dryly delivered declaration for truth.

"How can you be sure?"

"I have seen him kill."

He leans back in the chair, taking a drag on a cigarette. The sun has set as they sit outside at this café. Their prior engagement had ended with far too many questions, so she had agreed to meet again. She is still cautious, having told him of this place none too long before the time of the rendezvous. He understands.

"Then why don't you go to the police?"

He gives one of his short chuckles, smoke escaping with it.

"I used to be the police. You know that, don't you?" He studies her. "I was the police when I orchestrated your kidnapping. I worked for criminals. I don't trust the police, and I don't think you do, either."

"Worked?"

"Well, yes, Denman Malkuth is a criminal, but … he is of a different class."

"What do you mean?"

She has taken a few shallow sips of her beer, as though out of some propriety. This has not discouraged Duilio, and he finishes his first glass of red wine. He gives an agreeable nod to the passing waiter, wordlessly ordering another.

"I encountered many international criminals when I was with Interpol. I used to work for a powerful crime boss right here in this city. I thought I knew it all. Even though I was cynical, I still had that hubris. How wrong I was."

Therese continues to stare, boring into him despite its lack of results. "I still don't understand."

"You don't want to."

"Try me."

"The Malkuths are powerful and sophisticated. They don't deal in petty things like extortion or human trafficking. For all I know, they consider those 'bad' things. They don't even do what they do out of greed, though they are phenomenally wealthy."

"*What* do they *do*?" Therese persists.

"They …" Duilio's words trail into more of his chuckling. He barely stops when the waiter returns with a fresh glass of wine. He raises it to Therese, drinking off a good portion.

"Stop getting drunk, or I'll leave."

"Oh, Therese, I would like to get drunk. I have even thought of killing myself."

She blinks, showing little sign of reaction, but inside, she feels again that creep of fear.

"I am experiencing this new thing, this guilt. It rarely bothered me before. I feel a sense of responsibility, maybe even atonement. I want to do some good before I'm gone, but I worry I have made a deal with the devil."

"You mean Denman Malkuth?"

Duilio gives a slow nod. "Yes. He is a devil."

Therese watches him, continuing to closely observe.

"You mean that metaphorically?" she finally decides to ask.

The manner in which his eyes snap to hers again feeds that fear.

"Of course I do." He chuckles, and it sounds overly dismissive to her. He leans over the table, placing both elbows atop it. She does not like the proximity. "They are bad people, the Malkuths. I don't want to work for them anymore, but if I leave, I think they will try to kill me. And … well, I may be able to do more good if I stay where I am."

"Work from the inside," Therese says, gaining a nod from him. "Subvert their operations. If they're so sophisticated, that will also get you killed."

He responds with a chuckle. "Yes, you're probably right." He has another lengthy drag on his cigarette.

Therese finally has more of her beer, still keeping her samples small. Her eyes rarely stray from the man across from her.

"So, what was all that about when you kidnapped me? You said I was bait. We're you trying to trap the vigilante?"

Duilio has again leaned back in his chair, and he gives Therese a somewhat sidelong look, eyes narrowing. She can sense the wheels turning, but she says nothing.

"Yes, we were."

"That obviously didn't work."

"No, it did not. I will confess, I wasn't sure if you had survived. I'm glad you did."

Therese gives the barest hint of a scoff, a tiny pull to one side of her upper lip.

"What the hell happened there that night?"

"I … I am not certain," Duilio says. "It was already unpleasant business, but it turned more so."

"Unpleasant business," she says, giving him a stony look.

"Yes, yes." He tries to placate. "I have done terrible things. I am not washed clean, but I do wish to atone, as I mentioned."

"Do you know who the vigilante is?" she asks, and though she pitches this with the same dry forwardness as all else, her pulse rises.

"Oh, no," he casually responds, crushing out the remnants of his cigarette, then reaching for his wine. "That…" He gives a chuckle, holding the glass poised before his mouth. "Did not seem important once the night had ended."

"I'm sure the police would like to know, or maybe even some criminal organizations."

Duilio sets his glass back on the tabletop, drawing his fingertips down the length of the stem and holding them there at the base as he gazes at the young woman.

"Is that what this is all about?"

Therese does not answer.

"Are you hoping to sell that information and make a nice payday?"

"No!" Therese scowls, pulling back into her chair.

"Ahh, of course. What was I thinking? The vigilante is your friend, no?"

"No," Therese repeats, but in a much less defensive tone.

Duilio emits a low chuckle. "The vigilante saved you. *Twice.*"

"Because I was stupid and got caught. And you know what?" she all but taunts, and Duilio leans forward, curious. "The second time was a fluke. The vigilante wasn't there to rescue me."

"Then why was he there?"

"To bust up your operation."

"It was not mine!" Duilio pulls back from the table, shoulders scrunching up.

"Your boss's, then," Therese snips, eyes slit.

Silence resolves between them. Duilio fishes another cigarette from his pack, but he does not light it, merely rolling it betwixt his fingertips.

"There was more going on there than my *boss* knew."

"What do you mean?"

"Things were much worse than he thought. In fact, he thought things were about to get very good for him, but he was so very wrong. I wonder, though, did your vigilante know about those worse things, hmm?" He sets eyes on her, perking his eyebrows.

"How should I know?"

"Ah, excuse me, the question is … rhetorical. I just wonder how much the vigilante knew."

Silence again finds a place, but Duilio intercedes before it may take too much of a hold. "What is this really all about? Why are you looking for Denman?"

"You said you didn't want to know."

"So you keep reminding me, but I am like you – an investigator."

"That information is privileged."

He gives a shrug, tilting his head and pursing out his bottom lip. He then brings the cigarette up and slips it into his mouth. He grabs the lighter, flicking it to life.

"I will have to tell them something, and if it doesn't satisfy them, they will push me away and use other methods."

"What're you going to tell them?"

"I have not yet decided, but I'm not sure they'll be satisfied with the answer of 'rare books'."

"You think they'd come after me over something like that?"

"I really don't know. I have given up on trying to understand the Malkuths. But maybe we can help each other."

"How?" Therese challenges.

He fixes her with another piercing stare. "How good are you at *hiding*, Therese?"

Night. What illumination there is comes from the sporadic fires. Some lick up from within diminished barrels, others toil on the ground, quickly eating their fuel amidst a haphazard collection of rocks and detritus. Shadows dance to the fiery beat. Fog has rolled in, giving more disturbance to proper perception.

A series of coughs erupt. The grating sound rises to a wet crescendo. Several pairs of eyes stare at Pierce as his hacking disturbs the otherwise eerie quiet. A reflecting gleam flashes off the fresh blood at his lips. He wipes at with a bony knuckle.

He looks back at those watching him. Most avert their eyes. Others here are lost in a dreamy haze of drug-use. They hide clueless within their own shroud, separate from the one infusing the area.

"It's coming."

Pierce's eyes then find Lance, giving him a nod. He takes his compatriot by the arm, moving him into a darker part of this place they have all come to think of as some perverse home. Lance stumbles, limping, trying to keep up. He grumbles out some protest.

"Just sit down and be quiet!" Pierce all but hisses at him.

They both do. Their observance darts about. The fog further rolls in.

The sounds begin to seem louder, as though echoing off the condensing air. Some reposition themselves, or make some pitiful effort to do so. Others hold their place, eyes fixed, their entire aspect one of apathetic surrender. No one is standing.

Light grows from the westerly direction, the strange illumination finding the mist, giving it more life as though a restlessly weaving vibrancy to the very air. Some might say the radiance merely shows what had always been there, but they would be wrong. It is not blinding, this light, but it should not be there all the same.

Some of those gathered glance at the growing illumination, a few looking over their shoulders, others staring from across the way, transfixed. Two people scoot away, still not taking to their feet, merely dragging their rumps over the worn earth, uncaring of rent pavement. They find a discolored, cardboard box to hide behind, huddling in like frightened rats.

"Whu-whu-whu-?" one asks, bringing up a bent finger to point toward the light and swirling fog. The question remains unvocalized, a thick stream of spittle trailing down from the hanging lip.

A figure has appeared, something insubstantial in the haze. It possesses a humanoid shape, though it seems too tall, the arms far too long, very slender. Something waves atop the head, as though suggestive of hair but all too thick. There is no wind to cause the motion. No one screams. Many just keep up the hypnotic observance.

Some others try to get away, crawling about, generating a ruckus. They do not go far, only trying to get some distance between themselves and the nearing shape. Whimpers arise, people huddling together, watching, waiting. Whispers rise between some, the sound sibilant, and a word may be discerned: "sacrifice".

The figure in the fog continues its lumbering approach, becoming larger but somehow not sharper. The haze appears to embrace it and thread through it. It moves by two people huddled on the ground, trying to become insubstantial themselves. Their wide eyes watch the passage.

The creature displays no awareness of those here, that bright light continuing to eclipse any detail of itself, giving up no more than the strange, shadowy shape. The movement continues atop its head, the tendrils giving forth a crinkling, wet noise.

The eyes of the observers stay latched on it, magnetized to the happening. The thing walks by another, this one laid out on her back, completely lost to intoxication. It pauses, rising further, its height already impossible. It then strikes out with a preternatural speed that appears all the more shocking due to how lumbering and slow it has been up to this point. Voices cry out to punctuate the motion, but the one that proves loudest belongs to the man now held in the creature's unfailing grasp.

"No. No!" he protests, struggling. "Not me. I don't want to go!"

The thing brings him closer, evincing more of its own bizarre size now that is has captured a closer point of reference.

"No. Oh, God, *no!*" The man's voice tapers off to retching, the meager contents of his stomach pulsing forth, sputtering out in an impotent dribble.

The monster turns, back to its slow movement. The man spasms in its grasp, finally lulling after a croaking series of sounds heralding more vomiting. The audience remains tense, silent, those that are aware. When the beast has finally faded, peace and quiet return. It might seem that nothing terrible has happened at all. The discharged fluid from the taken man mingles with the ubiquitous stains about the place, becoming one of many and nothing special.

"I-I thought it was going to choose me," a voice finally rises into the tense quiet.

Pierce looks at Lance. What fear had been there is now gone.

"They wouldn't take you."

"How … how do you know?"

"I just know. They wouldn't take me, and they wouldn't take you. We're too important."

Lance gives a shaky nod, one that does not belie conviction. Pierce looks about the area, sensing the dwindling shock. What hope have they? They are used to being mixed in the shit of this world. They'd all sell their souls for a way out.

They've finally arrived at Scholomance.

Their presence proves impressive, and Lilja is again taken at how much influence the Felrafts seem to have. The only reason she has not grown used to it in the time she has known them is due to how rarely they make such overt shows of it.

Nearly a dozen of them are here, and they have brought equipment. They managed to get all of this in-country and secure approval from the local government to thoroughly 'study' the historical grounds. What's more, the authorities have only sent one person to accompany them, and the man, Mihai Ungur, seems well out of his league.

He stands aside, eyes darting about as he watches the Felcrafts unpack. He gives a slight flinch when he first sees weapons, but he knows the permits are in place. He has been tasked with menial observation, told in no uncertain terms to stay out of the way unless they commit serious violations. He is not even entirely sure why they are here, but his mind is merely occupied with making it through this.

"Mr. Ungur!" calls out a voice, and the delegate turns to see the approach of David Felcraft, a smile on his face. He clasps the man on the shoulder. "Everything is coming along just fine."

"Yes, but-"

"I want you to meet someone." David beckons, and a pretty blond woman approaches, her hair long and straight, her eyes a bright blue. "Mihai Ungur, meet my cousin, Kim Felcraft."

"Ah. Oh, yes. Nice to meet you."

"A pleasure," Kim replies, her voice honeyed with its American accent. She gives the man a bright smile.

"Kim is going to keep you company while we do our business. She's happy to answer any questions you have. Is that okay?"

Mihai looks between them both. He blinks somewhat rapidly. "Oh, well, yes, that seems fine."

"Wonderful!" David walks off, noting as his relative steps in a touch closer, immediately engaging the man in casual conversation. He quickly gains Skot's side, noting as his cousin observes the new pairing. "Kim'll keep him busy."

"I doubt she was even needed," Skot assesses.

David gives a nod.

"We'll have two teams," Skot begins, and though David knows most of this, he snaps to more focus. "I'll lead the first team, Alpha, and you'll lead the second, Bravo. Lilja will be with you. Zoe will be with me."

David nods, realizing the wisdom of this. There will be other Hunters along with them, of course, but none of them possess the same strength of abilities. They are fitted with communication devices. Some will also stay behind to handle monitoring and tracking. The main expectation is that they will find nothing, or at most, perhaps something mundane that may prove suitable for a museum. This place has been explored before. They have also experienced unexpected Infernal presence in seemingly unlikely areas, so full precautions are being taken.

There is one, though, who still thinks it is a trap.

Zoe looks across the way at Lilja. The redhead appears as calm and collected as ever. Quiet, too. She is not at Skot's side, but the proximity is undeniable. Both young women display a veritable arsenal – Zoe with her slung shotgun, machete, and sidearm; Lilja carrying her G36C, katana, and pistol.

Zoe thinks back to their stint at the Barrington house. This all started there – the easily found "hidden" closet, the word, finding a trail that had always been waiting, Lilja's upside-down shadow, and the possessed mannequin that called out to her. The young Hunter cannot recall a time when the Infernal showed such abilities. Still, she assumes that if such a thing were more common or known, it would have been dismissed. This all leads her to think they are walking into some trap, and Lilja is the bait.

Suitably kitted and briefed, the two teams head out.

The courtyard shows its age, the small island here on the lake being taken over by the ruins of the structure. Grass grows up between cobblestones, some areas showing a complete lack of the carefully placed rock. What had been found inside before generally suggests this place did once hold purpose as a school or library, but no convincing records exist. It could well have been some wealthy nobleman's island retreat, though what is left does not seem to fit the idea of a residence. Still, it is all conjecture.

Once up the wide staircase, they are presented with their first choice. Two paths lead inside. "We'll take right," Skot says.

The two four person teams split. Skot spares a glance toward Lilja, but she is focused on the mission. His squad heads inside, finding themselves in a large, dusty room. Remnants of furniture occupy the edges, though some spare and broken pieces of wood have become litter on the floor. Sunlight gets in through one sizable window, the thin wood covering so splintered and worn as to provide little shielding at all. The solar rays catch clouds of floating particles, more rising as they make their way further along.

A quick examination of the furniture shows nothing of interest. Whatever once resided in these cabinets and cases is long gone, nothing inside or atop them. Two of the team members are snapping photos, but Zoe is keeping a sharp eye for threats. She drifts into her keener sense, but nothing suspicious shows.

The room gives way to a short staircase, turning ninety degrees and rising to an elevated portion of the floor. A silent assent is given by Skot and one of the other two Hunters takes advantage of the dilapidated state of the room to investigate beneath the raised area. The tactical light of his weapon shines within, revealing little more than dust and cobwebs. The place has been plumbed.

"HQ, this is Bravo Three. We have a situation."

Everyone pauses. Skot recognizes the voice on the com, and it is not David's.

"Roger, Bravo Three. Situation?"

"It's David and Lilja …"

Tense moments pass. They've all been trained in radio communication, but Skot can sense the anxiety veritably dripping from the other Hunter's words. He knows the people back outside are waiting as tersely as he, wanting to hear the rest but fearful of interrupting the frequency.

"Bravo Three, this is HQ. Repeat."

"They're gone! They just disappeared."

All eyes of the team look at Skot. No one is moving.

"Bravo Three, say again."

"David and Lilja are *gone*. I say again: *gone*."

"Bravo Three, this is Alpha One. We're en route," Skot interjects. When he heads out, they all follow.

Their movement is much quicker now, footsteps bringing up clouds of dust. They backtrack in seconds, through the edge of the courtyard and the other door. Two members of Bravo team await them, both carrying etchings of worry upon their skin. A quick glance around indeed shows no one else.

Skot approaches Curtis, one of the two left from Bravo. Tension boils deep, threatening to rise, but Skot suppresses it. He speaks in a calm tone: "Curtis, tell me what happened."

"We were just walking in, moving slow, checking things out, and then they disappeared."

Skot moves his eyes in a quick examination of the hallway. Unlike the chamber they found going right, this route has produced a wide passageway. It arches at the top, showing a smooth curve, the walls once lined in a firmer stone now showing their age.

"They went that way?" he asks, indicating with a nod of his head.

"Yes, yes."

Skot gives a look to Zoe, then continues down the hallway. The others follow, taking up positions.

"David? Lilja? Do you copy?" he tries, but he knows they won't answer. If able, they'd transmit.

They move carefully, eyes constantly on the move. He knows he's never encountered anything like this before, and he can't recall ever reading of anything like this. How could they just disappear?

It takes him a moment to realize it, for Zoe is still there near him, but he looks back, and they are alone.

"Zoe?"

"Yeah?"

He motions with his head toward the way they came. She looks back, stopping, blinking as her head rises on stiffening spine.

"What the Hell? Where did everyone go?"

"Where did *we* go?"

She looks at him then turns back, staring down the hallway, reaching inside for that extra sense to her perception. "There's something there."

He peers, setting his own studied gaze on that throat-liked walkway. He mutters, speaking words in a secret language, bringing up his left hand to articulate the required gestures.

It bleeds in like oily water reflecting light, the edges like a dark halo, tendrils wafting about upon their own air. The center shimmers as though a bubble caught in a framework.

"A gateway."

"How did we miss that?" Zoe asks. "And-" she cranes her head about, grip tightening on her weapon. "Are we in the Infernal Realm?"

"I don't think so," he slowly replies, also giving the normal-seeming walkway a renewed inspection. "HQ, this is Alpha One. Come in."

Nothing.

"HQ, this is Alpha One. Do you copy?"

"Skot?" a different voice responds.

"Lilja? Is that you?"

"Yes, it's Lilja. Where are you? We lost contact for a time. Over."

"We came to find you, but we're lost now, too."

"What? Can you repeat that?"

"We need to rendezvous."

"Acknowledged. We're back-tracking. Hold your position. Bravo Two out."

Mere moments later, they hear the sounds and then David and Lilja appear coming up the hallway.

"We're not sure what happened, but it's good to see you," David says, giving a smile.

"What's that?" Lilja asks.

"A gateway." Skot experiences a fleeting sense of déjà vu, hearkening back to the time he discovered Lilja was the vigilante.

"So, that's how we got here," David concludes.

"Where's 'here'?" Zoe inserts.

Skot looks around then back to find all eyes on him. "I'm not sure, but this looks like the hallway we started in. What did you two find?"

David gives a perfunctory shrug. "Looks like the remains of a building."

"Not exactly."

All eyes go to Lilja.

"Look," she says, gesturing to the walls. "It's not all dusty and worn."

Skot nods, walking over, daring to place a hand on the stone. "You're right."

When he turns back, the team is again focused on him, waiting, wondering.

"I don't know what's going on, but we need to find out if that gateway will allow us to return. They're back there scrambling and worried right now, just like we were when you two first went off the radar."

They all eventually nod, though he can clearly see the reluctance. This feels unprecedented, and they all want to explore.

"Right. We need to be sure we can return, then we can set up-" David begins.

"No." Skot halts him. "Just see if you can get back. Let them know we're alright."

David nods.

"And I want to be sure you're alright, so once you do that, come back to us."

David gives another nod, terse, confident, then heads back toward the gateway.

They all watch, collective breath held. He gets to the shimmering portal, as though the gently waving surface of a lake held on its side, and he moves through, disappearing.

Silence as they wait. Thoughts rumble through all of them. Where are they? Can they get back? What else is down the hall? Very little time passes before David returns.

"It worked."

David nods to Skot. "Sorry I took so long. Things are pretty chaotic, but I got them all to calm down. They didn't like me coming back, figured we should all go back and plan better, but I told them what you said."

"Could you see the gate from the other side?"

David shakes his head. "No. Still invisible. But I explained it to them and told them to hang tight on their side."

"Good. Alright, let's see what else we can find. Zoe, take point."

The young Huntress nods, moving out. The others quickly follow. Skot pauses to examine the walls. He looks over to find Lilja staring at him.

"I'm coming," he says.

They move further down the hall to find themselves in a spacious room. Much of the walls here are occupied by recessed bookcases, though they are empty. There is only one other avenue out - a large staircase heading down. The broad steps are covered by a dark fabric running up the middle, the sides and railing looking polished and pristine.

"There's something down there."

"What?" Skot looks over to Zoe as the quartet holds place at the top.

"I'm sensing something. It's faint, but it's there."

"Infernal," David comments.

"Stay sharp," Lilja offers, her eyes scanning what they may.

Skot gives a nod to Zoe, and she proceeds down. They all follow, David, keeping to the rear. Everyone keenly observes, though the light here proves none too terribly bright, showing up within strange colors as though diffused through pale, stained glass. There is little noise or scent.

"This is not our world. Expect anything," Skot advises, and though no one falters, a weight descends.

Zoe gets to the end of the steps, heading right into a large chamber. There are more empty bookcases. The room shows a recessed floor in its center. Though everything feels odd, it does not seem like another plane of existence. This is nothing like Skot thought the Infernal Realm would be, and considering David made it back safely, this does not fit with what little information they have on Hunters who went through gateways. Everything seems too still, as though a model or something artificial.

"Is this a replica?"

"What?" Zoe halts, looking back.

Lilja also sets her eyes on her boyfriend. He returns her gaze.

"What if we had kept going back there and missed the gateway?" he posits. "Not even all of us went through. Is it like this back there only showing its age?"

"I thought something like that," Lilja says.

"The walls," he mentions, and she nods in return.

"What do you mean?" David asks, his own wrinkled brow belying his confusion.

"I'm not sure," Skot admits. "It's a theory, but this looks like it could be the school, but it also doesn't look old enough, and we know we went through a gateway."

"We don't know what happens when someone goes through a gateway," Zoe says. "Only demons use them."

They all hold position for a moment, the stale air suddenly thick with tension. Skot finally looks toward the only way left to go – a rectangular opening in one wall.

"Let's keep going."

They are not even all in the room when a loud explosion rocks them, as though an artillery shell landing nearby.

They immediately go into action, crouching or dropping completely to the ground, returning fire in the direction the attacks seems to come from. There is no furniture in the room, but several large concrete blocks hold place, as though caskets covered in simplicity or smooth stone grown from the very floor.

Zoe rushes forward, hiding behind one, squatting low, peering. She sees it, something there, unleashing a barrage of magick unto them. She points her shotgun around from the covering, firing blindly. Skot had been a few steps inside, and he dashes to safety.

David rushes in, also heading to a source of cover, unloading his rifle in three round bursts. Lilja steps in calmly, legs bent to make her less of a target as well as to stabilize. She moves in a steady line, her compact assault rifle tucked in tight to her shoulder as she squeezes off precise shots. The air is a riot, filled with the amber tracers of their bullets, but there is something else. She sees it and holds fire.

Whatever the thing is that is ambushing them, it has projected a shield. The air coils with energy, the large, disc-shaped manifestation alive with a whirling of bright light, and the shots of theirs which might hit the target instead ricochet away. The averted bullets find the walls, creating marks and lines as they crack and hiss and kick up dust.

"Shit!" Zoe curses, ducking down, realizing that they are likely making things worse by shooting the magical projection.

She is not the only who comes to this conclusion, and the thing takes advantage of the lull to unleash another attack of its own, bolts of seeming fire lobbing out, raining destruction where they fall. Skot stays huddled back, but his mind races with what they are facing. He cannot recall any demon that displayed such powers, and he has scoured their records more than once.

David sights in, all four having taken various positions throughout the room to better effect attack and defense. He spies the thing, and it shows a vaguely humanoid shape. This does not concern him in the least, and he squeezes the trigger of his M4 carbine. It happens in a split instant, but the thing turns to him just as he pulls, as though sensing the attack, and it shifts the spiraling shield to block the incoming bullet.

The thing is not quiet, either, giving up its own grunts and retorts as of common sounds of combat. The room is immersed in a cacophony, but Skot hears something, something off. He angles his head, trying to pick those sounds apart from the rest.

Lilja is silent, and she creeps about, having slipped and dashed to the far side of the large chamber. Her rifle is now strapped tightly to her torso, and she carries her katana at the ready. She is bare meters from the thing and also notes the shape. It reminds her of any number of demon-possessed humans she has faced, though it seems larger, somewhat distorted. She wonders if it is another powerful skin wearer. It still bothers her to kill humans in the throes of such control. Still, a threat is a threat. Having gained enough proximity, she lunges.

The thing is fast. Too fast. It turns to face her, extending an arm, fingers of the hand splayed, shouting, "Regredior daemon!" Lilja is flung back, colliding roughly with the wall.

Skot moves out of cover, standing to full height. He quickly draws in power, ushering forth with great force and magick: "Non sumus daemōnēs!"

Everything halts. Everyone looks at Skothiam. He looks back at their opponent, hoping his suspicion will be confirmed. He sees what indeed does look to be a man, though radiating with such preternatural energy as to rival his sister. This thing, this man speaks Latin, and though Skot is not fully fluent, he hopes he knows enough.

Eyes study with an outré awareness, hands yet aglow with the promise of further lethal release. Skot steps further into view, arms open in a non-threatening way.

"We are not demons," he repeats, still speaking Latin.

"You do not have the demonic cast," the man finally utters, and though Skot has some difficulty with the enunciation, he does understand. "But you are unfamiliar to me, as are your weapons. Strange sorcery. Whose side are you on?" The last shifts from the guarded, conversational tone to one of demand.

"The humans' side," Skot says.

The others have not strayed from their positions. Lilja has recovered, paying close attention, able to pick up some on the exchange. She moves nearer, noting how Skot exposes himself.

Curiosity courses through her now, but she is ever-watchful for a threat.

The man moves his head back. His eyes dart again over the assembled.

"We fight the demons," Skot continues, still keeping to Latin. "We thought you were a demon."

"Of course, I am not! I am the Guardian."

"Of what?"

The man again takes time to observe. His aspect has muted, but Skot can still sense the power.

"How fares the battle outside?"

"The battle outside?"

"Yes! The one for the school."

Confusion has now found all of them, though the others remain patient and watchful. Zoe moves to peek through another open doorway as the conversation she does not understand continues.

"There is no battle outside."

The man looks upon Skot for a moment, then sighs. "It is over, then. Are they all dead?"

"Is who all dead?"

"The defenders! At least this means the demons could not breach the gate."

"You there put," Lilja says, trying to venture into the Latin conversation.

The man drills his eyes into her, and she stares back, unfazed.

"The gate," Skot elaborates. "You opened it?"

"We created it."

"Where are we?"

The man looks again at those who have entered his domain. Though he looks guarded, the conversation continues.

"This is a separate place, but it is based on the school. It is in-between dimensions."

"Time?" Lilja asks.

"Time is also affected," the man answers, "but the battle is finally over?"

A moment passes, and the air feels to fill with the weight of it.

"Yes," Skot finally replies.

"The demons are gone, then?"

"Yes."

Those eyes again drift over the others in here.

"You are not here because of the battle," the man concludes.

"No," Skot admits, "we were not sure what we would find."

"Why are you here?"

"We seek the book, *Ostia Tenebrosa*."

The man reels back, eyes widening. He brings up his hands, fingers crooking a peculiar way as he begins to murmur. Lilja notices, legs bending as she hefts her weapon.

"No!" Skot calls out, raising his hands, palms out. He speaks rapidly, switching between English and Latin. "Do not attack," then, "We are not possessed. We are not demons. You must know this. We have the other two books."

The man's eyes go even wider. "Is it true?"

Skot nods, soberly, standing there, letting himself be scrutinized.

"You *do* speak truth." The man looks from Skot to the others, seeming to suddenly see them in a new light. "And the battle. You said it was over."

Skot looks at the man. He pulls in a breath. "We don't know when it happened, but it ended more than five hundred years ago."

The man stares. He finally blinks. His lips part, and Skot expects him to rebut. He does not. "You speak truth," is realized instead.

"What power this?" Lilja interjects, having managed to keep up with the basics of the conversation.

The man looks at her, brow furrowing.

"This in-between place. The gateway. Being outside of time," Skot expands.

"You do not know these magicks?"

"No."

He heaves a sigh. "We created this school to properly train people, but it all fell apart."

"What happened?"

The man looks upon Skot then turns, as though defeated. That undeniable potency that filled him looks gone, deflated. He moves into an adjacent room. The others follow.

This one looks more comfortable. The shelves are not entirely empty, and there is furniture in good condition. The man has taken place in a large, wooden chair, cushions on the seat and armrests. They also notice sigils painted on the walls, the aspect and intricacy very deliberate.

"Please, sit," the man invites. "There is no need to rush here."

Skot nods, explaining to the others as he finds a place near the guardian. They do not appear so eager to relax, looking around, slowly finding some degree of calm. Skothiam introduces himself and his companions. The man's eyes move to each, piercing, not as bereft of promise as the rest of him has so suddenly become. Skot looks upon him, thinking of a piano wire that has finally been cut.

"My name is Kuzma Nasht." Silence finds them for a moment, but it feels weighty.

"The battle?" Skot prompts.

"Yes," Nasht replies, the question having broken his repose. "It was only a matter of time. I am surprised it took as long as it did."

Zoe stands near David, watching the exchange. Though the two are unable to comprehend it, they study in their own ways. Lilja also pays close attention, picking up enough to follow the basic thread of the conversation.

"You know there is real magick here," Nasht continues. "Superstition is rampant as well. We took on students, but so few of them showed any real promise. This sparked jealousy. The rumors began. We do not sell our souls to Satan!" The others look over at the sudden rise in volume. "Those are foul lies begun by the demons themselves to thwart us."

Skot nods, contemplatively. He will not share with the man that the school still bears the shadow of that reputation.

"The *inquisitors* began to infringe on our undertaking. What does it mean that the Church was doing the business of the Infernal?" He heaves a sigh. "I am not sure they even wanted to steal our secrets. They just wanted us to burn."

"The demons were after the book," Skot says.

Nasht looks at him, finally nodding. "Of course. That is why we took such measures to protect it."

Skot glances at Lilja, and her eyes meet his for a brief moment. He contemplates the situation. Might it be better to just leave the book here? He hesitates to think of this guardian's lot. Is he stuck here forever? What might happen to him if he passes through that gate?

"Where is book?"

Both men set their eyes on Lilja.

"Ahhh, that is also part of our defense," Nasht answers. "We expected the demons to breach the defense, even make it through the gateway. I was waiting to give my last fighting them."

"It's not here."

Nasht moves his eyes to Skot, nodding.

"We made another gateway, and it was carried away for further safety. I know only where that passage led but not where the book ultimately found its repose."

It is Skot's turn to sigh. The guardian nods again.

"I understand. It is better to know where it is for that protection, but we were desperate."

"Of course."

"Where?" Lilja asks.

The man sets his eyes on her, again studying. "You. You are also a guardian." She nods once. Skot fights the sudden twinge he feels inside.

"Leng," Nasht finally reveals. "It was carried to Leng."

"Leng?" Skot asks. "That is a place of myth."

"Oh, no," the elder man replies, shaking his head. "You should know that such places do exist. Think where you stand even now."

"Between place."

They both look to Lilja, and Nasht nods. "Yes. Unlike here, it is a permanent connection to our world, but it is not a land native to the Infernal. It disappoints me that such knowledge has been lost over time."

"How do we get there?" Skot asks, bringing Nasht out of his sudden drift into thoughtful melancholy.

"You must go to Tibet."

Chapter Seven

It is past 2:00 AM. The dark, stillness, and quiet work to paint a strange dimension over that which feels known. Eyes creep unto the solitude, looking for hints of danger. Is something there, or do they create it with their concern? Fingers scratch at the blemished flesh, dirty, cracked nails working, working, finally breaking the surface for that rich treasure of blood.

"Are you okay?" Lance asks, looking at Pierce.

"What? Yes."

Lance is not convinced. He thinks none of them are okay. He truly knows this, but something in his innate defense mechanism conceals that in hopeful doubt. He looks up, trying to find some other light besides the seep of distant street lamps and fading oil can fires.

"How's your leg?"

He looks again at Pierce, surprised at the sincerity in that voice. "It hurts."

"Here," Pierce says, producing a small pill bottle like a street magician.

"What's this?"

"Aspirin."

"Thanks."

He pops the cap, crunching then dry-swallowing one. He peeks inside, shaking the container, hearing very few left. "How'd you get these?"

Pierce shrugs.

Lance looks up as one of their shadowy brethren shuffles by. He is not sure who it is. He is not even sure of their gender.

"Do you ever wonder if you'll be next?"

Pierce looks at him, face pinching with annoyance. "Next for what?"

Lance stares back, stretching the silent moment. He finally answers, speaking in a fearful whisper. "The next sacrifice for when that … *thing* comes."

"Don't be stupid," Pierce retorts. "You know we're special, and they won't-" His voice disappears into a stream of coughs. This gains a look of worry from Lance. The sickeningly wet sound continues, breaking up the peace of the night, becoming a terrible clarion in the quiet.

"Are you sure you're alright?"

Pierce glares at him, then gets up and stalks away at a pace he knows his lame companion cannot match. He hunkers in a shadow. He hears someone close, some raspy breath. The person is probably asleep. He doesn't care. Lambs for slaughter.

He doesn't know why he and Lance were chosen. At first, it seemed like even more bad luck heaped upon this curse called life. They both became ill, which can easily turn into a death sentence for street people like themselves. Sure, they could go to some free clinics, but there'd only be so much effort given for dregs like them. At least, that was his take on the matter.

The symptoms had worsened, then stabilized. It can't possibly have been that long, but to him, it now feels like forever. As though history stretches far before his birth, and he was always there, hacking up blood as some bizarre toll to draw this fetid breath. His memories have been compromised, just like his body.

He feels a tickle, but this one is not to a herald of another coughing fit. No. He moves from the shadow, shuffling toward the twenty-four hour internet café. Time for more messages.

Fingers hold poise over the keyboard, and it might seem a ready lurking were it not for the slight tremble. The fingernails could use a cleaning. A blur as the digits move, speeding over the keys as a sudden maestro. They stop, hanging there, occasional twitching taking one or another.

Eyes do not notice the time, now nearing 3:00 AM. He's been paying close attention to other things, many other things. He has pieced together some of the puzzle, connected some dots in the hazy, fog-shrouded web. One of those pieces is another person, and he composes a message to her.

It's not a long message, but he keeps worrying over it, trying to pick the right words. The intended recipient will be unhappy to receive this and might immediately move to cover the small holes in her careful approach that allowed him to find her in the first place.

He does not cough, at all. His name is not Pierce, for many still avoid sleep at this hour, coursing around in cyberspace or the meat world. He decides to send her some links and details but not all of it. This is too sensitive for that, even if both of them hold abilities beyond the norm.

He hopes he will hear back from her. This is important. Too important for Sparrow to ignore.

Zoe brings the glass of bourbon to her lips, taking a generous swig. She swallows it with no outward sign of any burn. The glass is somewhat large, and there is some ice in there, but the measure of whiskey is generous. She is too young to legally be drinking in the U.S., but she is a regular here. She's never been asked for I.D. She also usually drinks beer, but this time, she opted for something stronger.

The burly, bearded bartender already had a bottle pulled from the cooler when he saw the shorn-haired girl walk in. She stopped him with a small shake of her head and steely-eyed gaze, uttering her desired drink. The slightest rise of his unkempt eyebrows had been his only reaction.

One might think of this as a biker bar, maybe a metal bar. The clientele and music suggests both of those, but that is not the entirety of their visitors. The bartender has seen Zoe coming in here for a good while. He knows she doesn't hold any interest in idle chatter. He thinks she's in the military or possibly a vet, but there isn't a base that close, and she sometimes comes in on weeknights. He also wonders if maybe she partakes in criminal pursuits, what with her aspect and the thick folds of cash usually pulled from those pockets.

He's seen some guys hit on her. As far as he knows, none have ever succeeded. There's never been any trouble, but it's clear she brushes them off quickly. She's a pretty girl, even if her hair is so short and she doesn't wear make-up and dresses kind of masculine. Hell, he's thought before of trying to get in her shell, but he's past his prime.

He notices it now, though, and a part of him knew it the first time she walked in. There's an edge there. She's seen things. That's why he thinks she military and part of why he's never bothered to ask her for I.D. Hell, some local cops came in once, and though one of them gave a bit of a curious look, they didn't ask about her at all. They didn't talk to her, either.

Zoe knows she could throw around the Felcraft weight. Her extent of that is to collect a very nice paycheck, really more of a stipend, and use it to live on her own away from most of the central family. It's not that she doesn't love them, but she feels like something of a black sheep.

She's been given a short respite before they head overseas to continue looking for the third and last book. She wonders about that, still worried that all of this is a trap with Lilja at its core. When Skothiam had been talking to the centuries old guardian they'd found, she and David spent the time basically watching and waiting. Lilja, though, had been right up in it, even throwing in some comments from time to time. It chapped Zoe. Skot is the Head, so it was his place to talk to the guardian.

It bothers her to know how little time Lilja has been among them and yet how much privilege she gets. She's had the woman's skills and experience hammered into her head as they all seem to spring to her defense. Even Nicole thinks something special lies inside the redhead, but Zoe doesn't care. They're *all* special, every single Hunter, and as Zoe is quick to point out, she's been training for it her whole life.

She just doesn't get it. She's the last one to follow rules for their own sake, but the amount of leeway given is obvious. Lilja's the main reason they didn't push harder to get the book out of the university's library! If it weren't for her, that book would be in the Felcraft's private collection.

Zoe doesn't look up when she's approached. The bartender obliquely notices, seeing the man walk up from behind and casually slip atop the barstool beside the young woman. There are plenty of available spots in the place, so he assumes this is another one who is going to try. Zoe still doesn't look over when the man up-nods to the keeper.

"A refill for the lady, and I'll have one, too."

He shifts his eyes to Zoe, and she finally seems to give some outward attention, nodding lightly to the bartender with closed eyes before focusing on the newcomer. "David, what are you doing here?"

"I came to have a drink with you," David says, smiling as good-naturedly as you please.

Zoe shakes her head with a barely noticeable motion.

"You'd think we hadn't just found out something huge. Why are you so grumpy?"

The bartender sets the two whiskeys in front of them, eyeballing the exchange as if he expects something bad to happen. Zoe slits her eyes at David, then has a deep draw on the fresh drink. "What did we find out?"

Now comes David's turn for a light shake of the head, then angles with a gesture. "Let's go sit somewhere more private." He heads off to a secluded table, and Zoe follows. "What's in your craw? Wait, don't tell me. Lilja."

Zoe gives him a cold look from beneath her brow. He smirks, having more of his own drink.

"You really need to-"

"No. Did you go to the debriefing with Skot and Nicole?"

David just looks at her.

"Did you?"

"You know I didn't."

"But *she* was there."

David says nothing, because they both know this as well. He readies to resume speaking, but she again cuts him off.

"I don't care how good she is. It's one thing to use her in the field so much, but she basically is involved in command decisions now. And you know what, if she's good enough for that, then where has she been all this time?"

"What?" David asks, looking at Zoe with an etching of confusion on his features.

"How many wild Hunters do you know out there? If we don't find them, then usually the Malkuths do. Or they're really unlucky, and the demons get them. How many wild Hunters are just out there, doing their thing, with no one bothering them, and then we just find each other when they're in their twenties? No one survives that long."

"She did."

"Well, doesn't that worry you ... even a little bit?"

"Why should it?"

She looks at him, incredulous. "Because no one does that. *No one.*"

"*She* did."

Zoe looks upon her cousin, lips parted as though to say more, but instead, she shakes her head.

"Okay, Zoe, then what do you think it is? Why did she survive that long?" No answer proves forthcoming, so he carries on. "Do you think she's in league with the Infernal?"

"Nnn- I don't know."

"Is she being manipulated by the Malkuth?"

"No."

"Then what is it?"

And again silence rises for an answer.

"You can't keep thinking it's just because she's Skot's girlfriend. Do you think Nicole would put up with it if that were the case? They both obviously see something special about her, and maybe that's the *exact* reason she survived as long as she did on her own. She didn't need us to rescue her, and she still doesn't. She's helping us. We're lucky to have her."

"Maybe," comes out like a petulant child.

"Maybe? She's saved Skot's life on more than one occasion!"

"And I've saved yours, and you've saved mine. That's what we do."

David takes in a breath, readying to say something in response, but an exasperated shake of the head is as far as it gets.

"Okay, okay." Zoe nods. "She's talented. *Very* talented. She's had years of training, even if it wasn't specifically related to being a Hunter, but you have to admit that too many *big* decisions are made because of her or with her direct input. David, you're one of the most senior people in the family, and you're less involved in that."

"Hmph. I don't want to be in charge."

"I knew you'd say that, and you know that doesn't matter."

David takes some time to drink, eyeballing Zoe. "You're still sore about that mission and Skot not putting you in charge."

Zoe gives one of her cold looks, the kind the bartender thinks do not bode well at all for the recipient. David, of course, fails to be cowed.

"Forget who was in charge, and think about everything the Infernal did specifically to her."

"Zoe, we've been over this."

"So! They didn't do it to *me*. They did it to *her*. *Why?*"

"I don't know why," he forcefully answers. "They also left Charles' body in a bad state specifically for Skot, or was that targeted at Lilja, too?"

No answer arises.

"You know they needle us. You *know* it. Maybe they see her as an easier target due to her lack of experience."

"Exactly!" Zoe almost shouts, making David wonder if he hasn't stepped into a trap.

He opens his mouth to again say something, but he thinks the better of it, deciding instead to stick to his drink.

"So, you are going to meet with him?"

Therese looks Duilio in the eyes, her fingers playing over the mug of coffee. It is in the evening, but she prefers the stimulating brew over alcohol. Her companion's preference is firmly established, and he looks back at her over a glass of wine.

"This is a dangerous thing, Therese."

She still says nothing, just looking back at him. He figures he should be thankful she even told him, even agreed to meet again. He sighs, taking a sip of his drink.

"You are going to do this."

She nods, slowly, though the words proved no question.

"You were captured twice!" he suddenly exclaims, but his show of passion gains none from her in return. "What if they have guns, or they are better trained, or they have many people?"

A moment passes as Therese ponders this.

"It's just one guy."

"How do you *know*?"

She gives a meager shrug. "He's like me, a hacker. We're typically loners, not the best trained or suited for offline encounters."

"Then let me go with you."

"Eehhhh-"

"I found you again, because you are, *again*, getting into very dangerous situations you don't know the full extent of. I want your help to hide from the Malkuths, to perhaps work to thwart them in some ways, but this could be them. I am most assuredly not the only tool in their box."

She has a sip of her coffee, her eyes still unafraid to latch onto his.

"You keep telling me how dangerous they are, but you won't tell me exactly why. You don't just want my help to hide; I suspect you could do that just fine on your own. You want my help to screw with them. How dangerous will that be?"

He exhales again, nodding. "Sì, sì, you are correct. I just …"

"You just what? Want me to do dangerous things on your agenda but not mine?"

"It is not like that! I want to help you, not use you. I can protect you."

"The best protection would be for me to not fuck with these Malkuths at all, wouldn't it?" she challenges.

"Oh, yes, but it is too late for that. You are on their radar now. I am still reporting to them, and I am worried they are unsatisfied with what I am telling them."

"Then why don't we both hide?"

He looks at her, then closes his eyes, emitting another sigh. "If that is what you want, then fine. I will leave you alone. I will do my best to convince the Malkuths that you are no threat, that you happened on their name by accident. Is that what you want?"

"No," she finally answers, then shifts in her seat, leaning closer toward Duilio. "What was Malkuth doing at the university, anyway?"

"I don't know. Why were you looking for him in the first place? This cannot just be about rare books."

Now it is her turn to express a sigh, and he blinks, surprised at the crack in the usual 'tough' exterior.

"It *is* about the vigilante."

He blinks again, studying her.

"You don't know who the vigilante is, do you?"

She slowly shakes her head.

"But you *want* to know?"

The motion changes to a nod, equally slow.

"I see, I see," he says, becoming thoughtful.

She knows he doesn't grasp the full picture, but she feels she's trusted enough.

"Thank you for being open with me, Therese. I will tell you this – there are things going on that are well beyond anything … *normal*. The extent of what the Malkuths do has shown to be much more than I ever suspected."

There blinks twice, brow pinching. "What? How is that telling me anything?"

"I am trying to protect you and warn you."

"Thanks," comes her dismissive response.

"If you are insisting on meeting this fellow hacker, then please let me come along as protection."

"I don't know. He wants to meet with me alone."

"Of course, he does!"

"It's not like that."

"What? What is it not like?"

"He's paranoid, okay? Worse than me. Hell, he managed to get past some of my securities, and *no one* has ever done that. He's also said things to me that remind me of myself. He's not a threat."

"Hmph. Do you think he will decline the meeting he wants if you say you are bringing someone along just to feel safer?"

She ponders this. "Maybe."

"Do you want this meeting so bad that you are willing to agree on his terms? Hmm?" he pushes, raising his eyebrows.

116

"I … guess not."

Duilio nods. "He has come to you. He wants something of you. You are in the stronger position for negotiations. Doesn't it even make sense that you'd bring someone along?"

"I guess."

"Good. It is settled," he says, reaching for his glass.

"We continue to see."

What her eyes see is a sky shedding itself of color, dark, sickly tones roiling about as though the entire atmosphere swells with a seeping infection. A terrible emptiness might lie beyond, but this does not concern anyone here. There are those who know, and those who do not.

She finally turns to look upon him.

He is struck by her beauty, though what drives that concept here is quite different from others. He can feel the power inside her, the vitality, the promise. He feels a stirring, a needful coil. It causes him suspicion.

"We do," she finally speaks in response.

A sudden punch of doubt. He wonders why he has even come to deliver her this news. How does assuredness so crumble in her wake? After some time of just looking at him, she turns back to gaze out over the bleak landscape.

"The Immaculate Machine."

He moves nearer her, and he knows she does not speak of this world.

"We are of the fallen host of the builder. We deserve our time."

"Time is something of which we have much, and thus are we punished to know how long we linger from that beauty. Such a waste."

He looks at her. Both, for a time, seem of stone.

"They do not even know they have lost their own rebellion. They boil in the crucible, the heat a thing they welcome."

"Fools."

She cuts a sidelong gaze to him. He has already looked away.

"We are all fools."

"Even you, Loviatar?" he asks, speaking smoothly on the trail of her declaration.

"Why do you seek to flatter me, Satariel?"

"If you truly believe that, then I have gained against you."

"Surely you do not think me the champion of our kind."

His eyes give forth one slow blink. She sees, and she knows. As much as they fight amongst themselves, as much as jealousy and envy plague them, without a focal point, they shall wallow in doom.

"You are the nearest we have to a mother."

"Careful that you court weakness."

He does not avert his gaze from hers.

"I understand our transcendence. We are not the things we once were."

She gives him one nod, then looks back out unto their world, glancing up into the sky.

"This place befits us. It is a world so full of hunger that it eats itself."

"Do you see an end for us if we remain here?"

Time passes. Wind slips through sharp places.

"No. We have been abandoned."

His nod is slow, leaving his head hanging before he lifts his chin again.

"All we shall do is open our own throats and leave behind emptied corpses."

"It is much sweeter there."

"Yes," he agrees, drawing out the sound in a sibilant cadence. "We just need our gateway."

Chapter Eight

Therese lurks back in the shadows. It is night. This is not a parking garage or a bus stop. The place is more out of the way, more in the dregs and back alleys of the City. This acts as something of a buffer zone between the clean city proper and the subterranean refuse. She doesn't actively confront it of herself, but she does not feel out of place here at all.

She waits, having deliberately shown up early as she is wont to do.

She'd argued more with Duilio. Their compromise consists of her being wired up and broadcasting for sound as he observes from a distance. He expressed his dissatisfaction at even this, but she'd threatened to carry out the rendezvous without even telling him.

Duilio watches, unwilling to use the small binoculars he's brought for fear of drawing too much attention. She's back in the darkness anyway. He doesn't like this. Doesn't like the time or place. He told her to push for a meeting in some public café in the middle of the day. He doesn't know if she tried, or if she doesn't even want it. Here they both stand, waiting for this person who has contacted her. He's convinced it's nothing but trouble.

She looks off to one side as she hears a rasping cough. It carries on for some time, but she is more surprised at how close it is. She knows she's not alone out here, and apparently she is not the only one lingering in less-illuminated places. She finally sees as someone huddling on the ground shifts position, seeming entirely uncaring of anyone else's presence, their own ill health evident.

Her eyes then find the person walking up. He looks like he could be the one- tall, thin, though paunchy about the belly. He's dressed too meagerly for the weather, as though uncaring. She notes a jitter about him, but it's not that cold. Therese can guess many different reasons for such subtle animation. He also looks around too much. She almost rolls her eyes. If she were a cop, this guy would definitely ping her radar for being suspicious. He finally stops in an area vaguely close to the one they chose for this encounter. He glances about more, looking at his phone to presumably check the time or for messages. His impatient jiggling almost holds a rhythm.

She moves over to him, not trying to be silent. The cadence of her heavy boots finally gets his attention, and he looks upon her with a mixture of relief and excitement.

"Hey," she greets.

"It's you. Sparrow."

"Yeah, and you're Kettle," she replies, giving his hacker moniker. He nods, though it had not been a question.

"Oh my god. This …" He trails off, taking in a calming breath. He nods more. She just looks at him. "You know, it's frightening, right?" She wrinkles her brow as he carries on. "It can feel like you're all alone, like you're the only one who knows, and everyone else is against you. It's … it's really lonely like that." He shifts his eyes to her, then a wane smile finds his lips. "I'm not alone anymore."

"What are you talking about?"

"The monsters," he answers, a hint of incredulity touching his tone. "Out there," he adds, flinging one arm to indicate.

Therese nods, slowly. She feels like she is beginning to get it, and she thinks this guy is late for the proverbial bus.

"I found you because you were running searches similar to mine. I've got a script that checks for that, basically to see if anyone is hunting for *me* that way. I mean, of course, I've heard of you, but I didn't know you *knew*."

She keeps up her slow nods.

"The demonic killings?" he leads, eyes popping.

"Right," she says.

He leads with more exuberant nods. "You know about the *monsters* out there."

"I do," she agrees.

He emits a single, breath-filled chuckle. "I thought I was the only one."

She narrows her eyes. He sees this, waving a hand as he shakes his head.

"I *know* others know. Of course the authorities know. They *have* to. Right? Of course, they do, but you know how corrupt the police are."

She almost grins, knowing that Duilio is listening in. She cannot help but nod to this.

"It's tough," he says. "We can find out about it, but it's hard to know what to do." His focus then jerks to her. "So, how do you *really* know? I mean, how did you find out?"

"I saw them," she says, which gains a start from him and more wide eyes. "I was kidnapped twice."

"What!"

She reels back a bit from his exclamation, just looking at him.

"How? How are you still alive?"

"I was rescued."

And now it is his turn to narrow his eyes. Kettle studies Therese, mulling over this information. "I didn't realize they ever caught anyone."

"They're bad people. They kidnap all the time for their sex trafficking and..." She trails off as Kettle begins waving his hands.

"I don't mean the people. I mean the monsters. The *demons*."

Therese blinks into a wrinkled brow. Her lips part, but she doesn't say anything. Kettle looks back at her, also flummoxed. A tremor takes his head as though he tries to force words out.

"Yeah," Therese finally manages, her lips approaching a sneer. "Whatever you want to ca-"

"Therese! Therese! Stop talking to this man!"

She looks over to see Duilio jogging up to them. Kettle shifts his attention to Duilio, reeling back in place. His eyes return to Therese. Duilio reaches them, inserting himself between the pair, his back to Kettle.

"Therese, you need to stop talking to him. He is clearly unbalanced. We should go."

"Who are you?" Kettle demands. "We're supposed to meet alone."

"You're right," Duilio whirls on him. "She is not alone. Perhaps you should go."

"What the fuck!"

Both men top, setting their eyes on Therese.

"What's going on?" she pushes.

"Why is he here?" Kettle demands again.

"I wanted protection. You think I'm just going to meet some strange guy at night in some isolated place? You're paranoid. You understand."

Kettle blinks, taking a half step back. His lips curl into a frown, whether from being hurt or because he did not take more of his own precautions is unclear.

"And you're supposed to just *watch*." She stabs a finger at Duilio.

"You will have to forgive me, Therese, but this man is unbalanced and dangerous. I must insist-"

"Oh, fuck off with your 'insists'," she bites. "I'll talk to whoever I want to talk to." So said, she moves around Duilio and to Kettle.

"You were supposed to be alone," he mutters. "I should've … I shouldn't have gone offline." He then scuttles off.

Therese turns her attention back to Duilio, giving him a scathing look. He shrugs, pointing with open hands toward the empty space vacated by Kettle.

"Therese, I-" He stops as she brings up a hand of her own.

Before he may speak further, she stomps off.

They sit, catching their breath. Sweat glistens on flesh. Zoe takes another pull on the water bottle, exhaling deeply. Lilja gives her a sidelong glance. They have completed an intense training session, one that has included some sparring. Lilja had been surprised when Zoe suggested it. Zoe had even seemed sincerely grateful to be shown some effective self-defense moves.

"Who else have you sparred with?"

Lilja's eyes move back to Zoe, noticing the girl studying her.

"A lot of people."

"No. I mean other Hunters."

"Oh." Lilja goes quiet a moment, thinking. "Skot and Anika."

"Anika?"

Lilja nods. "Yes. Anika Malkuth."

"When did you spar her?"

"It was a while ago. She came to the City to inspect the Book's defenses. She said I was one of the defenses, so she wanted to spar with me."

Zoe blinks beneath a furrowing brow. After a time, she speaks again. "Was she any good?"

Lilja gives a quick nod. "Yes. She'd been training in martial arts for a long time."

"And?" Zoe leads, drawing out the word as those eyebrows rise. Lilja does not take the bait. "Who won?"

"I did," Lilja says after a brief hesitation. She'd thought of explaining the situation, how Anika had basically forced the match.

"Wow."

"You've never sparred with her?"

"No," Zoe says, her tone sharp. "The first time I met her was during a hunt, and the demon just about killed her."

"I heard about that. You know, it's funny …"

Zoe waits, then blinks after a time, moving her head nearer to Lilja. "Funny?"

"The Felcraft and Malkuth are rivals, but you saved Anika. She ended up coming to the City, and she saved my life."

"She did?"

"Mmhmm."

Zoe licks her lips, pulling the lower in for a short chew. "I didn't know that. And anyway, we may be rivals, but we don't hunt each other. She needed help, so …" Her voice dwindles as her thoughts are claimed of those lost that day.

Lilja looks at her, noting the change, sensing the curtain of darkness that falls. She says nothing, asks no questions, instead taking to her feet to stretch her arms and lower back before having another pull on her water bottle. She ponders the various situations since finding out about this secret war with the Infernal and suspects many of them have been saved and saved others. Such is the nature of the beast.

"What'd you see in that fountain?"

She looks down to find Zoe's eyes staring up at her. "Hmm?"

"The old fountain at the Barrington house. Remember? You were looking in it, and you thought you saw something."

"Sorry."

"What?" Zoe replies, her face again pinching up.

"I don't remember," Lilja manages. Her voice holds more than a murmur, but it lacks conviction, nonetheless.

Zoe stands, staring intently, but Lilja does no more than look back. Zoe finally exhales loudly through her nose, giving a shake of the head.

"It's hard to trust you sometimes."

"Sorry."

"See?" Zoe exclaims, flinging a hand toward the other woman as she then steps away. "It's stuff like *that*. You don't even ask me why or act shocked, you just … apologize?"

"Sorry," Lilja murmurs yet again.

Zoe looks back, her lips pressed together in an exasperated smirk.

"You can stop saying you're sorry. It's not camouflage, you know?"

Lilja blinks rapidly, confused.

"We know about something very dangerous, and we're doing very dangerous things. We need to trust each other."

"I know."

"I'll admit, back at the Barrington house, you kicked some serious ass. You can handle yourself, just like everyone says," she tacks on, and it doesn't sound like a compliment. "But you saw something in that fountain, and that attack was directed at *you*."

Lilja's jaw moves as though she fights to speak, but all she finally manages is a meager nod.

"That's another thing. You're skilled, *obviously*. You're brave. But with something like this, you look like a scared child. What the *hell*?"

Zoe stares, drilling into Lilja with the weight of a non-verbal attack.

"I don't know."

Zoe rolls her eyes. "We've seen attacks before that were directed at a specific person. The Infernal like to try to get under our skin, undermine our confidence. They want us to doubt, to be afraid. One way to deal with that is to own it. You're just trying to hide."

"I'm sorry."

"That doesn't make any difference. What matters is if that comes out at the wrong time, and one of us gets killed."

"It won't."

"Are you sure?" Zoe asks, steeling her gaze against Lilja's own sudden solidification. "You froze up when that demon came at us."

Lilja backs down, parting her lips as though to respond, but all she does is swallow.

"That's what they *do*," Zoe presses. "I don't care how skilled you are, or how well you're taking to this, you don't know our enemy that well. You just *don't*. I was raised knowing about them; so was Skot. And we're still not impervious. They're picking on you for a *reason*."

Lilja gives a mute nod. "But I want to help," she finally says.

Zoe sighs. "That's great. Then help. Don't hurt. You know that putting us at unnecessary risk is a bad thing."

"You don't want me to go to Tibet."

Zoe cocks her head, eyeballing Lilja. She purses her lips as she considers.

"I didn't want you going with us to Scholomance. I didn't like being junior to you at the Barrington house. This isn't about my ego, okay? It's about your obvious inexperience. I don't get why I'm the only one worried about this."

"You're not."

"Oh?" Zoe challenges. "Who else is worried about it?"

"I am."

Zoe prepares another push, her lips part, the top curled a bit in a nascent snarl, but she pauses. The expression smooths instantly as she blinks.

"Then why go? Why the risk?"

Lilja shakes her head. "I can't let it keep me from going and trying to help. Don't they win that way, too?"

Zoe struggles with stifling another quick response. Silence ensues as both young women stare at each other. "Maybe? I don't know," she finally admits. "But that's because I don't think any of us really know their plans."

Lilja nods, slowly. "Maybe they don't want me there," she says without a trace of pride.

Zoe just looks at her, words failing as thoughts tumble in her mind.

Pierce eyeballs the guy sitting on the ground near him. Several others also hold place here, and all of them look like washed-out collections of rags and disuse.

"It's for something better!" he finally says, all but spitting in the end. A sharp gesture of his hand accentuates the revelation along with the wrinkle of exasperation on his face. "Do you want *this* to be it?"

"No," the guy responds, the word elongating. He glances about him. No one else says a word.

"You gonna get a job… and a home?" Pierce stabs. "You think any of that will make a difference? We're on the bottom rung. So what if you go up a few! All of this … *all* of it … is just *bullshit*. I know, I know," Pierce gives, nodding into the words, "we're in hell: agony, loneliness, depression. You think others aren't the same? They are, but theirs is wrapped in a prettier package. It's all *bullshit*."

"Yeah, but …" the guy continues trying, again looking to the others gathered around, all of them in various repose on the ground in their derelict congregation. "The tax."

Pierce stares back at the finally uttered word, latching on with a seeming laser-guided precision.

"You want to leave? Go out on your own? Go ahead." Pierce gives another quick gesture of his hand. "See how long you last."

"I just … I don't want to be taken by … one of those … *things*."

"Me, neither," one of the crowd mumbles, and this gains agreeing nods from many.

Pierce scans them, his discolored teeth revealed through disgusted lips. He stands, taking in a breath, and unleashes a torrent of wet coughing. Lance quickly gets to his own feet, wincing in the continued pain from his leg. Pierce pushes away from the efforts at comfort, spitting on to the ground. The expectorant shines in the meager light.

"You all disgust me," he says, wiping at his mouth. "This world is shit, and they offer us something better, and you get *scared*? You know why? Because they're *honest*. That's right. You should be scared of a lot of things, but you're not, because those other things hide behind acting like they care or sympathize, and that is all *bullshit*. We're all heading to slaughter. *All* of us. Do you want to do something, or just lie back for the knife? *Huh!*" He adds to this last with a startling jerk of his own body, getting some reels and quick intakes of breath from the group.

As he stands there, looking them over, they say nothing more. Heads hunch into shoulders. No one even has enough bravery to scuttle away. He finally walks away, and Lance follows.

Another series of coughs takes him, halting his exit. Lance consumes the opportunity to catch up with him. He places his hands on Pierce's back.

"Stop trying to help me!" Pierce cries out, batting those hands away. He shoots a look at Lance and moves further off.

"Sorry," Lance mumbles when he again catches up, both slipping back to the ground. "It's bad, though."

"What is?"

"The tax. Well, I mean, how it's collected," he addends when Pierce gives him an angry stare, but he backs down no further.

Pierce nods. "Yeah, it's pretty fucked up, but that's just the way it is. We're generating a lot of energy here. You know that, and they need it. Besides, it's all coming together. We'll be leaving soon."

"We will?"

"Yes. I told you we got another message, didn't I?" Pierce asks, his voice full of frustration.

Lance shakes his head, apologetic.

"Huh. Well, we did. We're leaving soon."

Lance looks back toward the group. It's dispersed, but it's still there. Some have gone to their own little places, trying for something like sleep. Others pair up to share drugs or sex. Some even seem content to just experience each other's company. They are all expending time, finding some sort of opiate to stave off the crushing boredom, the pains.

"What about them?"

Pierce cuts his eyes over. Time passes. Lance wonders if there will be no answer. He'd not be surprised.

"That was a good speech I made, wasn't it?"

Lance blinks, having almost dropped into some sort of pseudo-sleep. He finds something unexpected on Pierce's cracked lips – a grin.

"Yeah. Sure."

A chuckle starts low in Pierce's throat, and to further surprise, it does not turn into a sputtering fit.

"It was all bullshit."

"There is only so much we are capable of seeing."

Skothiam looks over at Nicole. She stands there, calmly, returning his gaze. After a time, it may seem her words have become but wisps of wind. Though they sound like a platitude, he knows she carries real intent.

"The gate at Scholomance."

She nods, slowly. "That is one example. I fear my own eyes have been closed to too many possibilities."

"I wouldn't figure you to have hubris."

He notes the slightest press of her lips and narrowing of her eyes. He grins, knowing this is as about as much of a smirk he may get from his sister. She finally turns away, her usual, otherworldly expression returned. Her eyes fall on the Book, one of the three. It lies open on the nearby table, a fine, leather bookmark resting atop the verso page. An intricately-designed piece of cloth lies below this, giving the whole thing an appearance of an altar.

"We know much of the Hidden," she intones, moving nearer the table. "Yet we must not fall into the belief that we know all merely because we have pierced some small part of that veil.

"We have gleaned further clues from the books in our possession, enough to feel confident that all three form some sort of puzzle, a key to unlocking the ability to manipulate the gateways. Or so we assume."

She looks back at him from having moved nearer the open book, reaching out slowly with one hand as though she might learn more through this gesture. He knows the things of which she speaks, and he wonders why she brings them up. Her tone and manner have become such that she acts more as one in reverence to the object as opposed to really speaking to him.

"Hundreds upon hundreds of years of records and information, yet we did not know of these … pocket dimensions and the gateways leading to them until we stumbled upon the one in Scholomance. Do these small places exist on their own, and those of the school found them, or did they possess the very power to create them? I will visit Kuzma Nasht and ask him."

He finally blinks himself out of his own quasi-hypnotic state, realizing his sister's oration has drawn him there. He finds her having turned back, peering at him with an unfettered gaze.

"Of course," he says, knowing his permission is merely a formality.

"One wonders at the metaphysical rules of such places. Clearly, they are somehow locked out of the normal passage of time. If the Guardian leaves this sanctuary, he would likely die."

"He didn't realize so many years had passed," Skot offers.

She takes time to reply, giving forth another of her single, slow nods, then shifting herself to partially face the book. "We all plunge into the unknown, then, all to fight the Infernal."

"How much did the authors of the Books know?"

"That is the question," she answers. "Another is how much can we learn from what they knew? They speak of many worlds, many peoples. They speak of vast civilizations that rose and fell before ours ever came to be. Is there truly so much out there?"

"Do others harbor us ill will?"

She cuts her eyes to him, head tilting slightly as she ponders. She gives no answer, returning her full focus to the tome.

"If those of Scholomance did such a good job of protecting the third book, then perhaps we ought to let it remain so. We would truly fall to hubris if we easily presume ourselves to be the most qualified to guard the books."

"Are you advising me to call off the trip?"

He senses indecision in her, and he realizes it gives him a simmer of anxiety.

"Does it not strike you as odd that after so many years of our searching, all three books are suddenly in our grasp?"

"We don't have the third yet," he reminds her.

She waves off the point with a graceful gesture of a hand. "I do wonder," she muses, "will you be seeking another guardian or a corpse? Regardless, it makes me consider the possibility that the Books *want* to be found."

He narrows his eyes. "Do you truly think them possessed of such power?"

"We cannot let our knowledge give us to believe in anything, and we cannot let our knowledge keep us from believing."

"I know that," he almost snaps. "But how do we practically know which actions to take? This mystery has remained for this long because it's so difficult."

She nods, giving him this, and perhaps also offering her own sort of apology for her prior remark.

"I'm worried this is a trap," she finally says, and the grounded sincerity in her voice moves him.

He realizes she has not sounded so human in a very long time.

"How could it be a trap?"

"I don't believe the guardians have laid a trap for us, but it may prove wise to leave it be."

Skot refrains from replying, realizing they have completed a circle. As usual, his sister has given him much to think on.

Chapter Nine

Lilja has never been to Tibet before.

She has her vivid red locks in a long ponytail and under a drab green ball cap, the rest of her clothing of similar dark, earthen shades. The expected quartet has come here, and she sticks near Skot, Zoe and David bringing up the rear. They've already settled into their rooms and set out to explore Lhasa.

Nasht had given them a pendant and a name. He had said the necklace with its curiously engraved black stone would draw them to the courier. He could not explain how, and Skot holds his own measure of skepticism, especially due to his recent talk with his sister. Centuries have passed. Who is to say the courier, Kuranes, deposited the book in Tibet at all? Skot tries not to feel despondent after such an amazing discovery at Scholomance, but he cannot shake the sense of hopelessness in this endeavor.

"This is where a great Buddhist master bound an earth demoness to build the foundation of a temple over her heart."

Skot looks at Lilja, blinking. A gentle curl touches his lips. "You are amazing."

She grins in return, blushing a touch, and he reaches in to give her a hug and kiss.

"It's just folklore," she explains.

A smirk is his reply. "You're cute."

She gives a little roll of her eyes, parting from him with a playful push. She immediately goes back to looking around, surveying their surroundings.

The area crowds with pedestrian traffic. The locals navigate easily through the density, stopping or angling off where they wish, plodding along with forethought. Lilja notices many eyes upon them, but few linger. They are not in the most obvious place for tourists, but their singularity doesn't seem to gain them much notice. They still spy many signs in English, these promising a variety of services or even enlightenments. A motorcycle rider honks his horn nearby, hoping to hurry the throng that holds little regard for streets and crossways.

Colors stand out here and there, attempts to gain notice for shops and stalls. Lush saffron shades mingle with honeyed yellows as though the vibrant, pulsing veins of nature's best offering. They are here to shop, in a way, but they hold no certainty on how they shall find what they seek.

Time creeps like the shifting of dunes. They find a place to have a quick meal, enjoying some butter tea. Thoughts collect, but they share little. They are still gathering information, letting it simmer. They make their way back out unto the avenues, finding themselves in a tangle of people backed-up from a procession of pack-bearing horses. A few people squabble over direction as a darkly-colored mastiff keeps watch. They take the opportunity to change theirs.

Lilja's eyes light up and she heads over to the tree. It sprouts up in the otherwise dusty, urban area like a vivid reminder of the earth beneath them, its yellow leaves giving off a distinct scent.

"A ginkgo tree," Skot says as he comes up beside her, smiling at her exuberance. She nods. He reels back, blinking rapidly. "Quite the smell."

He watches her as she moves about, not seeming bothered at all by the odor, more eager to peer and touch. The tree stands between two apartment buildings, those tucked in right behind the small stores and open stalls of the street.

"It doesn't smell that bad," Lilja comments, that youthful smile still claiming her lips.

"I haven't seen any others," Skot notes.

She nods, all but bounding over. "It does seem out of place, but it's *beautiful*." She then furrows her brow as she studies it.

"What is it?"

"I wouldn't expect it to have such yellow leaves this time of year."

"Maybe it's the altitude."

"It's starting to get late," David interjects, upnodding toward the sun.

Skot looks. "Where did the time go?"

The shops and general traffic don't appear to be abating in anticipation of the coming night, and none too far from the tree, they find a curious store. Amidst small bottles and bowls, the place shows an abundant population of moths. They seem to have free run of the place, flittering and settling where they like. One alights on Lilja's offered finger, and the shopkeeper gives a toothy grin, chattering in Tibetan.

"I'm sorry. I don't understand you," she says.

"American?" he asks.

She shakes her head, and the man narrows his eyes. "English?"

"Close enough." She chuckles, gaining a similar response from Skot. "What kind of moths are these?"

The man doesn't seem to understand, so she gestures with the one still on her hand as well as indicating all of those around.

"Ah!" the shopkeeper gives eager nods. "Ghost. Ghost!"

"Ghost moths?"

"La-reh, la-reh."

Lilja shakes her head.

"Yes!" the man says, extending a finger sharply into the air, motivating a scurry of nearby moths before they quickly re-settle.

"Why are all of these here?" Skot asks, finding Lilja's smile and energy contagious.

The man points to a wide and shallow wooden bowl filled with what looks like dried out seed pods. "Yarza ğunbu!"

"What?" Skot peers, leaning closer.

The man quickly brings up a handful for better inspection. Skot pulls back, chuckling softly. Lilja reaches in and picks one up.

"It looks like a dead caterpillar with a plant of some kind growing out of it."

The man gives eager nods.

"Caterpillar fungus," the man manages in heavily-accented English.

"Fungus?" Lilja arches her eyebrows and quickly drops it back into the bowl.

The shopkeeper continues nodding. "Very *strong*." He makes a fist, shaking it. "Make you strong." He points at Skot, then David, then does an unmistakable pantomime in front of his crotch.

"It's everywhere," Zoe pitches an observation, and though it is not the only item for sale, a good deal of it shows in promising heaps in various bowls and dishes.

"No, thank you," Skot replies, giving forth a brief smirk.

They make their way further, now beneath a dark sky, having found themselves away from the streets. The clutter of stalls shows a denser promise now. People mill about, some engaging in terse negotiations, but their numbers show to have declined in seeming direct inverse to the number of shops.

"Doesn't this seem off to you?"

Skot glances to David. He suppresses a sudden urge to give a quick negative. "What do you mean?"

"Look up. It's like we're covered in blackness. Where are the stars? And look at all these people? Most of them are wearing some sort of hats with face coverings."

"Like they're hiding who they are." Skot notices.

"Or *what* they are."

Skot steps back, gesturing, and the other three move in tight, close to him.

"Zoe, do you notice anything out of the ordinary?" he asks, whispering.

"You mean Infernal?"

He gestures with his head, and she turns, looking out on the assembly. It doesn't take long before she turns back.

"Something is definitely off about this place, but no, no Infernal."

"Should we get out of here?" David asks.

Skot takes a moment to reply, surveying their surroundings. He's not sure what is going on, but he does remember what brought them here.

"No. Let's look around, but stick together."

"An in-between place," Lilja muses once they get back to their exploration.

"Maybe," Skot replies. "If so, think of what that means," he continues, gaining a curious look from his girlfriend. "We know something of how gates may appear, and some may stay in a rudimentary state, but all of that ties to the Infernal, and as far as we know, there is no 'in-between'. You are either in one realm or the other."

The various people milling about the bazaar give them no more scrutiny than might be expected from strangers or those spying the generally unfamiliar. They keep to their business, engaging in their commerce. If unwanted intruders have entered their domain, they make no movement to indicate any retaliation.

"Are they human?" Zoe asks within a pitched whisper.

Skot finds himself again stifling the sudden urge to jump to conclusions.

"I don't know," he finally admits, feeling the coiling of paranoia on the end of the statement. It feels silly to him to say that, and he is forced to push aside the sudden conflict of impulses inside him.

"There."

They all look to where Lilja points. There is a store of a much more substantial appearance than the rest of the booths, stalls, and wagons making up the area. Tall, narrow windows mark its front, the flickering of gas lamps sending out their glow from within. But what has caught their attention is the sign above the doorway. It does not bear any words, merely a symbol, and it is the same etched on the dark stone given them by Nasht.

Frescoes greet them inside, along with rows upon rows of books. The place looks more a library than a bookstore, judging from the bindings and apparent age of the tomes on display. The paintings depict grotesque, surreal scenes, but they are not given long to examine them before someone arrives from the hidden interior of the building. He emerges and stands as though always having been there.

"Welcome," the man says.

He is slender and tall, carrying himself with a great poise. He wears a long robe with hues of dark red and bronze, nothing obscuring his head or face. Though he has the cast of a native, something of him hearkens to the exotic.

"Thank you," Skot finally answers him.

135

"Please do come in," he continues, coaxing with the subtle gesture of one hand.

They go further inside, some curious glances spared to the wares, though most attention finds focus on the proprietor. Skot wonders how open he should be with their search. Though this man holds an aged appearance, he speaks English with but a slight accent. He also looks as though he is from this area, not like one displaced from Eastern Europe and come here to run from demons.

"Help yourselves."

They see two metal bowls filled to the brim with what looks like small discs of bread. It is difficult to tell exactly what they are, though their shape and thickness is like a large pill. The man stands atop a dais, a short barrier going around that provides an entryway just where he waits. Two short pillars to either side not only mark the end of the barrier but also provide support for the bowls.

"What is it?" Zoe finally asks.

"Medicinal ambrosia."

They all look at him.

"Think of it as a sort of communion. It is akin to honeyed bread, though there are some herbs and spices to enhance the flavor and potential benefits. As you may see, the amounts are small. This is more a ritual of hospitality."

"Thank you," Skot replies, though none of them partake of the offering.

"How might I help you, then?"

"The symbol outside, over your door," Skot begins, and this gains sharp notice from Lilja.

"Yes?"

"We've come looking for it."

"You have?" the man replies, arching his thin eyebrows. "I am a purveyor of books, as you may note."

"Well, we *are* looking for a book."

Lilja steps in closer, grabbing Skot's arm. Zoe and David have fanned out, ostensibly to browse the shop, but they also keep watch on the goings-on.

"Then I hope to provide," the man says, giving a slow, shallow bow from the waist.

"A rare book," Skot continues, "one of a kind."

Those eyebrows perk again.

"Ah, I see. Something *very* valuable, then. Please, come this way," he invites, extending his right hand, turning it and adding a slow fan of his fingers. The entire gesture is slow, graceful, deliberate.

They follow to a door, one they had not noticed, such do the angles and lighting effuse a surreal, dreamlike quality to the place. From outside, the building looked common enough, at least in structure, but now that they are inside and moving about, hidden depths reveal themselves.

They move into this next room, the ceiling angling down and away, giving the far end a hidden section of shadow. There are less books here, all shown front forward, some behind glass.

"The pride of my collection," the man says.

Skot gives a dip of his head as he and Lilja begin scanning the stock. David and Zoe continue to keep an eye on the man and the rest of the store.

"It's not here," Lilja soon announces.

"Ah, I am sorry," the proprietor offers. "What is the title? I might be able to procure it, and I confess I am burning with curiosity to know."

"The symbol outside," Skot says.

"Yes?"

"It has meaning."

"Yes."

"Why display it so prominently?"

"Ah, because only those who are friendly would know of it." The man gives a polite smile.

Skot's brow furrows slightly. He finds the answer spurious, almost pandering.

"Then you know the book we seek," Lilja concludes, coming up near him.

"I know there is reason for some things to remain hidden." He gives his smile to her, then looks back to Skot, the expression gone. "Why do you seek this book?"

"Protection."

"Protection? From what?"

Skot produces the pendant, showing it to the shopkeeper. The man fixes his eyes upon it, widening them as he does.

"We have this. Does it not give us credence?"

"This is entirely unexpected," the man says, speaking quicker than he has until now. "I would ask something of you." His tone also drops, closer to a whisper. "You must know that no place is safe. Safety comes not only in protection but also keeping that place *secret*, yes?"

Skot gives the man a single nod.

"Good. Good. Will you return tomorrow? I will have it for you then."

"It's not here?" Skot asks after a moment of thought, his eyes never leaving the proprietor.

"It is not here."

"Where is **Kuranes**?"

"What? That is not the name of the Book."

"Nevermind," Skot dismisses. "We'll be back tomorrow."

"You know," Therese begins, not fully looking over from the barrage of windows on her computer's monitor, "some of this demon stuff might make sense."

Duilio gives a nervous laugh, the expression causing a jig to the unlit cigarette held in his lips. "Come now, Therese. Surely you don't believe in such things?"

"I don't mean *literally*," she carries on, still focused on the screen. "Hell, Satan can be some imaginary character, but a Satan-worshiping serial killer is still a bad thing."

"Yes, yes," Duilio agrees, nodding emphatically. "Is that what you think this has all been?"

She finally stops, pushing back from the table and looking up at him. Her eyes pierce into this man who once kidnapped her and now is a guest in her scant apartment. He steps away from the proximity he had gained during their talk.

"Is Denman Malkuth a devil-worshipping serial killer?"

A quick pinch flits across Duilio's face. He then sighs.

"I don't think so."

"Which part are you not sure about?"

"I don't think he actually fits the definition of a serial killer."

"But he worships the devil?"

"Therese."

She continues looking at him, waiting.

"I don't know his personal … *religious* beliefs, but I doubt he does."

"Why is it that every time I dig more into stuff related to the vigilante, *you* turn up?" She stabs a finger at him.

"I …" he shakes his head, holding out his hands as he inches further away. He then blinks, looking aside, brow furrowing.

"What? What is it?" Therese presses, standing and moving closer.

"I just … thought of something," he says, still looking away, his voice low, measured.

"What did you think of?"

He finally looks back at her.

"Why *does* that happen, Therese?" he asks, and as she begins to reply, he waves it off. "I am being rhetorical, but why? Is the vigilante somehow connected to the Malkuths?"

"What?" Therese recoils. "From what you've told me of them, then no."

Now it is Duilio's turn to affix a pressing stare.

"You do not know that, Therese. You are defending him." He waves his hands again as she prepares to speak, the gesture more emphatic. He then takes up his cigarette as he gesticulates. "You were working for the vigilante, and you were caught."

"By you."

"Uhm, yes, but I was then working for Gnegon, or I assume I was."

"Both times."

"Yes, *yes*, I *know* this, Therese."

"*What* is the connection to the Malkuths?"

"That is a very good question."

Therese narrows her eyes at Duilio.

"And you said this all began from you doing research on rare books?"

"Yes," she finally replies.

"Did it, or did it not?"

"*Yes*. I was researching the rare books collection at the university, and the name Denman Malkuth came up. Apparently, he visited it."

Duilio nods, for they have gone over this. Still, he tries to the let information percolate into something new.

"Yes, but this research of yours into rare books was really about trying to learn the vigilante's identity."

He has not asked, and she says nothing else, merely watching as he continues to walk the pathways of his mind's library. He finally looks back at her.

"The vigilante came the second time and rescued you, but you said you did not call him."

She nods.

"Presumably he was there to dismantle Gnegon's operation or disrupt things and summon the police."

Therese nods, wordlessly.

"I wonder … what else the vigilante found there."

"*You* were there," Therese flings at him. "You said something bad was going on, and there was all that … chaos outside."

"I don't think the vigilante caused that."

"Neither do I," Therese says, again slitting her focus. "Look. The vigilante rescued me, got me out, and then … went back inside. All that … *shit* was going on, but the vigilante didn't leave."

A weighty silence descends as both ponder.

"Did the Malkuths have anything to do with what happened there?"

"No, no. Well, I don't think so. Maybe they did. I don't know."

"What the hell is going on in this city?"

Duilio looks at her, but she has now found her own way into the inner paths of her contemplation. He is not inclined to give an answer, even though he knows things she does not. This knowledge has not given him more confidence that he is any closer to an answer. On the contrary, it has pushed him further away, as though shoving him back from a dark abyss.

The darkly-garbed figure moves through the throng.

She had thought the crowds might thin by this late hour, but then she just as quickly wonders why she assumes. They had all been here some hours ago, and once settled back into their hotel, she had snuck out. She has her own ideas about what is going on, and so she risks a second trip, going it alone.

As she moves about, trying not to garner too much attention as she peers out from beneath the dark hoodie, she notices that the market does seem to have lessened somewhat in business. It's still dark, of course, and she is left to wonder if the sun reaches this place at all. She spares a glance to the black, starless canopy overheard. What do they really know of the in-between places? How have they been so left in ignorance, when all these people here know of it? Are they even people? Her senses are running wild with this place, but she tries to calm them.

She hears the sound of a cough. It continues, growing. She glances around, but then as quickly decides against such notice. When she lowers her eyes, she sees a person at an empty stall staring back at her. She freezes, trying not to appear to be unsettled. The shape appears that of a man, but she does not feel certain of anything here. A knit cap on the head sports a meager bill, but it proves enough to cast shadow over the eyes. Regardless, she holds certainty of being this person's focus. She finally looks away.

She continues, trying not to seem too suspicious, but she doesn't waste time playing the role of shopper at any of the stalls. She finally reaches the structure, the one holding the books and the curious proprietor who claims to have *the* Book. She doesn't trust him.

She wanders, keeping an eye out without appearing to do so. She's broken into buildings before, but there are more people in the area than she had anticipated. They don't seem to be giving her undue notice, but she is still left to wonder what she really knows about this place. Are there security measures she has no idea about?

She finds a shadowed corner, standing in it for a short time, just observing. A sort of isolation meets her, and the occasional passing of a person does not see their attention turning anywhere near her.

Is this worth the risk?

She's come this far.

The glass gives easily enough and with minimal noise. She carefully deposits the pieces in the nearby grass then opens the window. Once inside, she pauses, standing there, attuned for any sign or sound of her entry having been heard. Quiet. She proceeds

The place is dark and presumably closed. She again feels a scratch at her own expectations. Still, if the place is yet open for business, she doesn't want her presence known. She creeps further in, finding her way through this satellite room of atlases and into the main room. She had hoped to avoid this area, feeling it riskier, but a quick assessment shows her no other route. She remains crouched, moving slowly, senses on high alert.

She finally hears it.

The muted sibilance becomes whispers as she gets closer. At first, it sounds like a one-sided conversation, but she finally hears the other voice. Feminine. The other is the proprietor.

"This may not be unexpected to you, but it is to me. What do I do when they come back?" he asks.

"You know the plan. Your courage is failing now that you are being tested. Did you think we wanted this to never happen?"

"No, of course not, but-"

"But what?" the woman asks, her voice insistent yet holding an underlying calm cadence that is unsettling. She speaks again when nothing is further said. "They are prepared to take the bait. Eager. Now is the time."

"I told them I would have the book for them tomorrow."

"Everyone holds the shovel that digs their own grave."

"Even you?"

A stretch of silence, and it bleeds the very air with its weight.

"You do yourself a disservice by letting the place in which you dwell lead you to think you are safe," the feminine voice finally speaks. "You are yet mortal, and the trail may be found without your help."

"I ... apologize."

"Your contrition means nothing to me. Be useful, and I see no reason to end your stage of existence."

A bowed head is the only response.

She finally hears more sounds after a time that feels to take forever. There is no more discourse, only the noises of the shopkeeper going about some business. She burns with intention, unsure if she should confront him now, continue the surveillance, or head back. She decides to play it safe, knowing that she needs to tell Skot of this as soon as possible. She waits a short time longer as quiet descends, then Zoe makes her exit.

Therese sits at the distant table, sipping her coffee. She likes this place. The saucers and mugs are all bland bone white, showing some stains and lines of age. The furniture is mismatched wood, plastic, steel. Everything carries a deliberate weight of no-nonsense. She appreciates the irony. She also finds it amusing that though the shop carries a none-too-subtle simmer of catering to a subculture, it finds an array of clientele. The people more on the "normal" spectrum usually just get their brew and muffin and leave.

It's somewhat crowded, though she has seen it more so. She did manage to get this out of the way table, and she takes her time, hardly tasting the coffee, looking over information on her tablet. She looks up and catches some guy across the way looking at her. He averts his gaze instantly, looking down into his own lap. He wears a dark hoodie. Therese blinks once, slowly, and though the unerring line of her unamused-seeming mouth makes no change, she smirks inside.

She doesn't leave right after paying the check, instead taking some more time to deal with some analyses and messages, then she stands. Out of the corner of her eye, she notices the guy's piqued attention. She takes a last gulp of the strong brew, then slips into her light jacket before heading out.

Her tablet now in the black rucksack, she lets her attention go to her phone as she walks down the street. Or so she pretends. The guy is following and too closely. She wonders that she made such a bumbling "investigator" on her first attempts. She decides to engage in some play.

She crosses the street to a bus stop, acting all the world as though she had been so engrossed in her phone that she almost misses the crosswalk. She rushes across as the pedestrian light turns red. Her tail rushes, too, proving horribly obvious, but he gets stuck on the other side. He finally finds a chance to catch up, jaywalking to do it, even though she has now stopped well in sight.

He hangs back, keeping a shadowed eye on her. A bus arrives. She continues messing with her phone, then acts as though she is going to board the vehicle. She sees a twitch in him as he prepares to rush to try to also get on, but then she turns on her heel and marches away, continuing on foot.

When he turns the next corner, she is standing right there, waiting. He comes up short, feet skittering, the jerk of his body more of a telltale sign even were the hoodie not insufficient. There are others around, but not too close. This is how she planned it.

"Kettle, why are you following me?"

"I – ah. Sparrow. Uhm ..."

"*Why* are you following me?"

"I ... ah, ah ..."

She just looks at him, and he finally takes a reasonable breath.

"I *really* need to talk to you. I don't think you know what's going on. Especially with your bodyguard."

"My bodyguard?" She narrows her eyes.

"Yeah, that guy you brought with you when we met."

"You're paranoid. I'm paranoid. I told you I was kidnapped *two* times, and I came close to being killed. So I brought along someone to help protect me when I'm meeting a new person. If you don't like it, tough shit."

He shakes his head, moving his hands.

"I don't mean that. Fine. You brought somebody, but I don't think he's protecting you."

"What?"

Kettle roots in his pockets, then brings out a clasped envelope. He opens it, producing glossy prints. Therese balks.

"Not digital. This is safer," he says, proffering them.

Therese begins to scan through them. She recognizes the photos as from that fateful night when the vigilante rescued her the second time. These appear to be captures of what happened in front of the compound.

"Something big happened at this place. Your bodyguard was there." Kettle points, and Therese does indeed see the face of Duilio.

"I know." This gets a sharp look from Kettle. "He ... ugh ... it's *complicated*, okay?"

"You knew?"

"I was there, too."

"Wha- ... so you *have* to know what's going on!"

"Keep it down, okay?" She waits a moment, and he nods, going silent after a quick perusal around them. "Sure I was there, but how does that mean I know what all was going on? And *you* weren't there, were you?" He shakes his head. "Then how do *you* know what all was going on?"

"I ... come on, Sparrow, you know we can find out things even if we're not there. Sometimes we know *more*."

"Okay, okay." She gives in. "You said something before about demons. What were you talking about?"

Kettle just looks at her. The moment stretches. Awkwardness creeps unto her, and Therese reels back, slowly, the movement subtle, as though she doesn't even know she is doing it.

"You said you knew about the monsters," he returns, his tone laced with accusation.

She slits her eyes. "I do."

"Okay. Maybe. You just said you were there but you don't know what all was going on. I get it now. You're aware of what they're doing, but you don't really know the monsters behind it."

Therese feels her heartbeat try to pick up. *Is he talking about the Malkuths?* The question flies into her mind seeming of its own accord. She thought she had finally come to a point where she had things more under control, but she instead suddenly feels like she is a vulnerable, small thing in the path of a tidal wave.

"Are you sure you do?" she asks. The question is more plea than challenge.

"I'm sure I *don't!*" he exclaims.

She stands there, looking at him, finally giving him a blink of her eyes.

"I told you how lost I felt when we first met. I figured I was one of the few people who knew who wasn't ... somehow ... all tied into it," he manages, moving his hands about. He then ceases the motion, eyes set upon her. "Then I saw your posts, and I figured I wasn't alone. Of course, *Sparrow* knows." He tries a smile on her, and it feels unsettling.

"I know what?"

He opens his mouth, then just stands there. He finally closes it beneath a slitting of his eyes. "Is this all some kind of test? You still don't trust me?"

"I – what? Why would I trust you?"

He nods, slowly, inhaling.

"Fine. Demons are out there. *Literal* demons. Like from the Bible … maybe. I don't know, but inhuman, supernatural … *things*, and they are killing people."

"I've got to go," she says, turning and stomping off.

"Did I pass the test?" he calls after her.

She barely hears the words, but even as much as she wishes to immediately dismiss him as some lunatic, she feels a deep urge to interrogate her "bodyguard".

Chapter Ten

When they return to the curious book shop the next day, they are decidedly less polite.

"Greetings," the shopkeeper welcomes them, hiding any trepidation he may feel.

They say nothing, walking up close. Zoe and David move to either side and somewhat behind, gaining a hint of unsteadiness to the man's composure. He finally seems to notice the steely looks on the faces of his guests.

"The symbol is a trap," Skot says.

"E-excuse me?"

"You said those who recognize the symbol are friendly, but what you've actually set up here is a trap."

The proprietor's eyes widen and he leans back.

"What's going on?" he asks, his eyes darting to each.

"I came back last night," Zoe reveals, pressing in even closer. "I overheard your conversation with … whoever that woman was."

"Who was she?" Skot pushes, even as the man tries to speak.

"I … surely you must understand …" he stammers, then takes in a breath, trying to firm himself. "I will not be treated this way in my-"

"I don't know who you are, but it's clear you're trying to deceive us," Skot interrupts. "I seriously doubt whether you have the Book at all. Your usefulness is rapidly dwindling, and if you are a threat, we can't just leave you here."

"Wha … what do you intend to do to me?"

Skot glances to David.

147

"We can interrogate him here," David says, "just close up the place, so no one else comes in. We could also take him to your sister if things need to get serious."

"You can't take me away from here!"

"Why not?" Skot asks, his tone flat.

"This ... this." He looks again between those surrounding him. He takes a stuttering breath, then exhales, defeated. "This is an in-between place." Lilja gives Skot a knowing look before switching her focus back to the shopkeeper. "It is here to protect the Book. The Book is a part of it, and if you take it, this place will cease to exist. All those who have come to dwell here will suffer for it."

"I don't believe you," Skot replies after a short time of contemplation. "I do wonder thought what would happen to *you* if we take you from here."

"But you must believe me! The Book is safe here. Leave it be," the man pleads.

"Who were you talking to last night?" Zoe thrusts. "What's the plan? What's the 'bait'?"

"Where is the Book?" Skot adds.

"The Guardian is here," Lilja suddenly says, and everyone looks at her. She is no longer focused on the brewing interrogation, instead looking off toward the room housing the rare books.

"What?" Skot asks.

She points, her eyes appearing to have lost focus on the primal plane before her. "The Guardian lies in there. It's a tomb."

The other three drill stares into the proprietor. David and Zoe manage to close more of what remains of the scant distance, all but touching the man now. He sighs again.

"I will show you."

Duilio comes up short to the expression on Therese's face. Her eyes bore into him, her arms folded over her chest. She wears a white t-shirt hanging loosely over black track pants, and her entire aspect is one of having been waiting for some time. He has arrived this morning bearing what he'd hoped would be a welcome gift – coffee and breakfast rolls. He all but forgets the paper bag as he looks at her.

He smells a cigarette, but he doesn't see one in her hands. There atop the table rises a coil of thin smoke from within a coffee mug. How long has she been waiting?

"Therese? Is everything alr-?"

"I should have known."

He emits a forced breath through an awkward smile. "Should have known what?"

"That you were keeping secrets from me."

"Therese." He tries a placating tone. "I'm only trying to protect yo-"

"Spare me," she clips, finally moving away.

He breathes a touch easier, relieved to be released from that accusatory stare. She retrieves a packet of cigarettes, pulling one free, grabbing her lighter. She holds them both in her hand as she turns back to him. He has barely set the bag on the tabletop.

"The demons are real, aren't they?"

His eyes widen, and he manages to get out some semblance of the word "what".

She shakes her head, lips pressed together. "Jesus fucking Christ, they *are* real." She finally lights up the cigarette, taking a deep drag.

"Therese," he tries again, taking a half-step toward her, but she quickly raises a hand, silencing him.

She shakes her head, finally giving to again drilling into him with her gaze. "Unbelievable."

"Yes!" he agrees.

"Don't you keep lying to me," she demands, pointing.

He holds up his hands. "I have … done my best to not outright lie to you, Therese."

"What does that mean?" she asks, her lips barely moving, jaw clenched.

"I …" he begins, pausing with yet another heavy sigh. "I have been as truthful as I can."

She again goes back to the slow shaking of her head. She finally lights the cigarette, having a deep drag. He is thankful she does not blow it into his face.

"Are the demons real?"

It takes him some time, but he finally answers: "Yes."

"Do the Malkuths know about them?"

"Yes. That's how I found out."

She glares at him then fishes through some papers on the table, producing one of the photos given her by Kettle.

"This isn't how you found out?"

"What? Therese, no. I ... knew something very unusual had happened that night, but I had no idea it was ... demons." He looks at her, and she looks back, unflinching.

"You weren't going to sacrifice me to them?"

"No!"

She nods.

"Who else knows about the demons?"

"I am not sure."

"Our government? The police?"

"No, no, Therese. The only other ones I know of are the Felcrafts."

She shakes her head, brow furrowing. "The what?"

"They are a powerful family, like the Malkuths. They are, in fact, the Malkuth's rivals."

"What ... the fuck," she says, her head seeming incapable of stopping its slow movement of disbelief.

"How did you find out?" he asks, and she darts a look to him, eyes slitting.

"I met with Kettle again." She is satisfied to see but a slight reaction of displeasure. "Honestly, I still wasn't convinced. He gave me those pictures, too. None of it was any sort of evidence, but it all got under my skin." She has another drag of her cigarette. "That's all it takes, you know. So, I did some more digging, put together more pieces of the puzzle, and they began to fit."

"Began to?" he prompts, eyebrows raising.

"The way you reacted when I confronted you, sealed it." She gestures toward him with the hand holding the burning cigarette.

He sighs, realizing the trap. "I think I always expected you to eventually find out. I was trying to spare you." He huffs out a chuckle shortly after saying this. He finally looks at her to find her already staring back. "You realize this changes everything, yes?"

She nods.

"We are now both marked for death."

"Everyone dies."

"Of course they do, Therese, but do you want to be brutally murdered when still in your prime?" He pushes through her aloof façade. "Hmm? I have seen Denman Malkuth kill people in the blink of an eye, with no care."

"So he *is* a Satan-worshiping serial killer."

"Oh, no," Duilio quickly says, and Therese looks up at him from where she had been staring at the floor. "The Malkuths *fight* the demons. They have convinced themselves that they are better suited to protect *and rule* humanity than anyone else, and they are *coldly* pragmatic. They will end any number of lives for what they feel is the greater good."

"Jesus ..."

"Yes, as you say ... *unbelievable*."

And Therese whispers the word at the same time he speaks it.

"Do you think the vigilante knows?" she asks him.

He shrugs. "I don't know."

"So," she begins, and the tone gathers all his attention. "What are we going to do about it?"

They carefully follow the shopkeeper through a short hallway and into a medium-sized room that feels all the smaller for being cluttered. Pieces of forgotten furniture share space with boxes and crates, these covered in dust and filled mainly with books. Skot is given to passively wonder why these reside in refuse. They make their way through, helping to move some aside to eventually find the unceremonious resting place.

The sarcophagus lies on the ground. It is carved of stone, showing age, despite this ageless place. It feels disrespectful to have it discarded so. Burning questions crowd his mind, but Skothiam voices none of them. He merely works with the others to push aside the heavy lid. Zoe is the only one who does not help, keeping a watchful eye on their host.

The body inside holds little more than bone and the tatters of clothing. There is no book, but within the dark and dust, a worn piece of jewelry may be seen – a necklace that holds the symbol.

"How do we even know this is him?" David asks. He does not look at the shopkeeper, expecting nothing of assurance from the curious man.

"Where is the Book?" Lilja demands, stepping up to the proprietor, and though she shows no outward sign of aggression, her force holds a veritable weight.

"It was not buried with him." All eyes turn on him, and he cringes, shoulders crowding up as he tries to retreat. "I said I would show you the Guardian, and there he is!"

"We came for the Book," Skothiam reminds, his tone so casual as to sound conversational.

"I know ... but-"

"We've been very patient with you," Skot continues. "You have lied to us, manipulated us, and you are working with someone opposed to us. Where is the Book?" He enunciates the question more emphatically, though the volume of his voice retains its normal level.

"Please understand, we are also trying to protect it."

"I will not threaten your life," Skot says, moving closer. The others move minutely away, and this does not comfort the shopkeeper in the slightest. "There are ways to plumb your mind without your cooperation. They're not pleasant, but if we're stuck here, then we *shall* try another way."

The man looks between them, fright beading on his face with the sheen of perspiration. He begins to tremble. Skot waits a moment longer before turning back to the others.

"We'll need to bring in a larger team, but let's keep it small enough to not garner too much attention. We'll lock the place up and confiscate the books. We need to go through every inch of this place and see if the Book is here. And if it isn't," he says, turning his eyes back to the shopkeeper, "we'll see what clues we can find that will tell us where it is."

"No," the proprietor says, the word not much above a whisper. "You don't need to do this. The Book is not here-"

"Earlier you tried to dissuade us from seeking it because it is some sort of heart of this place," Skot interrupts. "Then that means it *is* here."

"Y-yes, but it is not in my store."

"Why do you have the Guardian here? Where is the Book?"

"This is the resting place. I have no choice."

"Who does have a choice?" Zoe joins, giving him a pointed stare. "That woman I heard you talking to?"

"Who is she?" Skot continues. "Who's doing all this?"

The proprietor's fright grows. He looks at each of them, perhaps hoping to find a crack, some solace, something, but he sees no condolence there.

"I can tell you how to get to the Book."

"No," Skot says. "You'll guide us to it."

Duilio remembers the place from his prior visit. He had not even wanted to come here, and his initial gut feeling had been to try to keep Therese from accompanying him. After recent events, he decided against it. She is persistent, and he wonders why it has taken him so long to understand and choose better when and how to try to influence her.

He had opted to call David Felcraft, hoping he might be able to reach out and find something like … sanctuary. He is not sure, but he and Therese must do something. They are in deep, but they will not give up on looking for a way out.

Therese, though, has proven impatient. Now with the cat out of the bag, her anxiety has understandably grown. She smokes like a chimney, making him feel sometime uncomfortable with it. She had initially questioned his idea about contacting the Malkuth's rivals, but once his assurance had set, she dove all in.

Unfortunately, phoning David had yielded naught but voicemail and no return calls. Therese had grown more agitated as the minutes turned to hours, and then after only one day, she had taken a visible turn for the worse. Duilio wondered if she had slept at all, and he spied her popping a pill into her mouth before chugging coffee. He can't blame her. How does anyone handle this sort of news in a healthy way?

So, here they sit, the car idling, outside the house that ostensibly belongs to Skothiam Felcraft. At least Duilio knows this is the one he visited back when this all was in its early stages. He hopes the man is home. He hopes he forgives the unannounced visit. The gates don't open, so after unvocalized but obvious pressure from the somewhat jittery woman in his passenger seat, Duilio gets out and heads to the call box.

"May I help you?"

He gives a release of pressure that at least someone has answered so quickly.

"Uhm … yes. My name is Gaspare Duilio. I … apologize for coming without an appointment …"

"How may I help you, Mr. Duilio?" the voice politely interrupts.

"I have been here before. I … met Skothiam Felcraft. I- if possible, I would like to meet with him again. This is a matter of life and death."

"One moment, please."

Duilio stands there, waiting. He glances back to find Therese drilling holes into him with her eyes. He grits his teeth, preparing to hold up a hand to suggest she stay in the car, and that is when the gate opens.

He does not enter the property, though, as a smartly dressed young woman has come out to meet him.

"I am Victoria Felcraft."

"Pleased to meet you, Ms. Felcraft."

"We have record of your having come here. You also participated in a *field mission* with some of ours, did you not?"

"Yes." He nods, a bit shakily. "I did."

"I'm sorry to inform you, but Skothiam is not here."

"Ahhh." Duilio looks away, then back. "Is David here, by chance?" He throws a sheepish sort of grin onto the inquiry, as if it might help.

"He is not. Skothiam and David are unavailable."

A moment passes. Duilio does not do the best job of hiding his disappointment, and Victoria gives a glance to Therese before fixing Duilio with a studied gaze.

"I wish I could be of more assistance. Our records also indicate you are in the employ of the Malkuths."

His eyes shoot to her, and he finally gives up another jittery nod. "That is correct."

"Then you understand the complications this presents."

"Uh … no." He exhales into a grin that he hopes is charming. "I don-"

"We're not sure how much we can trust you."

"Ah … yes. Well, I'm not … uhm … *gifted* like-"

"We know." She offers a polite smile.

"I … uhm."

"I will let Skothiam know that you stopped by," she says, slightly raising her eyebrows.

It is all the hint he needs.

"Well?" Therese presses after he has barely gotten back into the car.

"We're on our own."

Chapter Eleven

Their shambling through the throng does not go entirely unnoticed. As with others who come to visit this place, the regulars do not make it obvious that their focus has altered, their routine upset. The slower of the two stops at a stall, his pace less than that of his companion due to a pronounced limp. The other eventually realizes it and scurries back.

"Lance, what are you doing?" Pierce asks, ending the demand with a partially swallowed belch.

Lance glances at Pierce then back to the wares. "Something," he begins but stops to cringe and hold his lower back.

"You suffer from pain?" the shopkeeper asks in thickly accented English, his general suspicion drying up at the potential of a sale.

"We all do," Pierce quickly interjects, sharing an impatient look to both. He grabs at Lance's wrist. "Come on."

"Wait," Lance says, moving his limb to avoid being pulled. He shifts closer to the curious products on display, but he instead focuses his eyes on the shopkeeper.

The man reels back from it, moving his head to gain some subtle distance. He shifts his eyes from one to the other. Lance finally turns back to Pierce.

"They were here."

Pierce moves in. He takes a deep sniff, then, when the inhalation peaks, he erupts in a riot of coughs. The shopkeeper cringes, brow furrowing in a transition from disgust to anger.

"Get out of here! I don't want your sickness on my goods."

Pierce does not relent, curiously nosing about, getting a feel for the immediate area. Lance shuffles back, casting worried eyes at the owner. Some of those nearby take further notice, a few angling toward them.

"Pierce," Lance whispers, trying to pull at his friend, his own stability wobbly.

"Where did they-" Pierce begins, bloodshot eyes on the shopkeeper, but he stops himself, waving a dismissive hand. "You don't know."

He backsteps, then looks around, registering the growing collection of people. This time, Lance lets himself be pulled away as the two make a reasonably paced exit of the area. The crowd watches, all eventually going back to their business as if on some unvoiced cue.

The shopkeeper continues to scowl, taking away some of the items that may have been in Pierce's soiled path and putting them away for salvage or trash. He rearranges piles, hoping there has not been too much damage. He pauses, freezing, then looks up.

Nothing is there, but a sense of deep unsettling has seeped in like a furtive fog. His eyes move, trying to find what has changed, what has arrived. He then sees it, but for a flashing moment, and the yelp which begins deep in his throat is almost as quickly strangled. The sound is more like a failed breath, a wispy hiccup.

He is not sure what he has experienced, but even in this strange locale, it stands out. The passing moment gives way to a lingering sense of foreboding rather than any return to comfort. Those two have brought something in their wake that belies a greater power than originally thought.

The shopkeeper decides to close up for the day.

The landscape has changed from dense urban to a thick darkness. There is enough light to see, and what it reveals shows a tortured venue of once lush forest. Lilja and David use small flashlights to illuminate as needed. All are armed, save their guide. They have made their way here in a span of time that feels too rapid and yet expanded with tendrils of fatigue. Skot looks again to the dark sky, noticing the twinkling of even darker stars. It would seem impossible, yet that sight meets his eyes. Occasional sounds interrupt the eerie stillness, scattered coughs, irritating scratches, and even the gurgling of fluid. They come upon a narrow passage of water, its current slow.

"We must cross to the other side," says their guide, the book shop owner.

They have given up on questioning his every suggestion. It seems none of them possess sufficient sense to tell if this alien land holds promise or death. It is passive in its threat, giving forth nothing more than an unsettling grip as they delve further.

"No bridge?" David asks, shining his light along the water for the sign of any such structure. The darkness consumes closer than their vision would normally permit.

"No."

"How deep is it?" Lilja asks.

"Not deep enough."

They all look at him, curious. Is he making a threat? His aspect does not speak of such things. He appears resigned, as though having surrendered to his fate.

Lilja is first in the water, though Skot is close behind. They descend slowly, the liquid virtually impenetrable in its blackness, giving up the occasional glimmer of reflected outré light. They proceed slowly, crossing the languid flow.

The water is tepid, possessed of the same feeling of a lifelessness unrealized. The distance can be no more than ten meters, yet time is eaten by the laborious, slow trek. The water stops rising once it gets to Lilja's hips. She continues to lead the way, glancing back occasionally to check on the others. When she returns her gaze forward, the light glints, and she stops immediately, noticing a shape beneath the surface. She flicks on her torch.

"What is it?" Skot asks as he steps nearer, his voice just above a whisper.

"There's something under the water."

They freeze. The sound of churning liquid continues from only one – their guide. He comes up to pass Skot and Lilja.

"Corpses."

No words fall from their lips, but even in the still darkness, their inquiring gazes speak loudly enough.

"The stream bears them," he continues. "They drowned themselves rather than face a worse fate."

The Hunters look down, trying to pierce those depths, not for want of seeing but in realization of their surroundings.

"How do you know that?" Zoe challenges.

The man gives a noncommittal shrug, continuing to the other side. The hunters eventually follow, moving even slower now in hopes of avoiding the macabre occupants of the dark waters.

Once across, it does not take long to find themselves amidst trees and plagued by a foul stench. The wood of the plants shows signs of rot, the entire place decrepit and reeking. A buzzing reaches their ears. Lilja's flashlight again finds life, and she directs the beam to a hive of bees on a nearby tree. The honeycomb is exposed, whatever fluidity may have once been now dried into a miasma of crusty waves and droplets. Despite this, the insects continue. Lilja's light does not even seem to impede them. She quickly shuts it off.

"What is this place?" She asks the question on the forefront of all their minds.

"We are still in-between," the proprietor says. "The Book is vital to these lands, but its power is not unlimited."

Skot sets his gaze on him, but what is said next proves unexpected.

"Were it properly cared, vitality might return."

"What?"

The man blinks, looking to Skothiam.

"I'm sorry. Nothing more than proverb."

"That didn't sound like proverb," Lilja replies.

"It -" The man sighs. "This place is unsettling. Forgive me."

Another distant, coughing sound rises, as though drifting on fog.

"And what's that?" Skot asks as Zoe peers in the direction, using her keen senses to try to discern an answer to the inquiry pointed at their guide.

"I don't know," the man confesses. "I know some of this land, and I know the way to the Book, but I do not wish to know more."

Skot then looks to Zoe. She shrugs, so they carry on.

"How do you know about this land?" Skot asks, gaining a peculiar look.

"I have been told … by a compelling … source."

"The woman you were talking to about us?" Zoe pitches.

"Yes," the man finally admits after some time.

"I'd like to know who that is when you're ready to tell us."

The man stops, turning his full attention to Skot. The others halt as well, watching, cautiously.

"You might change your mind once you do know."

The noise of their guide's resuming steps comes all too loud in the fetid air.

The grounds of this place are well cultivated. The hills roll off toward the horizon, eventually giving way to less tamed growth. Trees clutter one border, swaying gently in the wind as though unafraid to remind of their presence. He has arrived here as summoned and walks some ways to get where he has been directed. He thinks of lighting up a cigarette but decides against it. He is anxious, and he is outside, but something prevents it.

He finally finds the man he is here to see standing just outside an enormous barn. Someone else is washing down the flanks of a gorgeous black horse. The beast stands there, content to be cleaned, pampered, its muscles occasionally twitching.

"Signor Duilio," his host greets, turning to him as he arrives.

"Mr. Malkuth," Duilio returns, dryly.

Denman quirks a brief grin, then wanders a bit away from the horse. Duilio follows.

"How are things with our little leak?"

"Fine. It was all coincidence."

"So you've mentioned in your reports, but that's hardly satisfying, hmm?"

"Coincidence is often not a good enough answer."

Denman turns to him, giving a little nod.

"And *always* worth delving deeper."

They stop at a nearby fence. Several horses graze in the distance. Denman relaxes against the barrier, eyes out toward the majestic animals. He watches them, noting how they interact.

"You've been spending a great deal of time with Miss Stendahl." Denman cuts his eyes to Duilio for a brief moment. "I imagine coincidence would not require such an investment."

"Always worth delving deeper," Duilio reminds.

Denman exhales a short-lived grin through his nose. He then resumes the languid stroll. Duilio wonders if the man implies that he is interested in Therese sexually. That would work in his favor, but he also doubts Denman would give too much time to something so banal. They work their way back to the barn. The horse has been stabled, the attendant gone. A chirping noise rises, four longer sounds followed by a series of rapid tweets. Denman has led them to a small workroom in the barn, and inside is a caged bird.

"A sparrow," he mentions.

Duilio stares, coldly.

The bird's feathers show tawny variations, cream at the breast going to richer browns of near red in brushstrokes along its flank and back. Its head is in near constant motion, focusing for several seconds on the two men before darting about.

Denman continues to give that direct gaze and lightly curled grin of self-satisfaction. He goes to the cage, opening the small door and reaching inside. The bird hops away, staying on the perch and does not try to fly until it is clearly too late. Denman brings the animal forth, holding it tightly in his right hand. It chirrups in an agitated fashion, head moving quicker now.

He moves to a nearby table, opening a drawer and retrieving a knife. With no ceremony, he quickly beheads the small bird on the wooden surface, giving a squeeze to encourage the already profluent escape of blood. He then releases it, letting the body twitch and flutter, the eyes blinking impotently as the loss of life eventually catches up with the animal.

"I have seen this before," Duilio remarks. "What are you trying to prove with this childish display?"

"How easy it is to do," Denman answers, more stoic than threatening.

The two meet eyes, neither giving a millimeter. Duilio's defiance bores into Denman's patronizing confidence.

"Are you thinking of killing me?" Denman asks.

Duilio blinks. Denman's smile grows by scant degrees.

"You don't have to pretend with me. I'm sure you have thought of it. Come."

Duilio follows as Denman heads back out to view the horses. They have wandered somewhat closer toward the fence. Duilio finds himself concerned for any lifeform under the "care" of this man.

"Are you a rider, Signor?"

"No."

"You've never ridden a horse?" Denman presses, looking at him.

"I have, but it was when I was much younger."

"Ah, then you've never been on a wild horse. Never broken one."

"I have not."

"There is something singularly exciting about riding a wild horse and that moment when you break it. Breaking is a rebirth, but it leads to something being lost. Look how late in your life you were reborn when we revealed the truth to you and put-"

"Stop right there," Duilio interrupts, and Denman does, though his gaze and condescending smile do not falter. "Part of this … whole thing," he continues, waving his hands about, the right moving more rapidly, rising, "is your doing – the Malkuths. You *enjoy* this power. You manipulate lives supposedly for some lofty goal, but you have also broken yourselves. You do this for its own sake. What would you be without the Infernal?"

Denman speaks through his sly grin: "You are correct. We have lost something. One thing we have not lost is caution, even paranoia. Thank you for your report, Signor Duilio. You will continue monitoring Miss Stendahl, *however you see fit.* We'll be in touch."

The buzzing has been left behind as has the deep, gurgling sound of the languid water, yet the unease lingers like wispy tendrils of an unwelcome curtain. Lilja considered herself a friend of nature, but the scents entering her nostrils prove strange. She moves slightly ahead of the team, even outpacing their "guide", and though the landscape is alien, she can tell the trees will stop soon.

Zoe continues her role of staying along their flank yet still ahead, using her highly attuned senses to spy for anything untoward. She spares occasional glances to Lilja, her attention unfaltering even as voices rise.

"Have you considered it is best the Book remain unfound and unread?"

"I have," Skothiam accedes.

"Yet you seek it."

"I do. Even if for no other reason than to lock it away from others."

"There is knowledge in the Book, and it may be terrible. Perhaps its own safety is written in its words."

Skot spares the proprietor a glance, though he mainly watches the placement of his footfalls. He also peers ahead to find Lilja. He lacks no faith in her ability, but his concern is ever-present.

"'Perhaps' is the key word. If we could be sure, then I would leave it alone."

"Would you?"

A brief smile takes Skot's lips.

"You suggest this is obsession. It is not. It is *duty*. For all our diligence, we Felcrafts are also pragmatic. The safety of humanity is our concern. If that means the Book not being in our possession, then so be it."

"Well spoke."

"And you don't seem like someone working against us," he admits. "You almost seem worried for us."

"Why would I not be? I am not a monster, regardless of what you may think."

"I have seen many monsters in my days, and I've seen those enslaved to work for them."

"You think me a slave, then?"

"You are driven by fear. That much is evident."

"Are you not also?"

"To some degree. Were it not for the predation of our adversaries, there'd be much less work to do."

"Again, well spoke."

"You are familiar with our adversaries," Skot concludes as they continue on their journey.

"I ... everyone has adversaries, do they not?"

The whispering hint of a smirk touches Skot's face. The clumsiness of the man's diversion is overshadowed by one that proves much more effective. They have come upon a structure, a manufactured change in the landscape, and they gather closer.

Stone blocks create a floor, some of it overgrown, but these rise to other levels, creating a series of steps that ascend some meters before ending with a wide platform. All of the place shows an age easily seen as they make way to the top. The statues begin before they get there.

They are humanoid, detailed, yet displaying that same smoothness of surface and fluid discoloration of having been here for some time. They explore this change from natural to unnatural forest. The figures show a variety, some depicted in a calm state as might be expected from contemplative art, others in the throes of pain, anger, fear.

"What is this place?"

It takes a moment of silence before their guide looks over to David, noticing all eyes on him. He glances from one to the other, feeling the expectation. His lips part, though no sound is immediately forthcoming. He swallows. "I don't know." Then after more time of the scrutiny: "Why would I know?"

"How long have you managed that store?" Skot asks him, coming closer.

This serves as a sort of cue as the others fan out, exploring the nearby area.

"I ..." The man pauses, then takes on an aspect of sincere consideration. "A very long time."

"Hundreds of years?" Skot presses.

"The measuring of time is strange here."

"So, you've not been here your whole life."

"Oh, no. I hesitate to think any who dwell here were born here."

Skot nods, solemnly.

"Even the deepest revelations may become commonplace."

He looks over, studying their guide.

"Is apathy our enemy, then? Do we merely need to seek change?"

"Shit!"

They all look over at the sudden cry to see David cringing at one of the statues.

"The eyes," he says. "They moved."

Once there, the statue appears as does all the others. The eyes of this one are indeed open, giving out the semblance of a calm stare. Zoe and Lilja inspect the stone even as David exchanges a look with his cousin.

"Those eyes were closed," he presses.

They wait, anxiously. Skot steals a glance to their guide, gauging the man's reaction. He seems as confused and distraught as all of them.

"Well?" he asks of the two women.

Zoe shakes her head, stepping back. "I can't see anything out of-"

"Something's not right," Lilja speaks, almost a murmur. The curious eyes all now move to her, but she takes no notice, drilling her own perception into the thing before her.

They all start when the eyes of the statue snick to her, carrying a scratching sound of too much weight.

"What the hell?" David speaks.

That noise amplifies as the shoulders struggle to move.

"Do we ...?" David tries, "help them?"

"They don't want help," Lilja states.

The expression on the stone woman shows hunger, anger, and though each of them would swear it was not that way before, it shows clearly now. The arms come up, the fingers deadly claws.

"Run," Lilja says, then turns to the others. "Run!"

They move away from it, Skot instinctively grabbing their guide, as the man seems frozen in place. They don't get far before realizing they have sunk deep into this forest of statues, and now eyes glare needfully at them from each and every one.

"Which way?" Skot demands, giving the guide a shake when the man shows himself locked in fear.

He finally tears his eyes away, trembling. "What?"

"To the Book! Which way?"

The man moves his mouth, licking his suddenly dry lips. He grits his teeth, again looking about. "There," he finally says, pointing a shaky hand.

"Come on!" Skot commands, and they rush toward hopeful safety.

The moving statues prove slow, and they are able to dodge and weave as the grating things close in. The other Hunters have drawn weapons, and the eerie silence of the place is ruptured by the careening report of David's revolver. The bullet shatters the head of a statue that had moved in too close. Zoe grunts sharply, swinging her machete to remove the hands and part of a forearm from another. This does not fully take the life from them, the headless one even struggling to regain itself.

They run.

What had once been a disturbingly lifeless place now erupts with motion, the numbers looking even greater now that these things have begun their deranged pursuit. Crooked fingers reach out on crumbling arms, scratching mewls emerging from deep within constricted throats. The eyes leave no doubt. These things have wakened, and they seek to harm those who have disturbed them.

Lilja and Zoe change tactics simultaneously, turning well-honed blades onto the legs of the things as they easily avoid the outstretched grasps and hack at the lower limbs. The statues fall, still driven as they continue to reach and claw. The high-pitched noises become more agitated.

Skothiam and their guide lead the way. David holds his position, changing his careful aim from body shots to trying for the legs. He misses some, giving himself patience to shoot when they are closer. The two women finally catch up, sheathe their blades, readying firearms. They all stop, looking, and they see a small army. Where have they all come from? Even as far back now as the top of the stepped dais, more of them clamber over, and as this new life moves them, they gain speed.

"Watch him."

The trio look to the guide, not sure to whom Skot has spoken, but they remain as he moves forward. He looks out over the coming throng, takes in a breath, then raises his hands. He begins to speak in that secret language of theirs, the one akin to Latin, the one of whose origins they are still not completely aware. His own fingers begin to curl, not entirely unlike the seeking digits of their pursuers, but where theirs are rigid and angry, his possess a relaxed fluidity until coming to that final poise.

With a sudden press of those hands, palms going forward, Skot unleashes a great force. The power is visible, glaring forth in the deep amber hue that accompanies their magicks. It spreads out as it leaves him, and when it finds the statues, they fall. The ones nearest do not so much explode as tremble and clatter, pieces leaving them until they also become debris. Those further back struggle against the powerful intrusion, slowing then dropping. But it does not take them all, and plenty more screech and lurch, driven to make up the distance.

"We have to go," Skot says, turning back to them. "We've got to lose them."

Lilja looks at him, knowing that such an expulsion of magick must have taxed him. He does well to hide it, but she sees it. Their guide is also not a trained man, and he will likely weigh them. No choice.

"Come on," she says, her tone calm, oddly conversational, and she leads the escape.

And yet it all proves unnecessary, for as they have gained distance, they hear the horrible rise from those stoney voices along with the crumbling. They stop and turn to see that the remaining statues have reached a limit, and once they find that invisible barrier, they shatter, tumbling into ruined piles.

They remain hidden, breath loud as they try to catch it, and they watch. Quiet finds this place again, descending like a fog over the blighted landscape.

"What were those *things*?" Zoe demands of their guide.

He blinks, looking between the accusatory stares like a bird surrounded by predators.

"I - I don't know."

"What did that? Were those people?" David adds in his own interrogation.

"I don't know!"

Lilja and Skot exchange a look, then Skot speaks, "You know which way to go to get to the Book. You've lived somewhere in this … dimension for many years. Yet you don't know what caused *that*?" He points back toward the concrete platform.

He shakes his head, the fear in him like a tortured scent.

"You know this is bullshit," David says, going up to Skot and hissing the statement into his ear.

"I know we're all being used," is all the reply he gives.

Chapter Twelve

Therese awakes, bed linens tangled within her gangly limbs. She blinks, trying to bring clarity. She glances at the clock. It's quite early in the morning. She wonders if it might be too early to call, but then she shakes her head - a mix of again trying to gain wakefulness as well as a decision to herself. She won't call.

Padding into the kitchen, not bothering to dress in more than the tank top and soft pajama pants worn to sleep, she doesn't try to be quiet but makes little noise as she begins the preparations for boiling a pot of coffee.

"Therese, are you alright?"

She doesn't even glance over her shoulder, knowing the voice all too well. She also knows she allowed him to sleep here on her couch. He had insisted and insisted, and it seems they've both gone so far down the rabbit hole together, they might as well just admit it.

She swallows her initial urge to quip that it is nothing, and instead she turns, facing him. He looks as disheveled and lacking of real rest as does she.

"I had a bad dream," she says, realizing in the instance of utterance how lame it sounds, as though she were a child.

He blinks into a greater focus, treating the report as seriously as he might any other. "What was it about?"

"My mother. Something terrible had happened to her. She had left me a rambling voice message, saying it was just her and me now, everyone else is gone … Dad … my father. She meant my father had died."

"I'm sorry, but it was just a dream, yes?" He moves closer, though still keeping his distance. He has learned how fiercely protective she is of her personal space. He studies her, the sound of the heating water a gurgle in the background of their thoughts. "Do you want to call her?"

He barely finishes the question before she gives a single quick motion of her head in the negative. She presses up from where she had been leaning against the countertop and heads to the fridge.

"He's dead already," she reveals. "Bad memories is all."

"I'm sorry."

She fixes a look on him, one he has grown to know quite well. "It's fine," she says, flatly. She moves back to the pot of coffee, carrying cream. Duilio is tempted to make a quip about how so bitter a person seems to really like sweet coffee, but he thinks better of it.

"What about your mother?"

"What about her?" she asks, not looking over as she pours into one of her many mismatched mugs.

"Is she alright?"

"I assume so."

"Should you call her?"

"Why?"

"To make sure she's alright."

She stops, looking over at him. He sees that iron willed guard there, but it flickers. She still has her eyes on him, but they have softened, relatively. Her lips are parted, her breath held.

"What?" he presses. "What are you thinking?"

"I'm thinking it's a nice thought. Thanks. But I don't want to mix her up in this." She returns to her coffee, finishing it. She moves to sit at the meager table, leaving him to his own preparations. He pours out a cup, black, and sits across from her.

"I was going to say it was just a stupid dream," she begins after a moment of silence. "Well, I was actually going to say it's none of your damn business."

"You are right, Therese. It isn't."

"I know, but you're concerned, not prying."

"Maybe some of both," he says, giving one of his short, huffed chuckles.

She shrugs.

"Just a dream?" he leads, peering at her over his mug as he tastes of the coffee.

"Well, with all that's going on with these ... demons ... and everything. Are dreams *just* dreams?"

"I've wrestled with it, too, Therese. This whole thing will try to break you. Don't let it."

The morning quiet resumes, underscored by muted sounds of vehicles outside and the slurping of their brew.

"When was the last time you talked to her?"

For a fleeting moment, she thinks he means someone else, but his intent proves evident enough.

"Some months. We don't have the best relationship. We lost my father years ago, and she sort of retreated and moved on, if that makes sense. She has her life now, whatever it is, and she and I don't interact much anymore."

He nods, solemnly, holding back yet another apology.

"Any siblings?"

She shakes her head.

"Aunts, uncles ... cousins?" he continues, raising his dark eyebrows.

"No," she answers after swallowing, not seeming perturbed. "What about you?"

"Oh, I am Italian."

A gentle grin flickers across her lips, a premature laugh exhaled through her nose.

"I have two brothers and two sisters, and I am smack dab in the middle. My parents also came from large families, so even though they are gone, I have many cousins. Many." He nods, thinking on this, and he is shocked to hear an actual chuckle come from her. It is short-lived, but it was, indeed, there. He looks at her, head quirking.

"I'm sorry," she says, and they both have a brief laugh at this.

"You are right, of course," he says, and they sober quickly. She nods. "We cannot risk dragging our families into this. No one else, actually."

"There are others already in this," she states.

"You mean the vigilante," he says, and she is not sure if it is a question.

"No. I meant Kettle. Do you think the vigilante knows?"

"I don't know, but why would we try to go back to Kettle? He's a liability."

"How do you know that?"

He takes in a slow breath.

"I don't, but my hunch is to stay away from him. I … I still don't know exactly what to do. Sometimes I think we should just run away somewhere far away and try to forget all this. But I don't think anywhere would be far enough."

She looks at him, really studies him. How much their relationship has changed. This man helped in her kidnapping, not once but twice. It was in attempt to bait the vigilante, yes, but it did happen. And for all she knows, they intended to kill her if the trap was a success. He claims to be seeking retribution, and with these new revelations, that past feels insignificant. It's not so much that she forgives him, but it just doesn't seem important anymore.

She also wonders of this running idea of his. What would it be like if they just picked up and left? Where would they go? They both are capable of taking care of themselves in their own ways, and their strengths and weaknesses complement. Would it be possible? She shuts the idea out of her mind, contemplating another.

"Could the vigilante be wrapped up in all this?" she posits.

The shaking of his head is slight, continuing, as though a conductor's baton lording over his indecision.

"What do you think?" he throws back.

A moment passes, their eyes locked. She decides to reveal something. "The vigilante is a woman."

"What?" He blinks, his head jerking minutely. He then emits a chuckle. "Come on, Therese. That doesn't make any sense."

She smirks. "Think back to the first time I was rescued." She perks her eyebrows, giving him a steady, open look. The expression is not angry, but it says much.

He shuts up and thinks.

"Remember when you got your ass kicked? You had some guys with you, too, and you all got your asses kicked? Remember?"

"Yes, Therese, I remember," he concedes, deflated.

"Do you remember how *petite* the vigilante was?"

He narrows his eyes, blinking into an attempt at deeper recollection. "I … was he?"

"*She*," Therese corrects. "I was the one rescued, so I was very close to the vigilante. When we got outside, there was a very nice motorcycle waiting. I took the chance to size them up, and I am telling you, the vigilante is not much bigger than I am. Then we got on the bike, and I took hold. The vigilante is a woman. I promise you."

She looks around, trying to find a cigarette, a seeming reward for her conclusive revelation. Duilio notices and fishes a pack from a pocket, sliding it over to her. She takes it with unvoiced thanks, lighting up.

"Do you know who … *she* is?" he asks, carefully, reaching for the pack when she is done.

Therese leans back, exhaling toward the ceiling, shaking her head. "No," she says, eyes returning to him.

He lights up, drilling her with his attention. His initial exhalation is less melodramatic than hers. With lit cigarette between his first two fingers, he points at her. "But you have a suspicion."

She sits, motionless, returning his focus. A deep part of her wonders why she continues to keep up her guard.

"I do."

"Who?"

Another shake of her head.

"I don't want to say until I know better. It's more like one of your hunches. A lot of coincidental evidence, nothing concrete."

The condition of her empty apartment wasn't concrete enough? She dismisses that thread as quickly as it crops up.

"That is what started all of this, isn't it?" he asks, waving about that cigarette-holding hand, the abstract pattern of smoke accentuating 'this'.

"Yes. Well, there's more."

He continues looking at her, having a drag, waiting.

"There's a network of people, like myself, and we feed information to the vigilante."

"Yes."

"I suppose you already knew that."

"There was sufficiently strong suspicion to … accost you in the terrible way we did. I am sorry for that, Therese. Truly. But it was really more that … *she*-" Therese hears the doubt in the deliberate choice of pronoun "-rescued you the first time."

Therese nods, slowly. "Yeah. I was really bumbling. I'm a lot better at investigation when it's in cyberspace."

"Well." He chuckles. "The way you handled me when I arrived at the coffee shop proves you learned something." He pauses, slitting his eyes at her.

"What?" she finally asks.

"Are *you* the vigilante?" he accuses, eyes widening.

"Of course not," she scoffs.

"I am joking, Therese," he reveals the obvious, his body moving with barely suppressed laughter.

He gets a shake of the head and roll of the eyes as reward.

They sit about a small fire of David's making. There is nothing to eat, though they do not experience hunger. It feels as though many hours have passed since the start of their trek unto this strange land, yet the normal taxes on the flesh have not arisen. Skothiam and Lilja are a small measure away, sitting in silent conversation.

"It is very dangerous for you all to be here," the guide says, feeling the need to speak to alleviate the tension of those two sets of eyes upon him.

"I think you might could help with that," David says. His tone and aspect are much more congenial than Zoe's, but the hostility is there all the same.

The guide shakes his head slowly.

"I offered my best advice back in what was once my shop. When I said to not come here."

"Was?"

He fixes his eyes on David's, neither blinking. Breath passes in a seeming calm.

"I'll never go back there."

"Why?" Zoe joins the conversation.

"It has served its purpose." The cryptic answer comes a short pause after the question.

David has noticed this about their guide, especially hearing it in the partially overheard conversation between him and Skot. There was distance, yes, but sound seems to travel further here, as though in a fog.

"Bait?"

"Of course." And this response is immediate, and it strikes David truer than others. "All of this is a trap. I will guide you, as best I am able, and we might make it. This is a very dangerous place."

Nothing more is said for a time. The man studies the two Hunters, noting at once their calm and intensity.

"He is your leader," the man says, glancing to Skot before looking back to David. "You are the second in command."

"I'm not sure I'd-"

"He's second," Zoe clips.

"What if you both perish out here? That would be bad for you, would it not?"

"Sure it would, but that's just the risk."

"Your … *organization*," the man continues, putting a question on the word, "would be in some turmoil were it to lose you both."

David shakes her head. "I'm not second in line to lead the Family, if that's what you're asking. We don't do it like that. Besides, he has a sister, and she's much more capable than I am."

"Ahhhh. I see." Their guide nods.

"Why do you care?" Zoe challenges.

"I'm merely curious. Passing the time." He puts on a warm grin, spreading his hand, supplicatingly.

"I heard you talking to that woman," she reminds him, "though you won't say who it was." She narrows her eyes, leaning in, and he instinctively leans away. "I think it'd be better for you to shut up."

The man lets forth a sheepish chuckle. "I see that youth does not mean a lack of confidence in your *family*."

Zoe moves blindingly fast, jerking her machete from its sheathe where it lies on the earth near her feet. Before anyone may react, the blade is at the man's neck.

"I'm watching you, all the time. Because Skot says we need you, you live, but just give me the *slightest* reason, and your head is mine."

"Zoe," David chides as the tense moment lingers.

She does not take her eyes off his as she finally sits back, returning the weapon to its resting place.

The guide takes a deep breath, trying not to tremble.

"I have made many choices in life, as have we all," he finally speaks. "I must live with mine, regardless of how poor they have proven."

Zoe scowls at the statement. "That doesn't make it okay."

"Of course not!" Their guide heartily agrees, gaining further attention from this uncharacteristic rise in volume. "It is merely a salve to myself. I was naïve. I thought this day would never come."

David fixes a look on the man, eyes squinting. "You do know you were in a place where time is different?"

"Were?" the man retorts. "We still *are*."

David gives a smirk. "Then why'd you think this day would never come?"

The guide exhales, heavily. "You see how easily I am trapped."

The conversation ceases as Skot and Lilja return.

"I'm sorry for that," Skot says. "I think it's a poor idea to wait here too long. Does anyone need rest?"

The Hunters all shake their heads. Skot then looks pointedly at their guide, the expression not wanting of an answer, more an unspoken command. He stands, nodding weakly. David stamps out the fire, and they resume the journey.

The area waits like a graveyard. Mist hangs throughout, wispy scars. Stone interrupts the landscape. The grass shows more gray than green, hanging on in untidy clumps, encroaching onto the lower rocks. The sparse coloring is within and without, belying the unnatural aspect of this place. Scatterings of gravel and detritus form a mess of disuse, beginning sparingly enough to finally end at one side in a great tumult.

Noises have found their way here - alien noises in an alien place. A shuffling drags, raspy breath bleeds into a wet cough. The two shapes finally emerge from unaspected gray blobs into unlikely people, and they halt, looking about.

The stepped dais occupies focus, rising to call on any who might pass to investigate. What else may linger holds little consequence. Trek to the top and come what may. The two continue, their method and motion slow and haggard. Whatever lies in wait here would find easy prey of them. They finally reach the top shelf of the arranged stone.

"Nothing's here," Pierce eventually notes.

Lance does not reply, overcoming the pain in his leg to move further in, scanning the vicinity. "There." He points toward the chaotic mess of broken rock down on the far side.

Pierce looks, slitting his eyes. He then shakes his head, swallowing with a grimace. A gurgling rises from deep within his gut.

"Help was supposed to be waiting here. There was supposed to be others."

"I-" Lance tries, looking around to finally settle his eyes on his companion. "Should we wait?"

Pierce gives another shake of his head, his frown deepening. A reluctant sigh becomes a wracking cough, and Lance finally reaches over to help as he may.

"Stop it!" Pierce finally cries, waving Lance away.

Lance hobbles back, eyes agape, his expression one of dejection. Pierce leans over, hands on thighs, and he aggressively clears his throat, finally hawking a dollop of blood-infused phlegm onto the ground, the color an obscenity in this drained land.

He rights himself, finally finding Lance's expectant eyes.

"We can't wait. We're slow enough as it is," he says, giving Lance's leg a pointed look.

The great weight of dejection grows greater still.

"How will we catch them, then?"

"I don't know," Pierce replies, his tone blunted of its usual edge.

They are lost, yet they follow unerringly. Their lives have become so consumed, they have no real recollection of what it was like before. Memories sometimes pry unto them like sharp attacks only to become a wet, abstract mess that quickly dries to nothing. They bob and float as refuse on polluted waters, yet they do so with purpose. Something of that oily shell is a balm to them, a comfort in this otherwise horrid existence.

Pierce walks to a nearby pile of the crumblings. Lance follows with his shambling gait. Pierce pushes through it with the toe of a worn shoe, finally crouching to sift with a hand. He finally stands, unsure, looking out again over the area. Lance joins the passive search.

As the two observe, their postures grow subtly more erect. Pierce's eyes gain more color and focus.

"Come on," he orders, heading forward.

"Did you see something?"

"More help ahead. There's a trap. We need to hurry."

The somber coloring of this place has taken on a darker cast, creeping slowly like the ignored seep of a chronic wound. Lilja flicks on the light attached to her handgun, and only then does the contrast fully reach them.

"Time does pass here," Zoe grumbles, slipping an accusatory glance at their guide.

"It does," he agrees, keeping in the center of the group as they traverse the strange environ. "It just moves very slowly compared to what you all know."

"Have you forgotten that pace?" Skot asks.

The man emits something of a sigh. He then nods, solemnly, eyes closing before he opens them and looks toward the gray sky.

"Still, if you think of time moving here based on the passage of some sun, then you are mistaken." He begins this statement like a professor, but the end point is angled to the young Hunter. Zoe just glares at him. "We're simply moving into an area of less light."

The petulant shake of her head is miniscule, but it does remark on her maturity. She hacks with her machete at a gnarled, low-angled branch that is not much of an impediment, continuing in their trek.

"I'd like to know who built that ziggurat back there."

The guide looks at Skot, noting the calm to the curious gaze. The man is brought up by it, feeling that he has been pierced in an unexpected way.

"I cannot say," he finally responds.

"Look." They all glance over to Lilja's bid then to where she points.

In the distance more concrete shows, this less deliberate-seeming than the prior building. Walls rise half-buried out of the ground, culverts angling out in an unfinished, haphazard manner. It is more of a chaotic mingling of structure and nature, there seemingly only for itself.

"I suppose you can't say who built that, either, hmm?" Skot pitches, eyebrows rising.

The man shakes his head, then moves forward.

Lilja continues in her role as advance scout, reaching the area before the rest of them. The light has dimmed, but she can still see. She stands there a moment, staring, wondering how Zoe's sense works, wondering if something of that nature is truly awakening in her. Surely this place is odd, giving up insistent questions as to how, who, and why. The others finally catch up. Zoe looks Lilja over, curious as to the sudden still repose in the redhead, then she moves on.

"It's a trap."

Zoe halts, and they all look at Lilja.

"As I have said," their guide interjects.

"It's a trap made to bait humans," Lilja expounds. "A lot of us are uncomfortable in too much nature. The manmade is our attempt to impose order on what we think of as the chaos of nature. Nature is not chaos; we've just alienated ourselves from it. Then, we see something that appears of human construction in this weird place, and we're going to investigate it."

"Should we not?" Skot asks. He begins the question looking toward his girlfriend, but he finishes it by giving a pointed expression to the guide.

Lilja looks back, noting the exchange. She then turns fully, waiting.

The man offers a meager shrug and shake of his head.

"Maybe make him go first," Zoe suggests, pointing at the guide with her machete.

He gives over more expression of the scratching fear that will not leave him, but he still says nothing.

"Let's go," Skot decides, gesturing with a casual upnod toward the tangle of concrete and earth.

They round an area obscured by the sloping wall of the culvert to find further stone-hardened ground leading to a dark opening.

"Is that the way?" David asks, caution in his tone. Skot looks at their guide.

"There are many ways. We can go through there or over."

Skot glances at Lilja, and she moves quickly, traversing the ground to climb back up and around to better see. The noise of her movement channels down to them as they wait. She returns shortly after.

"The overgrowth becomes much more dense up there. Thorns, too. I don't know if it's venomous, but if it is, there's no telling what it may do."

"Why would you even think of that?" Zoe asks.

Lilja fixes her with an open look, more questioning than anything else. "Nature works to protect itself. Some stinging nettles are that way to help them spread and grow, not even as a defense mechanism, but they can have negative effects on us all the same. This whole place is alien, tainted. We need to be cautious."

"Hmph," comes the only reply.

"I think we threw out caution by coming here," David speaks what's on Zoe's mind.

"Be that as it may," Skot begins, "we still need to be as cautious as possible." He looks back to the guide. "In *there*," he says, pointing at the dark opening, "is that the way to the Book?"

"Yes," he finally says, sounding defeated.

Skot indicates with his head, and they continue, everyone but the guide turning on flashlights to help show the way.

The darkness encroaches quickly, swallowing them a few paces in. The way is not unlike what they might expect to encounter back on their home place, the surrounding concrete walls relatively smooth at first, though showing signs of blemish and corrosion none too far within. Stains show where fluid has run, some giving forth an eerie reflection of fresh wetness, spots hither and thither showing collections of that effluvia. They try to make little noise, but even careful footsteps reflect, announcing them.

They navigate a curve then come to an opening. Their torch beams show a major undertaking, more cement floors and walls, railings, pipes, all arranged to create a sheltered and walled subterranean space.

"This is *huge*," Zoe comments.

"There are at least two other ways out of here," Skot notes, angling his light across the chasmic space to show a rusty ladder bolted into the wall leading to another opening and then moving to a deeper progress into another restricted passage.

"That's not it," Zoe says, having moved forward to inspect the area. "This way leads around a bend and a bigger tunnel."

"Let's check that one first," Skot says, nodding to Lilja and Zoe.

The two continue leading the way, looking and listening for anything that may indicate the Infernal. They round the short bend into an area of such blackness as to make the gigantic chamber through which they just passed seem well-lit. They slow their movement, shining the beams of their lights to see what awaits.

One of them finds a haggard face, a man with unkempt hair and beard just standing there in the total darkness. He does no more than squint his eyes against the sudden illuminated intrusion. Their guide gives out a yelp clipped short by a rushed intake of breath. The Hunters show their own startle by merely taking stance and shining the lights.

"Get those lights outta my face," the man demands, his voice gravelly. He waves a hand as though thus capable of dispersing the brightness.

The lights are moved from his eyes, but all keep their shine on him. The man takes a shuffling step away, but the beams follow. His clothing is bedraggled, robbed of most color, affixed to his thin form as might be sloughing skin instead of garments. His flesh is dark and appears more like ironwood than wizened.

"Who are you?" he presses, still squinting and holding up hands to ward off the intrusion. "What're you doing here?"

"My apologies," Skot finally says, removing his light from the focus. "We're simply passing through."

"Your apologies!" The man drops his hands, trying to peer at them beyond the lights. "Man, ain't nobody here just *passing through*."

"We are," Skot replies. "Sorry to have disturbed you."

Though the interaction and exchange bears oddity, this lone man appears unthreatening. They keep distance, but they move to go about him and continue. The way promises no further lack of the enveloping blackness. Zoe and Lilja keep their senses sharp, hoping to spy anything of the Infernal through any means possible.

Another noise arises, a shuffling, mumblings and murmurs. Zoe moves her flashlight beam to the sound to find a huddling of many more similar people against a nearby wall. She trails the light along them, revealing a sizable group of these disused denizens. Several of those not on their feet press against the dirty concrete walls to rise. They all show the same ashen skin, as though having lived their entirety in this place has covered any vitality with its oppressive darkness.

"As I said, we're sorry," Skot repeats. "We mean you no ill will." He looks to the others, moving his head back toward where they came. "Let's go." He issues the command quietly, but it carries over the eerie silence of this place.

"But you only just got here," the haggard man says. He smirks.

Skot takes their guide by the arm, moving him in his own retreat.

"But the Book is that way," he protests within a hissing whisper.

"Book?" the haggard man chuckles. "What? You think this is a library down here?" This gains some weak chuckles from the audience, but Skot is more worried by those who look upon them with predatory intent.

They almost bump into a small group that has appeared in the way of their exit. They stand there, mute, almost as if they were human bowling pins, waiting passively to be knocked down. Their aspect is not threatening in the least, but they do block the way and show little intent of moving. David flashes his light back over to growing sounds, and the larger force has indeed gone to motion, collecting toward them.

"Why'd y'all bring guns down here?" the haggard man asks, his tone at once patronizing and accusatory. "You planning to shoot us?"

"No," David clips. "They're for self defense."

The haggard one chuckles again, and this time it goes on long enough for several others to join in.

"Zoe?" Skot asks much in the single word, looking at the young Huntress. She gives a slow shake of her head. These are not possessed people, nor demons in the disguise of flesh.

They are being surrounded, but Skot doesn't wish to open fire. Though these people are malnourished, there are enough of them to swarm. He also clings to hope that they can get through unmolested if they just remain calm.

"Why don't y'all stay awhile? We don't get visitors often."

"Thank you, but we need to be going," Skot says, and the man grins, showing he can even tell how weak that sounds.

The Hunter party has gone as far as they may to one side of the passage, the edge not showing a wall but a yawning abyss of total blackness. They try to move along it in the direction of their original intent, hoping to bypass and get out of this.

"Watch your step." More chuckles.

Skot then realizes the potential trap. They can easily force them over this edge into no telling what sort of fall. He shines a light into that darkness. He does not see a bottom, the black eating up the illumination to show nothing.

There is a wet cough, which ends in a forceful grunt and growl of throat-clearing. The motion of the slow-moving crowd stops. Lights shoot over to reveal two other people that hold their own aspect of fitting right in with the tattered group, though something of that keeps them apart.

"You don't want to go that way," Pierce says, and where any malicious intent may have only been suggested on a fraction of the others, he gives forth a grin that brooks no indecision. "Come on," he then invites, moving his head and turning. Lance looks them over with a tinge of pity, then goes to follow, his limp causing him to wince in pain.

The crowd closes, dried hands like leather taking their weapons and then pressing them in the desired direction.

They follow.

Chapter Thirteen

They take a walk in the late afternoon sun. She is not much for this, even if the weather proves lovely, but he had insisted. Their day had been one of general silence, she working away while he stayed lost in his thoughts. He finally spent some time of his own in cyberspace, interacting on his expensive, sleek laptop. She had chided him once that he'd spent far too much money since he pretty much only used it to send messages to his employers. He retorted that he had spent nothing on it. She understood.

He bit his tongue when she emerged with her usual layers of dingy hoodie and short leather jacket over a t-shirt. She had agreed to the walk, suddenly, so he figured he ought not question her over-dressing for the weather. Besides, he knows it is part of her armor.

They walk down the avenue, an odd pair at best. She wonders if people think them father and daughter, despite looking little alike. Maybe uncle and wayward niece. She has noted the increased strain on him, finding subtle changes in their time together. She finds it odd, since being with someone so much generally gives less focus to such changes. The demands of all of this has aged him, and he was not young to begin with.

He had mentioned that when he had been summoned by Gnegon to aid with the vigilante, he figured he was on the downslope toward hopeful retirement. He had money hidden away. Not a lot, but he planned to live a modest life once done with all this. How we trick ourselves, they both had concluded, leading to more cynicism upon cynicism. They remain driven in surprising ways, and not just to protect their own skins.

And yet, through it all, she still looked barely old enough to qualify for the birthdate on her I.D. Hell, maybe people thought he was a probation officer and she one of his surly wards. She used to not care very much what other people thought, but now, knowing the truth of the precarious situation in which they all lived, she found herself obsessing over the delusions. This ignorance was a weapon, whether wielded by the Infernal or the Malkuths, and yes, even the Felcrafts.

"I found something," she finally says after some time of their quiet walk.

They've made it to a large pavilion. An ancient church stands far on the other side as people mill into the outdoor tables of cafés. He stops, and she does, too.

"What have you found, Therese?"

She motions with her head, and they head down another street, the way narrower, until they pass through the squat buildings and find themselves by the river. The world opens, the sun brighter here. She ambles to the railing along the street, leaning on it, watching the waters below.

"Information on the Malkuths."

"Well, yes, that's what started all this mess, isn't it?"

She gives a tiny shake of her head.

"More. Much more. I did a lot of digging, especially now that you've helped to show me what they truly are. I called in a few favors, did some manipulating, and I've put together a good amount of information now."

"What?" He blinks, turning from where he had been also watching the waters to better look at her. "What do you intend to do with this information?"

"It's enough to get the interest of the authorities."

"Therese," he says in that tone that might as easily come from a father.

She fights the reflexive bile that tries to rise in her throat. He is not being protective for the usual prejudices people have, the automatic way they marginalize. He is cautious for very real reasons.

"It can't be linked back to us. Well, it can *now*, but I would fix that before doing anything with it."

"Therese, this is very dangerous, *very*. You know that."

185

She says nothing, waiting. She's learned something of him in their time together.

He turns back toward the road, watching the people and cars. He lights a cigarette, exhaling a thick stream toward the sky. The moment carries, and she continues looking over the river, waiting.

"Is it proof?" he finally asks.

"No. The Malkuths are too well protected. It likely wouldn't even lead to a case, but it'd be enough to get the attention of the authorities."

"And you think that would help us? You don't think they'd move to find the leak and plug it, permanently?"

She finally looks at him.

"I know they'd want to do that, but by the time they can move their resources away from the inquiries and look for us, we'd be gone. If they even managed to find the trail."

"So, this is meant to be a smoke screen?"

"A diversion."

He shakes his head, sighing.

"If the end result is our getting away, then why? This may bring unwanted attention on us."

"It's too late, right? Once I dug, I opened that door. And now you've been tasked with keeping an eye on me to determine if I'm harmless. From what you tell me, the Malkuths prefer to remove anything *remotely* a problem. It's easier for them."

"This is true."

"Then when we disappear, they will look."

"And you think this … *investigation*," he begins, waving a cigarette-holding hand to accentuate his speech, "will allow us time to disappear?"

"Yes. The initial move will be the riskiest. If we make it away, then the rest will be fine."

"Oh, Therese." He chuckles. "You make it sound so easy."

She scowls at him.

"It won't be easy, but you know we're dead otherwise. How long can you keep them from doing away with me. Maybe even the same to you?"

"I have no delusion, Therese. They will kill me as soon as they see no further use for me, or if they sufficiently suspect me. I think they are already suspicious, but they think our chances of doing anything to harm them are so pathetic, they don't bother.

"I can't really imagine why they haven't already done so," Duilio continues, "No offense to you, but if they've decided to use me solely to keep a close eye on you, then they don't think much of the value I bring them."

She turns to look at him, squinting from the light, idly wondering why she forgot sunglasses, though it won't much matter soon. She sees him ruminating.

"I think they recruited me, because they were wondering how much I knew, and they thought they'd make use of my contacts and associations in the law enforcement world."

"Criminal world," she edits.

"Well, yes, those are one in the same." He looks at her. "Power. Those who use it, or think they do, and *enforcement*, I think is a much better word for what they do. They do not think of themselves as criminals."

"What criminals do?"

"Most of them." He gives her a pointed look. "I have worked with career criminals. You know that. They also do not give into the illusion. They know they are law breakers. The Malkuths think they are above the law. They actually pity government. They feel the entirety of humanity has lost its way, and they are the shepherds … and butchers."

"That's scary," she admits, rising to a more erect posture.

"It is. As I told you, I felt I had some understanding of how things are in life. I had convinced my conscience to shut up. I was very wrong, and a part of me wishes I had died ignorant."

"It's too late for that."

"Yes." He nods, seeming defeated.

"You once told me you wanted to take them down from the inside."

"Yes," he says again, not further confidence showing. "I wonder if they even sensed that. I was openly defiant to Denman Malkuth. He scoffed at any threats I made. Maybe they put me on this assignment as punishment, or because they wondered if I might actually be a threat."

"So, that goal has changed."

He sighs.

"As much as I would love to take them down, or hell, even just hurt them in a way that mattered, I don't think I am capable. They have been at this for *generations*, Therese. They are protected."

"They are," she agrees. "Their security is excellent, but nothing is perfect."

"Is what you have really that damning?"

"I said it probably wouldn't even become a case, especially considering how strong they are, but it will cause a ripple. It's just meant to be a diversion. We know we can't take them down. We just need to hide."

"Then why bother with this?"

She gives a sigh of her own, but where his hinted at dejection, hers is one of exasperation.

"This will be better than our just falling off the grid. Besides, I'd like to sting them once before giving up my life to their fear."

"Don't make this personal, Therese, or you will lose."

She fixes a steely stare on him. "The man who kidnapped me is sleeping on my couch. Have I shown I'm not taking this personal?"

"Touché." He smiles into one of those clipped chuckles, then fishes another cigarette from his pack. She shakes her head when he offers one.

"That's settled then," she says. "Do you know anyone on law enforcement who is high up? Someone who has managed to maintain their integrity, or barring that, who feels prideful or powerful enough to do this? Preferably someone single with no children."

"Yes. Yes, I might."

"We can get the report to that person. I'll also send it to some other agencies, but a good champion would help. We just need to get Kettle and then release the report before we take off."

"What?" The word is all but wrenched from him. "Why are we getting Kettle?"

She gives a low-voiced near-grunt of impatience, back to staring needles at him. "We've been over this. Besides, I won't leave him to the wolves. Too many people have died because of this ... because of me. I ... I have enough trouble sleeping already."

Duilio blinks, taking in a slow breath he had not realized had already begun. She changed so quickly from angry determination to vulnerability that his own fuse failed before being lit.

"Those deaths are not your fault."

She shakes her head, slowly.

"I understand your point, but it still weighs on me. And you don't know all of it. I have sent people directly to the executioner."

"Alright, Therese, but Kettle is different. He was already in this, and *he* came to *you*, hmm?" He perks his thick eyebrows.

"Maybe so, and maybe he'd also hide, but it would always nag at me. Look. I don't want to bring him with us, but he needs to be warned, so he can go into hiding. Or better hiding."

His nod holds weight, hidden bitterness.

"I don't like it, but I understand. This is your thing much more than mine, anyway, so do what you have to do. Find him, and we'll do this."

He watches, half expecting her to object to his being involved. He feels a great relief when she just nods her assent.

They have come to a place of abatement for that choking darkness. There is light here where they stop to rest, but diminished, as if an eternal gloaming cloaks the land. The entire place looks half-formed, painted with an unimaginative palette. The concrete yet lingers, but what might pass for more 'nature' gives way - crooked, leafless brush along with wane grasses. This change takes further hold as they rise along the incline.

The Hunters have been bound, but they are still capable of a labored form of locomotion. Reaching this point had been simple enough, though painstaking in passage. As with everything, all is slowed and weighty.

"Why have you brought us here?" Skot looks to Pierce and Lance, throwing out the question with an accusatory tone.

Some time passes, Pierce focusing on the captives while Lance gives a slow, rheumy blink to his companion. "They brought us here," Pierce finally says, moving his head toward the others.

"Aren't you in command?" Skot asks.

"No," Pierce states, flatly, then shuffles away.

Lance keeps looking at them, his expression one of pity, then he finally follows. Pierce remains standing, showing a pinched anxiety, impatience, but Lance takes the opportunity to plop unceremoniously onto the ground, giving his leg a respite.

"We have something exciting in store for you," the haggard man says, grinning a crooked grin.

"What!" Pierce turns his head suddenly, practically shooting the word at the man. The Hunters note his surprise, all registering it in their own ways. Skot thinks it does not bode well for any of them.

The haggard man turns that grin onto Pierce, stepping nearer. "It's very boring here, so we've come up with games to keep us entertained."

"The fuck are you talking about?" Pierce all but growls.

The grin does not falter. "Listen," he invites, bringing a hand to cup an ear. "Do you hear that?"

Pierce slits his eyes, drilling them into the man. The subject of his intensity just smirks back. He finally turns, beckoning with an unusual and sudden enthusiasm. "Come on!"

Those near them roughly bring the captives to their feet, and the laborious trek continues upwards. They finally reach an area of some leveling off, the cement gone, more of the thirsty scrub brush crowding about. A rise of the rock on one side forms a natural wall, then falls off a steep incline. They hear the rush of water.

Pierce looks around, noting what seems an end to their path. "Why did we come up here? You're supposed to-"

"There!" the haggard man points, gesticulating. He places a hand on Pierce's shoulder, and Pierce finds it revolting. He nearly shudders from the contact.

They all move over and then see it. There is a narrow bridge of rock connecting from their side over to a continuance of walkable ground. The brush there turns to trees, the land more inviting, in relativity to what else covers this realm. To get there, though, the thin walkway must be traversed. Its length is not as fearful as the lack of width, but below shows a deep drop into sickly-looking waters raging over ugly rocks.

"We have to cross *that*?" Lance asks, fear laden in his voice.

"No," the man chuckles. "One of them do." He points a gnarled finger at the Hunters.

Pierce again fixes the man with a slit gaze. "What are you tal-
"

"This is the game!" The man claps his hands together once.

Skot notes a charge rising in their captives. Some of them gain a fidgeting motion, others brighten with the look of genuine grins. It all resonates deep in his gut, and his sense of alarm heightens.

"One of *you*." The man springs lightly on his feet, giving forth the suggestion of a jig, as he points at the captives. "One of you will cross it, and then, we will be *fair* and wait a while for you to try to get help. If you don't return soon enough, then another will be forced to try."

They look to one another, knowing the futility of this. They have no clue what waits on the other side, much less if they can find help were they to successfully traverse the precarious walkway. It all feels designed to slowly end them all for the enjoyment of their wretched captors.

"This isn't *fair*!" Their guide gives voice; fear bubbling forth as he looks from the contemplative Hunters to their eager captors. "How are we to even find help if we cross *that*?" He points at the bridge, finger trembling.

"You?" the haggard man says, "You wish to volunteer?"

The guide goes immediately silent.

"Come *on*," he draws out, a perversion of a gameshow host. "Someone volunteer, or we'll choose."

Skot sees it then - the resolve on Lilja's features. He can all but read her thoughts. She harbors no doubts she can cross the bridge; the true test is figuring out how to get back unseen and provide help.

"I'll go," speaks a voice, though not the one Skot had feared.

"We have our volunteer!"

Most of the bedraggled group gives forth applause as David gets to his feet. Lilja reaches out to stop him, her hand grabbing at his arm. He looks back at her with a congenial smile. "Don't worry. I've got this."

"I can-" Lilja begins, but she is cut off by a swarming intercession.

"Wait your turn!" the haggard man commands, waggling a finger in Lilja's face. "And *you*." He turns, looking David over. "You're very healthy. You 'got this', huh?" He titters, then nods, and the swarm of people presses closer, hands on David, pushing and pulling and holding.

They drag him some meters away, others remaining behind and grabbing hold of the other captives. Skot figures this is to prevent them trying to intercede, but then a different sort of terror unfolds.

"What are you doing?" he demands, trying to keep a better watch as his captors hold and press upon him.

"We've got to make this *sporting*," the haggard man explains.

It takes many of them, but they manage to do it. Surprise is also on their side. They bring out David's right arm, holding his hand over the hard surface of a stumpy rock. The crude stone club swings down several times, fast, direct, and the sickening crunch is only overwhelmed by Zoe's voice.

"Stop it! Stop it! What are you doing to him, you fuckers! Let me *go*!" She struggles but remains held.

"Oooh. Spirited." The haggard man looks at the Huntress. "Maybe you'll be next."

"Fuck you!" She continues to try to press forward, baring her teeth.

David grits his teeth through the pain, whatever vocal reaction he had overwhelmed by Zoe's fury. He tries to extend the fingers of his right hand, but they don't all move as they should, and the sudden shock of pain reels into him. He mustn't pass out. He feels a tremor beginning to shake up from his ruined hand, and he takes several deep breaths, trying to calm himself. The haggard man gives a terse nod, and David is pushed to his feet. His bonds are cut. He stands there, taking in some more breaths.

"Go on, now," the haggard man chides. "You got this, right?"

David looks at Skot. Both tell tales with their eyes, but the training ultimately froths forth. David turns, and steps toward the bridge.

It looks as unnatural as this unnatural land, connecting to this edge with a span of one meter at best. It carries on, sloping inward deceptively to its most narrow part where David knows both his feet would not fit side by side. The composition even partakes in the trap, starting rough here, eager to offer hold, but the slender middle is smooth as though somehow shaped by the fluids far below.

And that water rages. David listens to it, letting it lull him from the pain. He then blinks, shaking his head, realizing the danger of this. That coursing river flows in from his left, picking up speed to go quickly from a gurgle to a angry crash where it is choked by sharp rocks and forced into a more narrow passage to finally course away again. He wonders that they did not notice it on their way up here. He takes a calming breath, then proceeds.

"That's it."

He hears the voice from behind him, close. It's the haggard man, and there is such desire in the tone, he wonders that they might just shove him off the bridge to get the death they want. He uses this as inspiration, stepping along, keeping himself low at the center, knees bent and passing his weight evenly. He has undergone hours upon hours of training, and he knows how to keep his balance.

A decrepit tree waits on the other side, coming out from the edge and rising aside the bridge in the perversion of a lover's embrace. More of the eager scrub comes up with it. It looks to David as though the growth of nature here is more *natural* there. That side holds the possibility of freedom. He must get there.

He slips, catching himself quickly, wobbling. He rights from the tilt. His 'audience' reacts accordingly, giving forth gasps and caught breath in anticipation of his possible failure. None of his own are in those voices.

He slides his right foot forward, feeling it catch on the smooth surface. His nerves are getting to him, the throb of pain in his hand coursing up his arm. He is very close to the tree now, nearly there.

When he sets his left down, it happens. That foot glides aside as though no purchase at all waits on the bridge. He steps forward quickly with his right, leaning that way, reaching for the tree. This foot holds, but not well. He tries to shove off, moving left to center himself, but he knows he is losing. He grabs at the tree, so close now, and he feels the riot of pain in his ruined hand. This will not hold, and he thrusts wildly with his left, finding a decent reach of branch and gripping tight as he falls.

The crowd gasps, calls, some even clap as David goes over the left side. He hears a stunted cry and call of 'no', and he knows it is

Zoe. He waits for the pull, holding tight with his left hand. He is not sure how he'll climb back up with only one good hand, but he'll find a way. His hope is that the branch is short, and he may not end up too far from the bridge.

And then the branch snaps.

The Hunters try to rise, to fight, as David falls, but they are held by too many hands. Zoe's surge of anger creates a tumult, but their captors are too many. Skot merely sits, resigned, that unfortunate familiarity of mourning already setting in.

The haggard man watches, standing right on the edge. David does not scream, little more than a forced grunt emerging when he hits the water of the river. It's clear the impact does not kill him, but his body is carried on the charged rapids, and he collides roughly with the rocks.

New red mixes into those gray waters, coiling together like a dark announcement in the already soiled river. David is turned, and he lets out another call of anguish, also trying to pull in a breath, then he is swept under and disappears beneath the rocks.

The haggard man turns, looking upon his captives with a satisfied grin. Though it looks of satiation, it takes not long for it to change.

"Who's next?" he asks, giving a single clap of his hands.

"Bastard!"

He looks to Zoe, the Huntress still struggling against the bonds and hands holding her.

"I'll kill you!"

"Oh my. You, then?"

Lilja suddenly squirms free, having been patiently working to this for some time now. She has the most experience of them all with this sort of thing, what with her grappling and self-defense training. She'd remained calm and subdued like Skot, but where his had been the true resignation of accepting the inevitable, she had done this to coerce her captives.

She rushes to the bridge. Skot sits up, gaining further attention from those holding him. He watches with deep fear as Lilja approaches the bridgeway. She is moving too fast. She has somehow slipped the bonds about her ankles, but her wrists are still held.

"Wait! No!" calls out the haggard man. "You can't go like that!"

Like that, Skot repeats in his head. As if the way were not precarious enough, their 'game' requires that the prisoner not be whole when going across. He slits his eyes, moving his fingers in a particular way. All attention is on Lilja.

She traverses the length with speed, using that momentum to her advantage. She gets to the tree, all but bounding across with such a show of grace as to awe many. Her hands take hold, using the plant to aid in her final movement. She does not stop, quickly gaining distance.

"Go after her!" the haggard man commands. "Bring her back! This is not how it's s'posed to be."

A good number of them hustle to it. None fall as they help each other to get across the bridge. They don't match Lilja's speed, either, but soon enough, a decent group is in pursuit.

The haggard man looks at Skot, angry. Skot gives it right back, though his expression is much more calm.

"I think we might just slit your throats," he says, no grin at all on his cracked lips. His face is pinched with need, his eyes boring into Skot's. "What!" he challenges, seeing movement at Skot's mouth. "What are you saying?"

Those left holding onto Skothiam cry out in pain, reeling back. They have felt a sudden surge of heat, like the shock of intense fire. Skot shuffles to his feet, straining, and he snaps the bonds around his wrists.

"Get him!" The haggard man points, hand waggling, but he moves away in the gesture, obvious fear gripping him.

Though Zoe's anger covers like a red coat, she does not fail to see the opportunity, and she takes advantage of the confusion to attack. She bares her teeth, lashing out at the nearest captor, and with an animalian snarl, she tears into the flesh of his neck.

He screams, trying to move away, and is only able to do so because she releases him. His hands shoot up to his neck, trying to staunch the flow of blood. The bite is not bad, but his fear makes it worse.

Zoe continues, pushing against another, getting to her knees, then using the improved stability to headbutt one who tries to take better hold. His nose erupts in a riot of blood, and he reels back. She shoves her shoulder into the solar plexus of a woman trying to offer assistance, throwing her back.

Skot rushes over, dodging, noting the reduced number of them now that most have left to catch Lilja. He collides with another, knocking the man down, and he then gets to Zoe's bonds. She is freed quickly and makes a beeline for their weapons.

They know not why the weapons were collected and brought when it would have been wiser to discard or use them, but she reaches the treasure easily, most of the remaining captors now reeling in confusion and fear. Machete in hand, she becomes an angry dervish of revenge.

It's over in seconds, and she stands next to Skot, both peering over the edge into the waters. She breathes heavily, painted in the blood of the slain. Skot gives her a look, his own eyes drooped.

"He's gone," he says.

"Let's find Lilja," Zoe replies, handing Skot his own and Lilja's weapons.

He gives a nod, and they are off, dragging their guide with them.

Moments later, the explosion of a cough having been forcefully held sprays wetly unto the scene. This is followed by shuffling, grunts and groans. Lance and Pierce emerge from their hiding place. Lance stays supported by the large rock, his eyes showing a wariness. Pierce marches to the bridge, angry. He observes for a moment, and Lance hopes he will not cross. He doubts he could make it, but he would try. They are both compelled.

"Fuck!" Pierce exclaims, turning. "That stupid fuck!" He looks out at the fresh corpses, the riotous stains of blood.

"What are we going to do now?" Lance finally asks.

Pierce looks at him, the anger mostly gone.

"We're all going to the same place. We'd better hurry."

Duilio feels relegated to nearly being borne carried along as baggage.

He still carries his sidearm from time to time, noticing those instances have increased in frequency as his involvement with the Malkuth has deepened. Therese has taken charge of their work, not only in determining what needs be done but doing most of it. Duilio has his contacts and experience in investigation, but all of this preparation has been taking place in cyberspace.

He also recalls when he encountered her in the coffee shop, and how easily she handled him. Where she has learned to better herself offline, he has done little to keep up with the radical ways the internet has changed the world of investigation. She even showed him how to disable the tracking in his smartphone, an option they have only just taken for worry it would cause suspicion.

Their destination is not terribly far from Therese's residence, but they take a few different busses just in case. A burning need to be done drives them, but they know they cannot be impatient. This is a game with terribly high stakes, and they hope to survive the play.

The apartment complex is a few blocks off the main road where they disembark this final bus. It gives Therese reason to wonder. She actually expected it to be more isolated, but she just as quickly changes her mind. It had been very difficult to locate the address in cyberspace, and that would be the main security. She figures there are likely some cameras and other intrusion detectors, but at this point, they don't mind being seen.

It is quite likely that Kettle will refuse to have anything to do with them, and if he is adamant in that regard, they'll go on without him. Therese had agreed to this under Duilio's incessant push to enforce some control over their final play. She knows he is entirely against including Kettle, but he seems just as against abandoning her. She wonders that he doesn't make the correlation between the relationships. Yes, they just learned of Kettle, and there is no real bond, but the sudden exposure of an internet investigator to possible harm is something that strikes close to home for Therese.

And there it is. They stand in front of the non-descript door to this unit, the only thing marking it as different from all the others being the numbers. Therese also gives a slight gesture of her head. Duilio looks, slitting his eyes. She rolls her own, pointing emphatically and showing the small lens of the camera there beside the door.

"Should we?" Duilio begins, feeling caught.

She shakes her head, looking directly into the small device and giving three steady knocks to the door.

"Maybe he isn't home," Duilio hopes after a short wait.

"He's home," she states, flatly.

She knows how little she used to leave her own place. Days would go by with her staying tucked into her dark hovel. Those who thought she might go mad from the enclosure had no idea of the magnificent scope of the virtual world. She felt more claustrophobic and oppressed when she'd go out for supplies than when expending hours in cyberspace.

She's changed, of course, grown, but she still prefers the online world to this harsher, more desolate seeming one.

She gives a raise of her chin to Duilio, then glancing pointedly at the lock. He passes a raspy inhale through slightly parted lips, shaking his head before producing his tools and bypassing the lock with some ease. He carefully opens the door, breaking the seal and waiting for any sound of an alarm. None comes.

"If he has one, it'd be silent, but I don't think he has an alarm. We're being watched, though," Therese says.

She again takes the lead, heading in.

The place is darkened by closed blinds and pulled drapes. The late afternoon sun manages to creep in, casting gray illumination everywhere it touches. She notices dust on several surfaces, barely any decor on any of the walls. The place is hardly furnished, yet it feels cramped. The condition belies age and a lack of care.

"Hello?" she calls, gaining a startled look from Duilio. "We're not intruders."

"Therese, we just broke the lock and entered uninvited."

"We're not here to try to harm him. We're here to try to help him."

"Good luck with that," speaks a voice with a cultured Transatlantic accent.

They both freeze, looking over to see the well-dressed, handsome man seemingly materialize from the shadows. It is done so well, and after all Duilio has seen, he wonders if the man has appeared here via magick.

"Denman."

"Gaspare," he returns, giving a single nod of his head as if this were a casual encounter. He then slips that gaze to Therese, and Duilio is not at all comforted by the shift to a more predatory look.

"Ms. Stendahl."

She says nothing, staying frozen in place, eyes on the man. Duilio steps forward, protectively.

"Denman, we're here-"

"Spare me," Denman holds up a hand. He then lets pass a lengthy breath, one suggestive of boredom. "You took long enough in getting here. I barely had the patience to wait for your conversation to give me the proper dramatic moment to announce my presence. It's all very tiresome, really."

"We..." Duilio draws out, spreading his hands, giving one of his short chuckles through a light grin.

"Oh, Gaspare," Denman says, a condescending smile on his face. "Have you fallen in love?"

Confusion takes both, though Duilio is the more expressive.

"Your taste surprises me." Denman gestures to Therese. "But why else would you risk yourself so? She's not your daughter, is she?"

"No!" Duilio clips, gaining a further grin from the Malkuth.

"Good." He nods. "I know you, Gaspare, but this does surprise me. Still, I doubt you've fallen far from the tree."

The man blinks, unsure what Denman means.

"And you, *Therese*," Denman continues, his eyes now on the woman. "Eve with the apple, hmm? And you managed to get our good Gaspare to eagerly partake. We let you find that information. How stupid do you think we are? It's really quite pathetic. You two actually think you have a chance, but why did you come *here*?"

Though Duilio would agree, he says nothing.

"Kettle is already dead," Denman says, no grin on his face now. He speaks with the placid calm of one completely sure and entirely uncaring.

Therese gives forth a barely perceptible tremble, her eyes drilling into the Malkuth.

"You're angry," Denman notes. "How could you possibly care so much for him? Well, you clearly see yourself in him. It's a shame, really. Why bother? You should take a page from the ex-inspector there. He is much more selfish."

199

Once done speaking, Denman brings his hands together near his chest, the tips of his fingers touching. He steps casually toward Therese.

"Denman!"

The man turns, still moving slow and casual, though Duilio knows well the lethal speed he holds in reserve. Denman sets eyes on Duilio, eyes which now show a complete lack of amusement.

"You didn't let me finish my job."

The Malkuth perks his well-sculpted brows, the only quarter he is willing to give. Therese has moved away, but little more than the wall of the room now waits her in this small space. She sweeps her eyes over Denman, watching for signs of an attack. She tries to remember the lessons she learned from Lilja so seemingly long ago, but something in this man's casual, predatory nature gives her terrible fear. She stands no chance against him.

"You sent me to see who was prying into your business, and I found her," Duilio continues, gesturing the obvious. "You told me to find out what she knows and determine if she is a threat, and if so, to plug the leak."

"You are a disappointment, Gaspare."

Duilio dares to move closer, and he notes the subtle rise in the already perked brows. Denman is not unawares.

"Let me plug the leak," Duilio bids.

"You?" Denman begins, and he chuckles. The sound carries, growing to a stream of low laughter. "You will slay her, hmm?"

Duilio stares at Denman with pleading eyes, and though the levity does not entirely leave, Denman gives another deep breath.

"I do hate to repeat myself, but you really are a disappointment. I can only presume that desperation now moves you. Why do you even care?"

Duilio steps closer, hands held out like a beggar.

"Pride in my work," he says, gaining a smirk from the Malkuth. "I am not entirely cynical, Denman, not yet. Let me have something."

"We let you live and work for us," Denman states, turning to more face the other man. "Call it your survival instinct, though I prefer to note it is merely a concentrated selfishness, but you possessed some meager value to us."

"Possessed?" Duilio gives rise to his own eyebrows, trying to sound hurt.

Denman shakes his head. "This is a waste of-"

Duilio moves as quickly as he is able, turning those beggar's hands to action. He has had years upon years of experience, but he has actually rarely ever unholstered his sidearm in the line of duty. Never has he ever tried to outdraw someone before. He has borne witness to this man's lethal prowess, so deadly that merely being within arm's reach of him is dangerous. He notes the flaw in Denman's thinking, though, and he hopes to have exploited it for the proper price.

The pistol is produced, a gleam of polished metal, pointed and fired. The sound is deafening, and Therese cries out, colliding with the wall as she moves back and tucks into a smaller form. She watches intently as Duilio and Denman part from that quick moment of near embrace. The Malkuth stumbles back, a thin tendril of smoke rising from his chest. No hole has come from his back. Duilio has used a hollow point load, figuring rightly that if ever such a scenario as this would take place, he'd have one chance.

In Denman's right hand, he holds his obsidian dagger, the blade a light-drinking black, and it drips with blood. He dabs at his chest with his left hand, coming up with more blood. He wobbles, slightly, looking at Duilio, and he grins.

"You…" he begins, then stumbles back, dropping to his knees before rocking and falling.

Naught but sheer adrenaline and shock has kept Duilio on his feet. He holds the smoking gun in his right hand, his left clamped tightly over his throat. He had not felt the strike at all, but he knows Denman's methods. Fluid leaks and seeps from behind his hold, and he also falls.

Therese rushes over. "No!" she demands, taking hold of Duilio. She slides her own hands in, displacing his, trying to staunch the flow of blood. Duilio quakes, trying to shake his head, wide eyes going toward Denman.

Therese looks over, still maintaining the hold. She watches, her body a taut purveyor of stress, but Denman does not move. She looks back. "You got him," she says, her tone gentle, and she even tries to crook her lips into something of a smile.

Duilio nods, though it comes out more as a shiver, and he gurgles, coughing.

"No!" she cries again, pushing harder, but it doesn't matter. What she may be preventing leaving through the slit in his neck is finding its way into his lungs.

He manages some control of himself, and he looks in her eyes. He tries another shake of his head.

"No. No," she says, and the desperation is indeed there.

It gives him sorrow, and he closes his eyes.

"No, Gaspare."

She leans down over him, still holding her hands over his throat, and her body gives into the convulsive wracks of terrible sobs.

She doesn't wait too long, a part of her analytical brain nagging at her that surely someone has called the police, and they will be here soon. She sits up, looking at Duilio, knowing he is dead - another casualty.

She doesn't even check on Denman, wanting to get no closer.

Instead, she stumbles to the kitchen, washing her hands. She wets a ratty towel she manages to find with a short search and wipes at where blood has gotten on her clothes. It is her fortune that the dark shades of her clothing manages to hide the stains well enough.

She doesn't bother looking for Kettle or his set-up. She knows the cameras saw them, and the police may be able to get this information. She'll deal with that remotely, once she is safely home.

Safe …?

She wonders if that is even possible anymore.

The land's fertility, such as it is, abates. They enter this area, colorless, lifeless. It feels incomplete. They have arrived.

Zoe and Skot had pursued the pursuers, their guide running along with them. Zoe's drive and harshness spoke much to the former storekeeper, telling him she'd just as soon further wet her blade on his blood and damn the consequences. He kept his mouth shut and followed.

It did not take them long to find Lilja. Or, to be more precise, for her to find them. The haggard ones did not prove effective as trackers or fighters. She had tangled with few of them before winding her way around and waiting. It had been her plan to disrupt them, separate them, then avoid. Those wasted people were only good at capture by deceit, and they had played their hand.

David was lost. They would mourn him, but they knew they had to carry on. The rites would be performed for a fallen Hunter as had been done many times before. He had been amongst their best, and the loss was deep, it's manner ignoble even though he had faced it with as much fight as any other.

Skot had felt that anger surging in him even as it expressed itself so openly in Zoe. She wanted to continue hunting those people, kill every one of them, but he managed to calm her. They were easily avoided, unworthy of any fight. Victory came with correcting their own mistake and being loose from them. Victory waited with the final Book.

And thus were they here.

"What is this place?" Lilja asks, bright eyes looking about, her voice not much more than a whisper.

"It is the end of here," their guide speaks, fatigue and more laden in his voice. "It is the *why* of here."

"It feels … *unfinished*," Zoe remarks.

Skot wanders, half-listening, senses eagerly open. Not only is the environ washed of color, but as he looks over his companions, they even seem somehow dulled. A perpetual gloom bathes this place, as if poised at the cusp of a held breath of creation.

He looks about for the Book, but he does not see it. He searches for signs of its resting place, but all that greets him is this strange landscape, again having gone from a crowd of brittle plant life to rocks somehow not natural but not precise enough to seem human-placed. As if it weren't confusing enough, a wet cough invades the solitude. He is quickly joined by Lilja and Zoe just as those two curious ones from before reveal themselves.

Lance looks upon them with an unerring gaze, difficult to read, suggesting he doesn't want to be there. Pierce wheezes, trying to catch his breath, and when he finally does, he sets a look on them clear in its intent.

"We-" he begins, straining suddenly, clearing his throat angrily, "we took a shortcut, but it wasn't easy."

Zoe's machete is held ready, appearing there so quickly it may have never been sheathed. She is halted in her steps by Skot's hand on her shoulder.

"Who are you?" Skot demands.

"Who are we?" Pierce repeats, smirking. "That's what you want to know? After all *this*!" His held out hands shake once with the volume of his last word, then he buckles over with coughing, finally ejecting a bloody expectorant with what force he may muster. A stubborn trail of it clings to his bottom lip. "I guess," he begins again, then pauses, blinking, and he wipes with the back of his left hand. "I guess that's actually a *very important* thing to know."

The transition begins, and though it is alarming, the trio of Hunters finds it not entirely unexpected. Their guide recoils, eyes going wide, and he skitters away to find a hiding spot.

The eyes take on a red hue, the glow beginning subtly, like the appearance of the full moon in the early night. Both gain a more erect posture, chests filling with vibrancy, shoulders moving back. Pierce takes a deep, untroubled breath, and Lance stands strongly on his swollen foot.

"Skin wearers," Zoe breathes.

"No," speaks a voice from Pierce's mouth. It is more powerful, laden not only with strength but a subtle echo and reverberation as if more than one speaking. "These vessels are human, though they have been changed."

"We are many within," says an equally chilling sound from Lance, and then he raises a finger to point at Lilja. "Ask *her* who we are."

"Lilja?" Skot dares as their eyes meet.

"I don't know them," she says, her firm tone showing the barest hint of desperation.

Zoe looks at the redhead, remembering their trial back at the Barrington house. That entire encounter had felt tailored to Lilja, and now, *this*. She grips her weapon more tightly, watching Lilja closer then the two who have accosted their progress.

"It is there," says Pierce, the cadence of the words off, inhuman. "Deep in your memory's memories."

Lilja stares at them, then looks to Skot, finding his eyes already on her.

"I don't know what they mean," she says.

"These shells do not do us justice," Lance intones, and the two begin to walk toward them. The three Hunters ready themselves for the fight. "But surely you recognize your own brothers."

"Brothers?" Lilja blinks, and the hold she keeps on her weapon slackens. She whispers, "I don't have any brothers."

"We are the ills and the plagues," Pierce says as the two continue their slow, steady encroachment.

"Colic and gout," says Lance.

"Consumption and ulcers," says Pierce, giving a strange nod. "These are the ways you choose to comprehend us."

"The ways you *fail* to comprehend us," Lance elaborates.

"We slip in through your weakness. What hope have you?"

Skot takes a half-step forward, bringing the murmuring of his voice to a greater volume, and he unleashes a force of magick akin to the one he used to dispatch the stone figures. It propels from his palms, divided in particular ways by the placement of his fingers, and it rushes over the two as a hurricane's wind.

Tattered clothing peels away first, followed by skin, hunks of viscera. The two halt, but in the end, they merely wait out the spell. When over, they remain, though not formed as they once were. The parts sloughed away show a taut, powerful musculature, a deep red hue seeming to coil within. The pair stands taller, bringing up clawed fingers, and they attack.

Lilja thrusts Skot back with one hand even as she propels herself forward, katana at the ready. Her strike is blindingly fast, but it misses Lance. Pierce takes a different angle, heading toward Zoe, lust in his features. Zoe pushes forward to meet the attack, her own desire for death still evident. She cries out when those claws rend through her bicep. She stumbles, colliding with a large rock, hissing in pain. Her opponent looks at her, having suffered nothing in his attempt.

"Zoe!" Skot calls out, then brings forth his sword-cane, sliding the blade free as he moves toward Pierce. He presses, whipping the air with the flexible, razor-sharp metal. Pierce retreats, dodging with preternatural speed, that insufferable grin still on the lips.

Lilja gives some attention to how Zoe and Skot fare, and in doing so, Lance attempts to strike her. She steps aside, almost casually, then swipes with her sword. The tip finds some flesh, giving forth a spray of blood. Lance stares at her, top lip curled in a smirking suggestion of anger.

"You wound me, sister."

"I am not your *sister*!" Lilja retorts, the final word not so much shouted as uttered with an emphatic force. She lashes out at the same time, but Lance avoids this easily, emitting a guttural sound, something that might be a titter were it not so disturbing.

"The games are all the same," Lance announces, dropping down low with bent knees, too low for a normal human to not break or fall. He swipes out with his clawed hands, and Lilja dances back and to the side.

She sees the trap and so remains silent, a skill well known to her. Questions and doubts sizzle and tangle in her mind, but she pushes them away. She has trained enough to know how to shove such things into their own compartment until the proper time to consider. For now, the fight.

She is distracted by a hissing noise, and she looks over to see that Pierce has wounded Skot. She makes to head there, but Lance shoots in, barely missing her.

"No, sister. I get this honor."

Her eyes go wider as she pulls in a slow breath, sliding her lagging foot closer for better balance. Her fingers show a minor adjustment to the two-handed grip on her sword. Lance licks his lips, staying light on his feet, a distinct change from his lumbering gait before. His grin grows even more as he stares in Lilja's eyes. That brilliant blue seems to shine, and it even hints at a different hue.

"I see you giving in to the embrace," he says.

Just as his sentence is complete, Lilja propels herself forward. His own eyes go wide with shock, for he had not expected such speed. The motion of her blade is carried upon the brief glimpse of an amber-hued force, and when she passes Pierce, his right hand is disconnected from his body at the wrist. A putrescent, black ichor jets out for a split second then settles to a seeping ooze.

"Sister, you wound me."

She looks toward the other fight, tired of hearing the same taunts. Skot and Zoe have gained some ground, though their opponents seem to show such an unnatural fortitude that doubt fills her mind as to the possibility of success.

Zoe sees naught but revenge, her anger growing when Skot is wounded. He continues as well, keeping up the barrage of distracting swordplay and unfurling of magicks. Pierce dodges down and away, missing Zoe's machete by mere millimeters. He then just as quickly rights himself, smirking at Skot.

"You throw such powers at me? Do you not even realize who we are!" he demands, the layered chorus of his voice chiming forth with renewed intensity. "You are but a weak perversion, but we were born in the same land where this power was created!"

He lunges out with both hands, though he does not close the distance. Instead, an infernal energy erupts and shoots out with tremendous force, colliding with Skot and carrying him away some meters before he collapses in a heap.

"No!" The word is shouted by both women, and though they wish to go to him, they are pestered by their opponents.

Lilja dodges away from a lunge of Lance's, the attacks wild like an animal. Skot gets himself up on an elbow, trying to breathe. The attack has left a weight on his chest, *in* it, and he feels a restriction to his respiration. He recalls these two mentioning they are ills and plagues, and he wonders what this magick has now done to him. But such concerns will have to wait, and he musters himself to his feet, rejoining the fray.

Zoe has renewed her press on Pierce, anger erupting on her features. She slashes out with her machete. Pierce keeps that half-smirk on his partially ruined face, but he is pushed back, stepping lightly on his feet until rock awaits him. Skot watches for but a moment, wondering what might happen if they managed to press either of their assailants out of this unfinished-seeming place. Is there something here that gives them power?

He comes in less blatantly than Zoe, striking high. Pierce sees it at the last second, raising both hands to block, uncaring if the blade cuts there. This is what Skot wants, and it leaves Pierce exposed. Zoe slashes out at the left side of his chest, dragging her blade up along his armpit.

Pierce emits something like a grunting growl that bubbles into a chuckle as he contorts and gyrates his way out of trouble. Skot and Zoe are left momentarily stunned, for such an attack should have at the very least, left their opponent without an arm. Pierce is wounded, slightly, and a fresh spray of the liquid foulness within him adds to his unworldly appearance. He is clearly able to continue the fight, and he lunges.

Lance is evincing his own preternatural abilities, and he ducks below a fast swing of Lilja's, barely missing being beheaded. In doing so, he turns and slams his elbow against her nose. She stumbles back, though still keeps her feet, moving the sword to guard. Lance merely stands there.

"I won't kill you, sister," he says, giving forth a confusing aspect of seething and amusement.

"I am *not* your sister," she replies, feeling a trickle of blood from her nostril.

"Your ignorance changes nothing."

"Then why send demons to kill me!" she challenges, her voice suddenly going to its authoritarian loudness.

Lance gives a sheepish shrug. "They are not always the most obedient of children."

This startles her for a moment, then she feels the infusing surge of anger. She lunges, striking forward, then slashing mercilessly with follow-up attacks. Lance dodges them all, dancing about, moving much faster than anyone should.

Still, Hunters are not without their own abilities, and Lilja draws further upon hers. She had undergone years of training with never knowing of the Infernal. But now, it seems as though it had all been done in preparation for this true battle. She inhales, setting herself on planted feet and strikes out yet again. This time, her blade is bathed in the outré light, the color showing a deeper hue toward vermilion. And this strike is true.

She cries out at the end of it, accenting the power, and she whips the blade and herself back to forward, ready to continue as needed. A splattering of rich ichor indicates she has found purchase. Lance looks at her, his expression more one of emotional pain, and he topples, his form nearly sliced in twain at the belly.

He does not die immediately, if any true form of death even awaits him, but the vast leakage of viscera and flaccid state of his body indicates he is no longer a threat. She rushes to the other melee.

Lilja's blinding speed is a shock to Skot. He registers her approach on some deep level, as if seeing it after it has happened. He wonders, briefly, if another of the Infernal has arrived, but then Pierce tenses, his body taut. A good portion of the katana has thrust through the back of his neck. Lilja twists the blade, then jerks it out in the new direction. Gore erupts from the hideous wound, and he falls.

The trio of Hunters stands there, breathing heavily, eyes all searching one another. Lilja drops her sword and quickly closes the distance to Skot, wrapping him in a hug. He returns it readily, the two of them showing relief and exhaustion. Zoe watches, a half-grin taking her lips against her will.

She looks at the two heaps on the ground, knowing the potency evinced by Lilja has proved something to her. The young woman is as good as they all thought, even better. Zoe's doubts have gone. She finds herself distracted, though she is not sure why, and when she turns her focus away from the pair, she sees the light.

Skot notices it, too, and he looks up from hugging Lilja. She feels the change in posture, and she turns, gazing upon it with her piercing blue eyes. "What is that?"

"It's the resting place of the Book."

They all look to their guide, having given him little thought once the fight had begun. Lilja notes the man's survival instinct.

The place waits there as if always having been, yet, until now, unseen. It is small, though its only barrier shows in a vague shimmering of the light. It bathes in the invisible, something that resonates on such a subconscious level that it requires no other declaration.

The trio walks toward it, their guide following. As she nears, Lilja makes out more, seeing a short pedestal upon which rests a closed book. She can make out the title from here, *Ostia Tenebrosa*. It has the look of the other two, but more than this, something palpable in the very air envelopes her as she nears, making it known to her that is indeed *the* Book.

"Lilja?"

She turns, seeing Skot and Zoe still off a short distance. They hold out their hands as if against the walls of a mime's box. Her expression asks the unvocalized question.

"There's some kind of barrier here. We can't get through."

"Is it another in-between place?" Lilja asks, moving back to them.

Skot looks at their guide. The man shrugs. "I did not make this place. I did as you demanded and brought you here."

"Just get the Book," Skot decides, turning to look back at his love.

"Do you think it's safe?" she asks.

"You've come this far. Why stop now?" speaks a voice, but it does not belong to Skot.

Where the chorused utterings of Lance and Pierce held a deep resonance that threatened to clench one's gut to the point of collapse, this voice holds a layered alien beauty. Zoe recognizes it as the voice she once overheard speaking surreptitiously to their guide, though that knowledge is within it, for now, the full scope of that sound comes forth.

Lilja turns quickly, and all of them gaze upon the figure. Just as with this place that holds the Book, the woman stands there as if having been there all this time, patiently waiting. She is on the other side from where they are, the curiously-lit space of the Book between them, and the ground she stands on holds such lack of visibility that she appears to be floating. It reminds Skot of his sister, and he shakes the thought from his head.

Lilja does recognize the woman. It is the one who approached her those few times so seeming long ago, the one who appeared as if from nowhere then cast an unsettling aspect in her congenial, unassuming tone. Though she does not look exactly the same, for here she wears a wrapped outfit that leaves to more ethereal hangings at her hands and feet. Her expression is one of benevolence, but her piercing eyes show a potency unknown to any of them.

"You," Lilja says, and the woman gives a single, slow dip of her head.

"You know this … woman?" Skot asks, he and the others still stuck on their side of the barrier.

"You are correct to hesitate," she intones, putting her eyes on Skot. He feels a discomfort from the direct focus. "You speak the word 'woman', and within it, you mean 'human'. I am not."

"Infernal," he says, whispering the word.

"I am the Mother," the woman continues, letting the illusion of a warm smile curl upon her full lips. "Where the others debase themselves within their appetites for destruction, I long only to create. I am Loviatar."

"The blind daughter of Tuoni?"

That expression increases, and it conveys a weighty condescension.

"Have you not now seen enough to know the falsity of such myths?"

Lilja merely stares, saying nothing more.

"Lilja? Lilja?" Skot speaks, his voice no longer a whisper but still carried on such breaths. "Come back. We need to get out of here."

Loviatar slowly shifts her eyes to Skot.

"You are stuck there, as I am here." She gently expands her arms, hands referencing the immediate area. "*There*," she continues, pointing at the Book, "is the final place created by the Guardians. They did their job very well. They made a place even they could not enter. They did not wish humans or … Infernal to be able to get the Book."

Lilja looks from Skot to Loviatar.

"You wonder what you are, then, if you are able to be where you are?"

Lilja nods, mutely.

"Don't listen to her, Lilja. She is a deceiver," Skot says.

Loviatar chuckles.

"Sometimes we deceive. Sometimes *you* deceive. Deception was a lesson you took so well." So said, she looks back at Lilja, the redhead still silently waiting. The expression on Loviatar's face changes, subtly, something more sincere. "The barriers around the book seek signs of humanity or signs of the Infernal. You, Lilja, *you* are the true in-between."

"What?" She barely vocalizes the word. "I'm … I'm human." The declarative comes out with little force.

Loviatar merely perks her eyebrows. The evidence of where Lilja stands is all needed.

Lilja looks back at Skot. They lock eyes, both pleading.

"Get the Book and come here," Skot says. "We need to get away from her."

"Yes," Loviatar says. "Get the Book, but come to *me*."

"What?" The word arises from Lilja as though of its own accord. When she looks back at Loviatar, the benevolent expression has returned. It holds a great power, a monumental patience.

"It is time for you to come home, child."

"What do you mean? Home?" Lilja continues in a whisper, having trouble even forcing this. Skot can barely hear her words, but Loviatar's attunement is far greater.

"Do you not yet feel it?" Loviatar replies. "You are my daughter."

"What? No." Lilja says, shaking her head the barest bit.

"Lilja, come back," Skot begs, the Book no longer a concern to him.

"I know my mother," Lilja says, walking toward Loviatar, a sudden defiance on her features. "You are *not* her."

"We see things with a longer view than do you," Loviatar replies. "True birth is a rare thing for us. We are able to mold some clay and breathe life into it, but true offspring are exceedingly rare.

"As you know," she continues, eyes settling momentarily on Skot, "We seek to create children not only amongst ourselves but also with *you*. It was our folly, truly, but once done, we could not go back. Thus, we sought *refinement*." Her eyes shift back to Lilja.

No one speaks, an audience held in thrall.

"Many ... *many* generations back," she carries on, nodding in recollection. "We found a family. There was a young man in this family, and within him, we sensed great potential. We slaughtered the others, but him, we took. I used him to create a very potent child. She also became a mother. And thus did I observe.

"I have always watched you. I have overseen as the souls move and new lives are born and born again. I have waited, patiently, for this moment, but you have naught to fear from me. Just as with all of us, you have free will."

"You've tried to kill me!" Lilja suddenly finds her voice.

"Necessity, child," Loviatar answers, unperturbed. "All of your ancestors were so tested. If any one of them had failed, you'd not be here."

"You play games with our lives," Skot joins the conversation. "You are *monsters*. Lilja, come back. Let us leave."

"Monsters," Loviatar says, contemplating the word, tasting it. "*You* are locusts.

My sons-" She gestures with a hand, vaguely, in the direction of the putrid remains of Lance and Pierce. "-claim to be the plagues, but humanity is the true plague. Your prolificness is proof of this. My people, and more other species than you realize, have been around much longer, but we don't destroy our land. Humans are like piranhas stuck in a small aquarium.

"With that book." She points. "They will have all three and be able to traverse new gateways and find new worlds. Do not let them have it. Let them fill to burst and eat each other, but do not release them unto the universe entire."

"Lilja?" Skot says after a time of silence, ignoring the wry hint of a smirk that takes Loviatar's lips. "Please, come back." Lilja turns her head to look at him, her expression showing the pinch of worry and turmoil. "The Book is safe here. We only wanted to make sure it was safe. Come back. Let's go home."

"That is not you," is all Loviatar says to Lilja.

Lilja again looks from Loviatar to Skot then back to the Book. She brings her hands to her chest, fingers curling into fists and holds them there at the bottom of her throat. Though no one speaks, she feels a tumult of voices, as though she stands in the maelstrom.

When she finally looks back, her eyes show a shimmer of burgeoning tears, forehead wrinkled over a trembling frown. Skot sees this, sees it directed at him, and he feels a crushing pressure envelope him.

"No," is all he manages, the word barely uttered, caught on its tail by a quiver in his lungs.

Lilja picks up the Book and chooses, going to Loviatar. The two disappear.

Epilogue

She ought to feel free.

She had not fully realized how close she'd become to Duilio until he was gone. Murdered in front of her. Even the death of his killer did not much assuage her. She wakes nights, sweaty and afraid, sometimes even jerking from sleep due to her own cries. She expects that man, Denman Malkuth, to be there, lurking over her, with that terrible grin, and then her throat would be sliced open.

She still wonders about Lilja and the vigilante, but in a way, that all seems so small now. How could any of it be related? And the doubts still scratch at her. Maybe Lilja does know. Maybe Lilja is the vigilante, and it's all tied together. Maybe there really are demons out there, waiting to savage us.

It's all too much, and she feels her hold slipping.

She decides to seek strength, not solace, and she rides to the university. As usual, she doesn't have too much trouble finding a parking space for her motorbike, and she plods to the gym where Lilja holds her self-defense classes.

She's seen the signs before, the precisely printed and laminated things that announce the delay of classes until a certain date. But this one catches her off guard, feels like a punch in her gut. This sign says the classes are suspended *indefinitely*.

She just stands there, looking at it, for a few minutes. It seems she's lost in it, but the voice finally wakes her.

"Therese?"

She turns, slowly, not her usual guarded reaction to having her name suddenly called when she does not expect it. She sees the security guard.

"Billy," she says, her voice holding little volume.

Both sound like they are in mourning, and she is so deeply there that she gives no thought to why he might sound that way.

"Uhm, hi," he says when she remains silent. "I guess … I guess you didn't know." He gestures to the sign.

She shakes her head.

"Yeah, it was a real shock to us all."

"What do you mean?" Therese asks, furrowing her brow, squaring herself more firmly in front of him.

"Oh, the …" he gestures again to the door and its sign, "the news about Miss Perhonen."

"What about Lilja?" Therese demands.

Billy looks at her, still showing signs of awkwardness with his inability to remain totally still. He finally exhales, shoulders slumping.

"She was off on another of her trips, somewhere exotic, out in nature. She does that, you know, and … she just … never came back."

"She's disappeared?" Therese asks, incredulous.

Billy nods. "That's what the official report says."

"What! Where?"

"Somewhere in the Himalayas."

"The mountains?"

He nods.

"There were searches, but they never … uhm found a … body. Maybe she's okay, and she'll come-"

Therese has silenced him with a shake of her head. He just looks at her. She can see it in him. He's crushed. She can also tell he is about to reach out to her, so she just turns and leaves.

She ought to feel free.

But she doesn't.

"She is varjolilja, shadow Lilja, because she has left a shadow over you, over your heart. What comes after such a woman? What can there be beneath the cast of such a shadow? Who is not eclipsed by it? You are broken, but do not give up. Do not surrender. The shadow may drown the light, but you are not yet done."

Skothiam looks at his sister. She sits with him on the couch, returning his sorrowful gaze with a strength he does not possess. There is silence.

He finally nods.

The End

Author Bio

Born in Houston, Texas into the temporary care of a bevy of nuns before being delivered to his adopted parents, Scott discovered creative writing at a very young age when asked to write a newspaper from another planet. This exercise awakened a seeming endless drive, and now, many short stories, poems, plays, and novels (both finished and unfinished) later, his first book, *Dance of the Butterfly*, is being published.

The seeds for this tale began with dreams, as many often do, before being fine-tuned with a whimsical notion and the very serious input of a dear friend. Before long, the story took on life of its own and has now become the first book in a planned series.

Having lived his whole life in the same state, Scott attended the University of Texas at Austin, achieving a degree in philosophy before returning to the Houston area to be closer to family and friends. During this time, he wrote more and even branched out into directing and performance art, though creative writing remains his love.

Please follow me for updates and information regarding new books at:

Scott's website/blog- www.scottcarruba.wordpress.com/
Scott's Facebook- www.facebook.com/AuthorScottCarruba/
Scott's Twitter- www.twitter.com/scott_carruba
Scott's Tumblr- www.scottcarruba.tumblr.com/

CHECK OUT THE OMP WEBSITE FOR
A COMPLETE LIST OF OUR TITLES

WWW.OPTIMUSMAXIMUSPUBLISHING.COM

BOOKS ARE AVAILABLE IN BOTH PRINT
AND ELECTRONIC FORMATS

RICKY FLEET
HELLSPAWN
SERIES

10.35 AM, September 14th 2015, Portsmouth, England.

A global particle physics experiment releases a pulse of unknown energy with catastrophic results. The sanctity of the grave has been sundered and a million graveyards expel their tenants from eternal slumber.

The world is unaware of the impending apocalypse, Governments crumble and armies are scattered to the wind under the onslaught of the dead.

Kurt Taylor, a self-employed plumber, witnesses the start of the horrifying outbreak. Desperate to reach his family before they fall victim to the ever growing horde of shambling corruption, he flees the scene.

In a society with few guns, how can people hope to survive the endless waves of zombies that seek to consume every living thing? With ingenuity, planning and everyday materials, the group forge their way and strike back at the Hellspawn legions.

Rescues are mounted, but not all survivors are benevolent, the evil that is in all men has been given free rein in this new, dead world. With both the living and dead to contend with, the Taylor family's battle for survival is just beginning.

Book 1 in the Hellspawn series.

Kurt Taylor and his family have battled the living and the dead and now find themselves on the run, their home reduced to ashes. With unimaginable horror lying in wait around every corner, the onset of winter and the plunging temperatures only add more danger to their precarious existence. They decide to forge ahead and try to reach the protection of others who have hopefully survived the zombie apocalypse. If this fails, their only choice would be to try and reach an impregnable fortress, a sanctuary that has stood for a thousand years.

Standing between them and salvation are the villages and cities of the damned, a path that will test their spirit and resilience unlike anything they have faced before. More companions are rescued from the jaws of death and join them in their perilous journey. Mysterious attacks befall the group and it becomes clear the dead aren't the only things that lurk in the darkness.

Tempers fray and personalities clash. The group starts to fracture and Kurt is forced to commit acts that cause him to question his own morality. Can they survive the horror of their new existence? Will they want to?

The Hellspawn saga continues.

BALLYMOOR, IRELAND, 1891

Patrick Conroy, a young American student of medicine in Dublin, decides to take a break from the hustle and bustle of the big city and spend a month in the quietude of the wild and beautiful Glencree valley, County Wicklow. However, surrounded by local legends and myths, he is soon dragged into an ancient mystery that has haunted the village of Ballymoor for centuries. Set on the background of the tumultuous years preceding the War of Independence, and colored by Irish folklore, the Haunter of the Moor is a ghost story written in the style of Victorian Gothic novels.

Meet Mason Ezekiel Barnes, former NFL tackle turned successful author of the naughty ninja adventure series Mia Killjoy. Mason is obsessed with winning a Pulitzer and is thwarted by his fellow author and nemesis, the twerpy little gnome Conrad Bancroft.

Perk Noir is full of comedic relief, pop culture, NFL, jazz, a little touch of romance, and flashbacks of Lightning and his family during both the first half of the 20th century and later during the Civil Rights movement. Mason and Shelly and their adventures is a fun filled thrill ride that will appeal to all readers, there is something for everyone at the Perk.

Two hunters pursue the same prey.

Fate has forged the slayer, Trey Thomas and the Sandrian vampire, Adalius, two natural enemies, into an uneasy alliance against an evil more powerful than either have ever faced. Only together do they stand a chance of defeating Anna; if they don't destroy each other first.

As they pursue Anna, the apprehensive Lycan watch as a confrontation looms on the horizon between vampires, the New Bloods and the Old Guard, which threatens to plunge the vampire world into civil war and trigger an all-out supernatural conflict which in the end could destroy them all.

Killing is the sole province of the religious fanatics, an axiom as true today as it was some five hundred years ago; and no nation, region or person is immune.

Europe had clawed its way out of the Middle Ages with the dawning of the renaissance, only to be plunged once more into darkness, as the dogs of war circled to destroy its resurgence during the 16th century. The Islamic successor to the Roman Byzantines, the Ottoman Caliphate, flexed its muscles to conquer much of Western Asia, North Africa and South-Eastern Europe. Christian Europe shuddered when the once invincible bastion of the Knight's at Rhodes were defeated; and now trembled as the Ottoman army rattled the very gates of Vienna. No Christian army, it seemed, could withstand the ferocity of the Azabs, the Akıncı, the Sipahis, the Janissaries, and ruthless Iayalar's of the all-conquering Islamic hordes.

This then is the cauldron into which Gideon de Boyne is unwittingly thrust with his small army of dedicated Christian warriors. On the hostile island of Crete, at the doorstep of the Ottoman Empire, Gideon must face not only the overwhelming force of Muslim warriors but his own inner conflicts of the futility of war and his very Christian beliefs.

Will he succeed and come out of it unscathed?

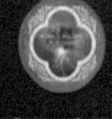

Collected tales of Madness and Terror

An OMP Magazine

Complete
Collection

MAXIMUS SHOCK

0

16 Mind-Shocking Tales!

RICKY FLEET   JEFFREY KOSH   EMIR SKALONJA

KEITH MONTGOMERY   SCOTT CARRUBA   CHRIS GARSON

LORRAINE VERSINI   MAURA ATKINSON BUTLER   MATT HAY

LEON BROWN   WK POMEROY

EDITED BY
CHRISTINA HARGIS SMITH

www.ingramcontent.com/pod-product-compliance
Lightning Source LLC
Chambersburg PA
CBHW020942180626
46814CB00003B/902